LAKELAND HEATWAVE

Elemental Fire

LAKELAND HEATWAVE

Elemental Fire

K D GRACE

Published by Xcite Books Ltd – 2013

ISBN 9781908262202

Printed and bound in the UK

Cover design by
The Design House

Surely there is no other place in this whole world quite like Lakeland ... no other so exquisitely lovely, no other so charming, no other that calls so insistently across a gulf of distance. All who truly love Lakeland are exiles when away from it.
– Alfred Wainwright

Like Lakeland Heatwave: Body Temperature and Rising and *Riding the Ether, Elemental Fire* is dedicated to the natural world, the true source of boundless magic and mystery.

Thank you, with all my heart!

THE LAKELAND HEATWAVE SERIES

9781908086877   9781908262789   9781908262202

Acknowledgements

Once again a very special thanks to Brian and Vron Spencer. Your boundless love and enthusiasm for the Lake District is contagious. Thanks for all you've taught me, and thanks for your help in exploring and experiencing and, I hope, bringing to life on the page, the magic of the English Lakes. Without your help, this trilogy could never have happened. You two are the best!

Thank you, Renee and Jo and all of the lovely Ladiez at Sh! Not only are you a fabulous fount of information, fun and encouragement, but you're an endless source of inspiration to me. Hugs and kisses and my deepest gratitude. You are my heroes!

Thanks to the amazing Miranda Forbes, who does the work of four people, and to the incredible Hazel Cushion, and to Gwenn and Liz and all the fabulous people at Xcite Books for making *Lakeland Heatwave* a reality.

Thank you, Lucy Felthouse, for cracking the PR whip, when necessary, and for staving off more than one panic attack for this neurotic writer. I couldn't have done it without you, EP! You rock!

Thank you, Kay Jaybee, for just being there for me and being your wonderful, encouraging, witty, kind self. The journey has been so much better because of you.

Thank you, Raymond, my Slatki, for believing in me and being proud of me and easing the journey. There's no one I'd rather have by my side. Volim te mnogo!

Chapter One

Seven Years Ago

Kennet ignored the pain, and it was strangely easy to do being as close to death as he was. There was little left to lose. It took all of his concentration to form the spell in his head. It might not even work, but at this stage it was all he had – that and the burning fire of helpless rage that kept him safe from his losses, kept him at arm's length from the grief until he could make contact or until he died. Whichever came first.

With a last push, his whole body tingled, and pain shot up his spine. Surely this was death. But consciousness remained in his broken flesh. He had managed to partition himself off from the pain and the drugs. This was too important. This was his only hope. Hope was a word that tasted bitter in his mouth. He meant revenge, didn't he? Surely there was no hope left. It had gone out of the world with Patrice and Annie. One last push, one last sting of pain, and he was there in the cave. He was naked, but he felt neither the cold nor the stones that should have been cutting his feet. Back in the hospital, would they think him only dreaming, or would he have slipped into a coma for his efforts? Made no difference.

The descent began gradually, then steepened until he had to lean back to keep from falling, but he imagined that was only necessary because he was still thinking in physical terms. Physical terms. If he were to survive this, he would be thinking in terms of physical pain once he returned to his body and probably more pain than he had ever experienced before. And the physical – well, that was really nothing compared to the rest of it. He kept moving downward for ever, it seemed, but he knew time passed differently in the Dream World, if that's where he was at. It certainly wasn't the Ether.

He saw the glow of her long before he reached the bottom of the shaft, and he wondered what guise she would take. The light danced like fire on the walls of the cave and was refracted off faceted crystals, like the inside of a geode, he thought. But he barely had time to think before he saw her, and he was relieved that she had taken human form. There were other forms she could have taken, other forms that he might not have found so easy to look upon. She stood with her back to him, and even so, he felt her presence through every cell of his body, both cold and hot, expansive and contractive, not pain as he knew it, but a force that made him feel like his own weight was suddenly collapsing in on itself like a dying star, too much to bear. Too much to bear.

And then she turned to face him and he knew he wouldn't survive. How could he possibly survive her? She eyed him for a long time, way too long for comfort. Even naked as he was, he felt exposed, as though she had peeled back his flesh and looked into the very heart of him, the very soul of him that now felt dark and fractured like an empty river bed. He couldn't look at her face. He desperately wanted to, for some unexplainable reason, but he couldn't lift his eyes from her beautiful feet. Botticelli toes, he thought. Such a stupid thing to think at a time like this. Aphrodite on a half-shell she wasn't. The dry heat of fire should have burned him to a cinder where he knelt. And he was kneeling, though he couldn't remember when he'd taken the position of obeisance.

She moved around him in a tight circle, so close that he was certain the heat of her would burn the skin from his body, so bright that afterimages of her danced behind his eyes when he closed them, and he had to close them. She ran a hand along the top of his shoulders to the nape of his neck and stood behind him, so close that he could feel her breath, warm and sweet against his ear. It was sweeter than anything

2

life had ever offered him, her breath, her touch. And he was suddenly, embarrassingly erect.

She came to stand in front of him. He would have tried to cover himself but the weight of his arms was terrible. He could tell she was looking down on him, and the feeling of arousal suddenly intensified, flashed bright and settled low in his chest into a tight knot of fear. And yet he wanted, deeply, irrationally, needed her to touch him.

Then, she did the unthinkable. She curled a finger under his chin and lifted his head until he knew if he opened his eyes he would die from looking into her face.

When she spoke, it was as though he were glass shattering, falling into tiny pieces in the ecstasy of her voice. 'We have met before, Kennet Birch. You had not grown so tall then. Adolescence is unpredictable, I am told.' Her hand closed around his chin to a nearly painful grip. 'Look at me, Kennet Birch. If you have come this far, then you will look me in the eye and tell me why you are here.'

Painfully aware of his vulnerability and his hard-on, he opened his eyes slowly and looked up at her. For a split second it was as though he were looking into the midday sun, but before he could shade his eyes, the light of her softened, dimmed, cooled. And the face he looked upon was achingly beautiful – young, slender, pale, with lips full and pink. Her hair hung in long golden ringlets around her shoulders and down over the robe she wore, which appeared like flames leaping to touch and caress her.

He groaned out loud as everything in him turned molten in the roil of fear and rage and helplessness all wrapped up in almost unbearable lust.

She relaxed her grip on his chin and offered him a smile that made all of his nerve endings sing with its beauty. 'I have not worn human form in quite some time, but if my form is to be the last you see before you pass beyond the land of the living, then I shall offer something that will not send you thence with terror in your heart. That would be terribly unkind of me, would it not, Kennet Birch?'

3

'Thank you … my lady.'

She laughed as though she had just heard the best joke ever. 'Your lady I am not, Kennet Birch. Nor is my ego so delicate that whatever you call me shall matter one way or another. I will ask you again. Why have you come?'

She turned and walked away from him, and for a second he felt as though the light had gone out of the world. As his gaze followed her, he realised that they were no longer in the depths of a cave but in a garden in high summer. He could smell the roses and the lavender. He could hear the insects buzzing. 'You know why I'm here.' The stab of pain nearly doubled him over at the reminder of his loss.

'Having nothing to lose has made you bold, Kennet Birch. Though I am not surprised. As I recall, you were already so as a youth.' She waved a slender hand. 'Yes, I know about the death of your wife and your sister. And though I am sorry for your loss, it has nothing to do with me. It is long since I have interfered in affairs of the flesh.'

'It has everything to do with you!' Pushing himself to his feet, with an effort that was gargantuan, he came to her side. 'The enemy of my enemy is my friend.'

She raised one golden eyebrow and turned to face him. 'I am not your friend, Kennet Birch, and even if I were, I hardly see how an alliance with you would help my cause.'

'Of course you see. Together we can defeat him.'

She absently plucked a blood-red rose from a bush that climbed tenaciously on a stone wall, sniffed it and studied it as though she had never seen anything like it. 'I fail to see how you could possibly be of help.'

'I could give you flesh.' The words were out before he could stop them, and his heart nearly exploded from his chest as she crushed the rose, raised an arm in a flourish that was almost like a flash of lightning, and they were once again back in the cave.

She stood close to him, so close that he could feel her breath coming fast and furious against his face. Her eyes were fire, her presence made him feel as though every fibre of himself were being shredded and being unmade even as he breathed. 'You are beyond brazen, Kennet Birch, to offer such a thing, as if I would want to walk among humans again, as if I would want to take up residence in their weakness and need.'

'But you do,' he found the courage to whisper, not even loud enough for her to hear, and yet she heard. He was certain she heard the very movement of his blood in his veins. 'You do want to take up residence in our weakness and our need. That's what you've always wanted, isn't it? And that's the only way you'll ever be on an equal footing with him.'

She studied him for what might have been ages, and he felt as though the pressure of her scrutiny would crush him.

'I have never worn man flesh.' She nodded down to his penis.

He blushed and surged and blushed again. His heart raced. 'Does it make a difference?'

She shrugged, still studying his cock as though she'd never seen one before. 'Not really. Flesh is flesh.' On a whim, she reached out and stroked his erection, and he gasped as the touch of her shivered up his spine and blossomed bright inside his head.

She continued to touch him, but her eyes were now locked on his face, and he tried desperately not to thrust against her. 'I am only touching your cock, Kennet Birch, and it is all you can do to keep from spilling your seed at my feet.'

'That is the most sensitive part,' he breathed. 'Of a man, I mean.'

She moved closer and ran a splayed hand up over his ribs. And he did spill his seed with a desperate gasp as though he could never get enough oxygen again. And he was embarrassed and terrified and angry, and it was as though the whole range of emotions exploded in his head in an instant. Then she leaned in and brushed her lips against his, and for a split second the world flashed before his eyes more vivid, more perfect, more complete than he had ever seen it before. He knew things, he saw things, he felt things, things beyond him. And he would have dropped again to his knees, but he couldn't, not held in her gaze as he was.

'I have barely touched you and you are overwhelmed, Kennet Birch. Do you really think you can survive my possession of you?'

He forced himself to hold her gaze, trembling suddenly as though he were in the grip of some powerful illness. All of him ached, and he knew the real world was bleeding through. There was very little time. 'I won't survive if you don't possess me. My coming to you has guaranteed that.' He wrapped his arms around himself as the shakes became more violent. 'You said it yourself, I have nothing to lose.'

'And why would I want a sick and broken male body?' She asked. Her eyes blazed in the dance of firelight that always seemed so close to her.

'If you possess me, you can heal me,' he said. 'And anyway, if you possess me and I die – well, it really doesn't matter at this point.'

For an eternal moment she studied him. She studied him until he looked away. His head was fuzzy, his body ached even in the dream world. He couldn't hold on much longer.

She lifted his chin once again so that he met her gaze, and the shakes stopped. The pain went away. He felt his head clear.

'If I do what you ask of me, even though you live, your life is forfeit. You know this?'

'I know,' he breathed. 'It doesn't matter.'

'You say that now in your hour of need. But when that passes, when you are whole and stronger and healthier than you have ever dreamed possible, when your heart heals and you learn to love again, you will not be so anxious to let go of what is rightfully mine when the time comes.'

He suddenly felt more pain than he knew existed in the whole world, and none of it was physical. He inhaled breath that felt like shards of stone. 'I'll never know love again. I'll never know life again, so there's really nothing you can take from me that isn't already long gone.'

Her gaze softened, and somehow he found that infinitely comforting. Then she moved closer and kissed him, slowly, languidly, as though they had all the time in the world, and his cock was hard again. She stepped back from him. One shrug and the robe of fire fell away, and the glow of her body flashed bright, then dimmed and steadied until he could see details, erect nipples atop high breasts, rounded hips, a golden splash of curls at the juncture of her thighs.

'I am not like him,' she said softly. 'It gives me no pleasure to make those who dwell in the flesh my puppets. You will be, how is it you put it these days, you will be in the driver's seat.'

She took him into her arms and kissed him hard, and when he feared he would disgrace himself again with his cock pressed up tight against the top of her belly, she pulled away. 'However,' she said. 'If I grant your request, then I will possess you. All of you. You will belong to me, your life will be mine.' Her gaze was painfully bright. 'And if you earnestly wish to be rid of Deacon, then you will do as I say for as long as it takes us to accomplish our task, and it will take time. I know him. You do not. I'm his equal. You are not. And one more very important thing, Kennet Birch.' She stroked his hair gently and whispered against his lips. 'Never, never forget how badly I can hurt you if you defy me.' Then she guided his hand down over her pubic curls. 'If my terms are not acceptable to you, then you must return to your body and face your fate.'

Boldly, brazenly, he slid a finger down low and circled her clit, and her eyes fluttered. 'If it weren't acceptable to me, I wouldn't be here,' he answered.

She took his hand and guided him back to a chair that appeared from out of nowhere. It looked like a golden throne with no arms. What? Was he to petition her? He didn't understand. But it was no throne at all. She pushed him down on it and stood before him caressing her breasts until her nipples were stiff and swollen. Then she raised one perfect leg and set her elegant Botticelli foot on his thigh, affording him a

7

view of her wet and fiery depths. 'I do not enter through your breath, Kennet Birch,' she said. 'As sex is your magic, so is it mine. You will go in through me, inside out. And your hunger for me will pull me into you when your libido surges brightest.'

And he was so hungry for her. She filled his head and his body with an aching want that even if he were not a practitioner of sex magic, he would understand was not mundane. And in his case, the fear that he would die if he didn't have her here and now was a very real one. That he might die even if he did, that her possession might be too much for him – well, that was a risk he was more than willing to take.

'Are you certain this is what you want, Kennet Birch?' she asked him as she moved onto his lap, positioning herself, opening her sex with her fingers.

'I've never been more sure of anything in my life.' Even as he said it, he realised how silly that sounded, since either way his life as he'd known it was over.

'Very well, then.' She settled to the point of contact, to the point at which he could just feel the head of his penis against the resistance of her opening. He reached for her breasts, and with the hand not busy between her legs, she cradled his head and drew him near so he could nurse. The electrical shock through his body caused him to jump and jerk, and at that very instant she settled onto him, sheathing him tightly, deeply, and he knew he was dying. This was the point of no return. It was as though the tight wet pull of her swallowed him whole. Then she cupped his chin and held his face again so he couldn't look away from her shining eyes. Her voice was like warm honey, thick and sweet, and he felt the sound of it in his very marrow, in his very soul. 'You are mine, Kennet Birch. No longer are you your own. I possess you, body, soul and life force. Even in name you are now mine, Kennet Lucian. You are mine until I have no further use for you, until I have used you up.' She gripped him hard and he exploded inside her and the world blew apart into tiny particles and disappeared like flecks of dust in the darkness.

'Bloody Hell! Dr Allen! Dr Allen! Get over here. Now!'

Kennet inhaled delicious, abundant air as though he'd just remembered how to breathe. Then he fought his way up from under an unruly sheet to sit up on the bed. A woman and a man in hospital scrubs stood on either side of him, holding him, and there was chaos and someone was yelling. It took him a second to register that it was him yelling over and over again, 'Where the hell am I? Where the hell am I?' And then the bright lights, the gurney with a body shrouded in a sheet next to him all came into focus. 'Jesus! What the fuck am I doing in the morgue?'

The woman in scrubs standing next to him looked pale and her hands were unsteady. 'Mr Birch,' she said, doing her best to stay calm. 'You were pronounced dead almost 15 minutes ago.'

Chapter Two

Seven Years Later

Tara Stone burst from the Dream World with a gasp. Everyone was dead except her, and Deacon wouldn't kill her. Deacon wouldn't let her die with her coven brothers and sisters. A dream! It was just a dream! Why wouldn't he kill her? Why wouldn't he let it be over? It was just a fucking dream, she reassured herself, wiping sweat from her forehead with a trembling hand. Damn it! She was supposed to be able to control her dreams, filter them. Dreams were her domain, her magic! Why couldn't she shut this nightmare out? She knew Deacon wasn't doing it. He was safely locked away.

Anderson! She needed Anderson. He could always calm her, make her feel better. And then the weight of the dream seemed only minor compared to the pain of the Waking World.

Anderson wasn't there. Anderson was still lost somewhere in the Ether trying to find his way back home to her and Cassandra and the Elemental Coven. Four months. Four long fucking months they had searched the Ether for him. She scrubbed her hand over her face and pushed the tangled duvet back. There were no tears left to cry. Her insides were like a desert, and yet as dry and burned out as they were, her heart still ached. There was no numbing it, no making it callous, no healing it.

She stood quickly and threw on her walking clothes. She had to get out of here, out onto the fells, out into the fresh

Cumbrian air. It was the only place she felt like she wouldn't suffocate. Anderson had chided her for walking the fells alone at night. When he feared for her safety, he followed her in non-corporeal form. And when she confronted him about sneaking around, he only ever shrugged and asked what was the point in being a ghost if one couldn't sneak around from time to time?

As she left her suite and pulled the door to behind her, she thought about checking Deacon's scrying mirror prison, but she knew he was still safely locked in his own private bit of the Ether. She would know immediately if he were free. Besides, she didn't want to be near him at the moment. She didn't want him in her house, really, but there was little choice for the time being, and it was the safest place.

She tiptoed down the stairs and made her way into the kitchen without turning on a light. There, she grabbed some of Fiori's homemade ginger snaps and stuffed them into her rucksack along with a bottle of water. She pulled on her walking boots, which sat neatly in a boot tray by the back door, then she slipped into the night.

In the Land Rover, she headed out along the Borrowdale Road toward Grange. The fells were dark and brooding against a sky spattered liberally with stars, and the night was unusually warm for early spring. She drove to the end of Derwentwater and along the River Derwent. The fells closing in on either side funnelled her into the Borrowdale Valley. It wasn't a long drive, and there was no traffic at this hour. She crossed the stone bridge over the River Derwent and pulled into the deserted car park in front of the Grange Methodist Church. From there it was an easy walk up onto Maiden Moore and High Spy and on around the entire ridge of the Newlands Horseshoe, if she were so inclined. That route was not advised in the dark, but though the moon was only just a waxing sliver, she'd walked it so many times she figured she could probably do it with her eyes closed. She took off along Swanesty How at a fast pace.

Spring had come to Cumbria warmer and dryer than usual

11

this year. But it was early days; there could still be frost and snow. They could hardly expect another spring heatwave like they'd had last year. Had it really been almost a year since Marie and Tim had joined the coven? In fact it was on these very fells that Tara and Anderson had first encountered Marie Warren. The young American had played the voyeur and watched them make love. The memory brought both a smile and a sharp pain of loss beneath her sternum.

Marie and Tim had breathed new life into the Elemental Coven. They had brought new hope. And Cassandra – no one had even known succubi existed until she had waltzed into their lives – well, into their dreams, actually, and into Anderson's heart.

It had all felt so hopeful, so full of promise. Even she had allowed herself to hope. A stupid thing to do, she thought. Anderson had been lost to them in the Ether in the battle to recapture Deacon. She'd wanted to believe they could end it. She'd wanted to believe that more than anything. She should have known it could never happen without a price. But dear Goddess, she'd never expected this price; the loss of her high priest, her dearest and oldest friend, her rock. She shook her head so hard her vision blurred as she tried to reassure herself. It was Anderson lost in the Ether. They would find him if he didn't find his way back first. No one knew the Ether like he did, though Cassandra was the closest second Tara had ever met. She knew Cassandra wouldn't stop looking until she found the man she loved and brought him back home. Tara had never known anyone more tenacious and single minded than the young succubus. And the Elemental Coven – well, they were the most powerful coven of witches anywhere. They often astonished even her with their brilliance. They would find him. They would!

She picked up the pace as she began her ascent, feeling the sweat break under her arms and low on her back. Then she picked up the pace again. Exhaustion was what she wanted, what she needed. She concentrated on her footing, navigating the loose rock of the ascent around Netting Haws, and that was a good thing. Right now, she'd do anything to keep her mind off Anderson's loss and off the dream she couldn't get rid of, even with Deacon in captivity.

By the time she reached the ridge between Maiden Moor and High Spy and followed it on to High Spy, she was hungry. She found a place on the moss just below the summit looking out over the broad, hulking shoulders of Dale Head and Hindscarth, separated from her by the deep abyss where Newlands Beck drained into the Newlands Valley far below. There she settled down, ate Fiori's cookies, drank some water and lay back to look at the night sky. She hadn't intended to fall asleep.

This time the dream was warm and sexy, and she found herself in a deep cave. She felt safe and comfortable. No one could touch her here. This was her domain. Caves were always her safe place, and they so often elicited a Pavlovian effect on her body. Caves were the place of powerful dream magic. Caves were the place where she always felt sexy by association. And even now, even in the Dream World, she felt deeply aroused, more so than she had since Anderson had been lost to her.

She undid her blouse and slid her hand inside to caress her breasts. It felt like for ever since she'd had a good fuck, and Goddess, she ached for her loss. As one hand tugged at her burgeoning nipples, the other worried open the fly of her walking trousers and slid down onto her mons. She'd left Elemental Cottage in a hurry, so there was no underwear to contend with. She stroked her soft curls for a few minutes, teasing, anticipating, her hips shifting and undulating against the ground. Then, when she could take it no longer, she slid two fingers deep into the gape of her pussy, wriggling and manoeuvring to where she was hottest and wettest. Just one stroke of her clit and she came in shudders and jerks. She hadn't realised she'd been that desperate for relief. But she had been distracted lately.

It was then she noticed the exquisite woman with long

golden hair sitting so close that her knees practically touched Tara's ribs. It came as no surprise to her, though surely it should have, but then this was a dream, wasn't it? The woman's robe pooled around her and ebbed and flowed like fire.

'You feel better now, do you not, my darling Tara?' she asked. Her voice made Tara feel like she was melting into warm, delicious nothingness and seeping into the cave floor.

Tara nodded and moaned softly, for some reason unable to speak, for some reason just wanting to remain in the presence of this woman, whoever she was. It brushed her consciousness fleetingly that maybe she should be concerned about the strange woman in her dreams, but the thought passed quickly, and she lay quietly next to her.

'Good,' the woman said, stroking Tara's hair away from her forehead. 'I need you to feel better. All of us need you to feel better. We have work to do, and we cannot do it when you are mourning your losses.' She nodded. 'Yes, of course I know about your Anderson. And I know that you do not fuck the living. Such a foolish girl you are to deny yourself the very pleasure you so willingly offer the dead. Elemental Cottage is not a nunnery, my darling.'

She leaned down low and kissed Tara on the mouth. Her breath smelled like the fells in high summer. Then she tisk-tisked and gently stroked Tara's pubic curls. 'You need more than you can manage with your hand, my sweet girl, no matter how gifted you are in the arts of pleasure. You practise sex magic, surely you know this?' She brushed slender fingers up Tara's belly and over the mounds of her breasts. Tara arched up into her heated caresses. 'Shall I bring you just what you need to make you feel better? Would you like that, my dear?'

Tara could only whimper and nod.

Once again she brushed Tara's lips with hers, adding the slightest flick of her tongue, and for an instant the kiss felt predatory, devouring. Or had Tara only imagined it? 'Do not worry, my love,' the woman said as she pulled away. 'I shall

send you just what you need. Wait here, and rest a little.'
Then she disappeared leaving Tara to writhe and moan on the
floor of the cave.

From far away someone shook her arm, someone called to
her in distressed tones, trying to bring her back to the Waking
World. But she didn't want to go back. It was safe and warm
and happy here. There was nothing but sadness in the Waking
World. She just wanted to sleep here in the cave and wait for
whoever the beautiful woman would bring to her.

But the shaking and jostling continued. She slapped the
hand away, but it kept coming back to shake her. She was just
ready to tell whoever it was to bugger off, when she opened
her eyes and looked up to see the outline of a man leaning
over her. Even in the darkness, the energy emanating from
him was magnetic. Everything inside her tightened with
anticipation, and Goddess, she wanted him. Surely she was
still dreaming.

'Are you all right?' His voice vibrated through her chest
and his touch felt electric, full of magic. 'I thought you were
dead, then I heard you moaning. I guess you were dreaming. I
was worried and then ...'

They both realised at the same time that her shirt was open
and so were her trousers, and one hand still rested on her
mons. She could feel the man's gaze taking in the situation,
and he twigged. 'Oh shit, I'm sorry. I didn't realise. I thought
you were –'

'I was! Dreaming, I mean.' She quickly jerked her hand
out of her trousers and tugged her open blouse across her bare
breasts. 'I was dreaming, and she said she'd send someone
and ...' She blinked hard and looked around at the night sky.
She couldn't have been asleep long, but everything felt
unreal, different. Was she still dreaming? Dreams could be so
powerful at times, so confusing. She reached up to touch his
face and felt a surge of magic – some new, some old. Some
very old. Had she enfleshed a ghost because of her horny
dream? When she walked at night, ghosts did sometimes
follow her onto the fells in hopes that she would enflesh them

and allow them to experience for a little while the pleasures afforded the living. And any other time she would happily oblige. But when she walked at night, she always sent them away. This was her place, her alone time. No one was welcome to disturb her here, and most ghosts knew that. Had she been that out of it? Was she that desperate for a fuck that her unconscious had broken her own rules?'

The man sat back on his haunches and looked down at her. In the darkness she could only make out his silhouette dominated by broad shoulders, but it was enough to make her own arousal spike. Certainly if she had enfleshed him, she couldn't leave him in the state he was now, no doubt, in because of her.

He gave a little gasp of surprise when she off-balanced him, pulled him down to her and kissed him. 'You shouldn't have come here,' she managed before she drew him into another kiss.

'I might say the same about you,' he replied.

Cheeky ghost, she thought, but she kissed him again. This time he returned the favour. And the power surge she felt went clear from her mouth down to the base of her spine and back again. His eyes fluttered, he gasped against her mouth, clearly feeling what she felt, and there was no disguising the press of his heavy erection against the fly of his walking trousers.

'What the hell was that?' She gasped, not entirely sure she wasn't going to come just from their last kiss.

He pulled back from her with a start, one hand against his lips and the other resting low on his belly. 'If you do that again, I can't guarantee what will … If you do that again.'

For a tightly stretched second, they froze in each other's gaze. Then she forced words up through her throat, struggling to breathe through her arousal. 'I can't … I need …'

'Me too,' he whispered. She couldn't see the colour of his eyes in the darkness, but his gaze was baking hot against her.

Focus. Damn it, she needed to be able to focus, to think. She forced a deep breath and then they were both speaking at the same time.

'I'm sorry … I didn't … I wouldn't …'

'I don't know what just happened,' he gasped.

'Me neither,' she managed.

Then they were on each other. He yanked the clasp from her hair and clawed it free from the ponytail. She curled her fingers in the front of his shirt and pulled him on top of her, down between her open legs, lifting her hips, wrapping her ankles around his waist and thrusting up to meet him. The sounds coming from his throat were deep-chested, wild, and she wasn't sure where his grunts and growls left off and hers began as he thrust and ground against her, shoving her arse into the soft moss with his efforts.

'I need to get to you,' he gasped, pulling away from her, tugging and fumbling at her trousers until they were down over her hips.

She toed one of her boots off and kicked it aside, and he lifted her leg free of the trousers while she pulled open his fly and slid her hand into his boxers until she could wrap her fingers around his heavy cock.

He gasped and pushed them away. 'Don't do that. I'll come in your hand and I don't want to come there.' He trapped both her wrists above her head with a large hand while he nuzzled his way into her shirt and battled with his trousers until his butt was bare.

Then he released her hands and kissed his way down her belly, shoving her legs further apart as he went, lowering his face, biting the inside of her left thigh just below the swell of her pussy. She yelped and drenched herself. He fingered her open and ran his tongue up from her perineum all the way to her clit and bit again. And she came, bellowing her orgasm into the cool night air.

'I want you in me, I want you in me,' she gasped, even before she could breathe again, even before the waves inside her had dissipated.

He positioned himself and pushed into her deep and hard and they both growled like angry wolves. She grabbed his

17

arse cheeks in an effort to pull him still deeper into her. He dug into the moss with his feet, shoved up onto his knees and lifted her until her shoulders rested in the moss and her hips were in the air, knees pressing upward against her breasts. Then he rolled with her and pulled her on top of him. With one trembling hand he shoved her blouse off her shoulders and her breasts bounced freely into his cupping fingers. With the other hand he expertly found her clit and, resting the flat of his palm on her mound, he stroked and rubbed with the pad of his thumb.

One wave of orgasm collapsed in on the next, like the waves breaking against the cliffs at St Bee's Head. Then both of his hands settled to her hips and he thrust up, nearly bucking her off in his efforts to penetrate still deeper. His grip on her hips was bruising, and she slammed against him harder and harder with each thrust, emotions surged – emotions that she didn't want to feel, emotions that she did want to feel, emotions that she had wanted to feel from the time she was a little girl. And somewhere in the midst of their thrusting and pushing, she realised that not all of the emotions were hers. But she couldn't think, she couldn't concentrate on anything but the in and out, push and shove, like a mantra, like a spell being woven in rhythm, in repetition, in sync.

And then they both came, screaming and raging and rolling in the moss until he was once again on top of her, his weight feeling like the weight of the world, and yet at the same time feeling like a blanket protecting her from the depths of her own pain. How could this be? How could she ever experience anything like this with some strange horny ghost on the fells?

She found herself with a million questions, and yet by the time she caught her breath, she was fast asleep. To her total surprise, he had crossed the dream threshold and they were chasing the dream together.

For a long time they walked hand in hand across the fells. It was dark with only a sliver of moonlight slicing the sky.

'Where are we?' he asked.

'I don't recognise these fells,' she said. 'I thought it was your dream. I thought you knew.'

'Honestly, I've never been here before, and I haven't dreamed with anyone in a very long time. Anyway, we weren't doing dream magic. How did we get here?'

'You crossed the threshold,' she said. 'I didn't know you could.' It was then that she noticed she was naked. They were both naked, and he was walking with an erection, trying to cover it with his hand, trying to keep it from interfering with their walking.

'You should really let me do something about that,' she said, nodding to his cock. And the minute she said it her own arousal became fully evident. How had she not noticed it before?

He cursed under his breath. 'I think she's doing this.'

'The woman in flames?' she asked.

He stopped mid-stride, his hand stroking his penis absently. She wished he wouldn't do that. It was so distracting. 'You saw her?' he said.

She nodded, her gaze resting on his cock. 'She was in my dream, the one I was having when you woke me up. Would you like me to take care of that?' She nodded to his erection.

'Would you mind terribly?' he said.

'Not at all.' She knelt in front of him and took his cock in her hand, and he grunted his appreciation. 'What does she want?'

'To destroy Deacon. You know Deacon, don't you?'

'As a matter of fact, I do,' she said. 'What a coincidence. I'd like to destroy Deacon too. Would you?'

'I certainly would,' he replied. 'Maybe we can do it together.' Then he added, 'Would you mind? I'd really like to fuck you, and I bet you're horny too, aren't you? Is your pussy wet?'

'Funnily enough, it is. Very wet,' she said. 'Oh look. We're back in my room. I'm glad. I much prefer to fuck on a bed, don't you?' She lay back on the bed and spread her legs,

19

stroking and tweaking the swell of her clit. 'I really am very aroused now that you mention it. I don't have sex with the living, you know. Only ghosts.' She chuckled cheerfully. 'I'm pretty fucked up.'

'Really? What a coincidence,' he said, climbing on the bed between her legs and lowering himself into position, taking over the stroking of her clit. 'I'm pretty fucked up myself. And I don't have sex with anyone. Well, she takes care of me. It's not proper sex, but with her it doesn't matter. I don't know why I'm so horny now.'

'It's OK, you can fuck me and we'll both feel better,' Tara said, admiring the size of his cock, anxious to have it inside her.

He pushed in with a sigh and she caught her breath. 'You're big,' she managed.

'And you're tight and wet.' He offered an embarrassed smile. 'I don't know how long I'm gonna be able to hold out in your grip.'

She wrapped her legs around his hips and reached up to grab his butt cheeks, feeling them clench with his thrust. 'It's OK if you need to come. It's a dream, remember? We can both come as often as we want.'

He laughed softly. 'Of course. I'd nearly forgotten. It's a good thing, because I feel like I could come a lot.' He thrust into her deeper. He tugged and fondled her breasts, then pulled a nipple into his mouth and began to suckle. She held his head to her.

'If you know how to destroy Deacon,' she said, 'I really wish you'd let me know because he's been giving me grief for almost as long as I can remember. Ridding the world of him would be a huge service to humanity.'

'It sure would.' He spoke against her nipple. 'She has a plan, and I'm sure she'd let you in on it if you want.' He raised his face to hers and kissed her with plenty of tongue. Then he pulled out, turned her over and took her from behind. Suddenly they were fucking in the cave where Tara had been earlier.

'I'd like that. Personally, I'd be glad to get him out of my house.'

'I bet you would. It gives me the creeps just to think about being under the same roof with that bastard.' He turned her on her side and took her from a spoon position, stroking her clit with two fingers. 'Great Goddess, you're wet,' he breathed. 'I think you're getting close.'

'I am, very close.' She strained back against his fingers. 'So does she know how to get rid of him, then?'

'Oh yes. As I said, she has a plan.' His words were strained and tight and she could tell by the tension in his body that he was as close to orgasm as she was. 'I need to come now,' he said. 'Will you come with me? Your pussy's all tight and ready.'

'Thank you, I'd like that,' she said, and they both orgasmed together, grunting and straining and chuckling a bit nervously as they began to calm, and breath came back to them.

'Strange dream, this,' he said, cupping her breast.

'Yes, strange. How did we get back on the fells? And look, the sun's coming up.'

'I have no idea. Amazing, really. Looks like it's going to be a nice day.' He ran his hand down to caress her mound, his cock still firmly sheathed inside her. 'You know, I wouldn't mind doing that again, since it's a dream. Would you like that?'

'I think I would,' she said. He hoisted her to sit on top of him still fully impaled. 'Anyway, you were telling me about her plan. You know, the plan to destroy Deacon.'

'Oh yes,' he said. 'Sorry, I was distracted by your lovely breasts.' He rearranged himself again until she sat facing him on his lap, their legs wrapped around each other. He nipped her ear playfully, bathing it in the warm humidity of his breath. 'It's simple, really.' Then he whispered very softly, so softly that if it had not been a dream she wouldn't have heard him. But in the dream she heard every word. 'Release him.'

And then they were falling into an abyss, dark and narrow

21

and bottomless. 'Wait. Wait! What do you mean, release him? I can't release him. Are you crazy?' She reached for him, but he fell farther and farther away from her.

'Release him,' he called up to her as he plummeted.

She woke with a jerk from the dream of falling. The smell of sex was all around her. Dawn was breaking pink over the Eastern fells, and she was alone. Of course she was alone. The ghost would have returned to a non-corporeal state once she had fallen back asleep. She sat up bare-arsed on the moss and felt the wet of sex seep from between her legs. One boot was kicked aside and one leg was free from her trousers. Clearly it hadn't all been a dream. Though certainly she'd never experienced anything like it before. Whoever this ghost was, he was brazen, and he was a damn good fuck.

And he practised dream magic. For a second she contemplated the dream they had shared. Sex was usually an integral part of dream magic, and what was revealed in the Dream World was often couched in a sexual context. That was no surprise. But what did the man mean about releasing Deacon in order to destroy him? The woman from her earlier dream and the woman he talked about were clearly the same. Who was she, and what power did she have to rid the world of Deacon? If there were any such woman with that kind of power, then she needed to find her.

She found the handkerchief in her trouser pocket and cleaned herself as best she could under the circumstances. It was then that she noticed the smell. The smell of sex was not just the smell of her female juices running thick, as she would have expected. There was definitely the base note of semen, and not just that, there was the smell of the man who had been in her arms. There was the smell of male sweat and pheromones. A chill ran down her spine. Ghosts had no scent. Even when they were in the flesh, even when they were totally corporeal under the enfleshment spell, the one thing they did not have, ever, was a scent of their own. She sniffed at the air again, then at the handkerchief. The man with whom she'd just had sex was definitely not a ghost.

22

For a second she felt as though the rock beneath her had fallen away. How could she have mistaken this man, whoever he was, for a ghost? That just didn't happen. Ever. Even a rank newbie at sex magic could tell the difference between a ghost enfleshed and someone living. And she hadn't had sex with a living male in more years than she could easily remember. Oh, there was no concern for unprotected sex. That was never an issue with those who practised sex magic with ghosts – ghost riders, as Fiori called them. The magic they did shielded them from disease and unwanted pregnancy even when they weren't with ghosts. It wasn't that. It was that it simply couldn't have happened. That was the point. Either the man was a ghost or he wasn't. She would have known. She couldn't have not known. And yet the scent of semen didn't lie.

Quickly she dressed, drank the rest of the water and headed back down to Grange, her mind racing at the experience she had just shared.

Chapter Three

Anderson had known what was happening to him the instant he had felt Deacon strike and, in truth, it was not unexpected, though he had hoped he could avoid such a fate. It was because he had known that he was able to reset the magical clock in his mind, the one that he always set when he rode the Ether. Had he not done so, he would not now have any knowledge of how long he had been trying to find his way out of the Ether and back to Elemental Cottage, back to Tara. Back to Cassandra.

His sojourn in the Land of the Living had already endured long after his death, and four months and two days in the Ether was as nothing really. In truth, he had been lost in the Ether before, though never for quite this length of time. Nor had he ever had such a pressing reason to return to the World of the Flesh before. Oh, he believed with all of his heart that the efforts to imprison Deacon had succeeded. He had no doubt that Cassandra was completely capable of carrying out the task set before her. He believed the rage she would have felt at Deacon's act of sending him, weakened as he was, so unceremoniously into the depths of the Ether would have almost certainly guaranteed Cassandra's success. Therefore he believed that for these past four months Deacon had been safely trapped in the scrying mirror prison, unable to do further harm. Thus he would continue to believe until he had reason to think otherwise. He was sure that if Deacon were still in the Ether, he would be ruthlessly hunting him at this very moment as a part of his ongoing effort to avenge himself on Tara Stone and those she loved.

Anderson knew Tara loved him as much as he loved her, and knowing how she would mourn his loss kept him sharply focused on his efforts to find his way back to Elemental Cottage. But it was Cassandra who drove him, Cassandra who filled his thoughts, Cassandra who made him ache in ways he would not have believed possible in this disembodied state. Anderson had had many lovers, in fact all of the other members of the Elemental Coven were, on occasion, his lovers, and in the 150 years since his death, and the 38 before, he had been in varying degrees of love. But no one had ever so completely possessed his heart as had Cassandra Larkin. And he knew her well enough to know that she would blame herself for his loss; that she would search for him night and day in the Ether, and that she would mourn his absence as he mourned hers.

Unfinished business. That was the term the charlatans who pretended to understand the ways of the dead used to describe the plight of ghosts and their reason for remaining behind in the land of the living. Anderson had never been concerned with unfinished business. Anderson had always lived in the present, before his death and since. But now, for the first time, there was unfinished business, and it all involved the people he loved beyond the Ether. Mostly it was the unfinished business of the heart that drove him, drove him as nothing else could have. His most fervent desire was that Cassandra was safe in the comforting arms of the Elemental Coven. His most fervent desire was that the young succubus had not withdrawn once again into herself, into the lonely world of books and vicarious lust that had been her plight before she had so unceremoniously pulled him into the Ether and made love with him. He could not bear the thought of her mourning his loss alone even as he knew she would blame herself for that loss. He could not bear the thought of any of the Elemental Coven mourning him. He was unharmed. He supposed it was comparable to being stuck in heavy traffic on Spaghetti Junction in Birmingham, or at least what Tim and

Tara had told him of the experience. He was just going to be stuck a little longer, that was all.

It was the reverberations of sex with Cassandra in the Ether that guided him, as much as it were possible to be guided in the Ether. As far as he knew no one had ever had sex in the Ether before, and the Ether held in its emptiness the memory of every spell, every whisper, every nuance that had ever happened within. Yet the void was vast, and it was rare indeed to come across an echo of one of those memories, and even when one did, reading those memories was difficult at best, and his circumstances did not, at the moment, qualify as the best.

The uniqueness of their shared memory made it somewhat easier to feel in the Ether than any of the other memories, almost as though what the two of them had done together had fundamentally changed the whole of the void – on a very minute level, it was true – but changed it nonetheless. He felt the memory of their lust like muscle memory in places where there was, at the moment, no muscle, for he wore no body during most of his sojourn. It was a waste of magical energy and a psychic weight he did not need to carry in his urgent efforts to get home to Cassandra. However, when the lust felt strongest, as though he may have found a sense of direction, he took upon himself the magical body he wore in the Ether and pleasured his manhood with all manner of thoughts of Cassandra and the delights they had found in each other's arms as well as with the fantasies his imagination could conjure of what liberties he would take with her upon their reunion.

The relieving of his needs not only opened him to the signature of their shared lust still remaining in the Ether, but created new memories of his own lust, which he hoped might attract Cassandra's attention as she searched for him. It was a risk, for it might also lure Deacon to him if Deacon had not been imprisoned by Cassandra and the Elemental Coven, but it was a risk he was willing to take, believing with all of his heart that they had succeeded in their mission to once again bind Deacon. And he hoped against hope that the final binding would end Deacon's reign of terror for ever. Thrice bound and once released, the aging books of shadows had said. Oh, that at last Tara could be free of his wickedness! Such was Anderson's fervent hope. That would indeed be cause to celebrate. The not knowing was a strain on even his patience, and he was a man well noted for patience.

Only once in the very early days of his sojourn had he been certain that his assurances of his safety and his words of encouragement had reached his dear friends, and especially Cassandra and Tara. He knew by his clock that it had been Full Moon at the time, a time when magic would have been high at Elemental Cottage. He had not counted on Cassandra and Tara sharing love to comfort one another. The sharing of pleasure between a succubus and the most powerful witch Anderson had ever known was enough to raise the level of the magic he needed to get a message through to them. Since then, he had not been so lucky, even on Full Moon.

At the moment – if there could be such a thing as a moment in the Ether – he felt the rise of the memory of their lust, and he was very near certain that he was following the ripple it had left in the Ether, growing closer to the familiar place of entry, though how close, it was impossible to tell in the void.

He had meticulously followed the ripple for nearly three days now. It was the longest he had ever been on the trail of the memory. Of course, shiftings and shudderings in the Ether could quickly and easily disorientate a rider. He had had luck in that the Ether had remained calm.

Even though he was certain the memory was stronger, there was still no way of judging just how close he was to the beacons the coven would have, no doubt, set to amplify the signal. In the Ether there was never really any certainty. But the success of the past three days meant that his own lust had grown heavy with his efforts, as it always did when he came in direct contact with the ripple in the Ether that belonged to Cassandra and himself. And even in non-corporeal form, the weight of it was immense.

When he could endure it no longer without relieving his needs, he magicked his ethereal body, a body which reflected instantly the intensity of his arousal. Gently he cupped his testicles and drew a heavy breath that was not real, though it certainly felt real at the moment. In his ethereal body, he felt more clearly the thread that drew him ever closer to Cassandra, and the longer he could hold his physical form and delay his release, the more powerfully his lust would penetrate the Ether.

For a length of time, which he did not bother to calculate on his ethereal clock, he cupped himself and controlled his breathing carefully, rhythmically as a lover from China had once taught him to do in order to prolong his pleasure and that of his partner. But his Oriental lover had never had to contend with lust in the Ether. The mere touch of his hand against his manhood caused him to shudder, and he gripped the head of his penis with the hard press of his thumb to prevent the emptying of his seed for just a little longer.

He set his mind to thoughts of his beautiful Cassandra, not just the exquisite sexuality that was hers as a succubus, nor the fact that her body was endlessly appealing to him, but that he loved her, that her mind was sharp and her imagination creative, that her hunger for knowledge was second only to her lust. The pulsating power of his need synchronised with his thoughts, with his ache for the presence of the woman he loved, for her smile, for her laughter, which was intoxicating and had been all too rare in the brief time he had known her. He longed to return to her and fill her life with many reasons to laugh. The ache and the arousal built together, swirling upward in a spiral of sexual magic, tightly controlled by his many years of training lust to do his magical bidding.

And for the briefest of moments, too brief even to register on his clock, he felt her, felt her with Marie and Tim, felt the three of them brush against the Ether, and his heart raced. Concentrating as hard as he was, he held his lust, held it tight, reached out to her with his fullness, with the depth and the

28

breadth of all he felt, of all the magic he could summon, then he sent it out along the pulse of his arousal.

Holding his breath, he waited, listened, opened himself to all he could remember of Cassandra, amazed at just how much he could recall. And when he felt himself on the edge, when he felt himself close enough that he could once again contact her, the Ether heaved and shuddered, and he lost the ripple.

He sat silently holding himself, careful to breathe slowly and cautiously, careful not to let his disappointment interfere with the spell he still wove. It was just as he regained his focus that he felt another ripple. And it was not the ripple of an old spell cast by a witch centuries before, though it had not the feel of new magic either. In fact, it had not the feel of magic at all. The shudder became a pulse, at first slow and erratic, then regular as a heartbeat through the Ether, and with a chill that rose up his spine, Anderson became aware that he was no longer alone.

'Who are you?' He spoke out. He had never walked the Ether in fear. Even Deacon he had not feared in this place. Deacon was no master of the Ether; he was only a trespasser in its realm. And this, this presence he felt was not one he recognised.

The brush of it was so close that he fancied he could hear breathing, even feel the brush of it against his ear, feel the scrutiny of the gaze that passed over him, examining him, lingering to examine his aroused condition.

'Who are you?' he asked again.

A soft sigh rippled through the Ether, and he felt it like soft lips caressing his manhood and he could hold off the inevitable no longer. He spilled his seed in convulsive shudders into the void.

Chapter Four

The three stood in a circle around the last of the second set of magical beacons in the Ether. They were casting the spell that would reinforce its power. It was only the second set from the originals and not the distant beacons that Cassandra and Tara had set at the last Full Moon. Only they had skill enough to reach the remote beacons safely. Once the spell was cast the beacon flared bright and steadied to a pulse that Cassandra knew Tim and Marie could only barely feel at this stage in their ethereal training. But she felt it like a resonant frequency low in her abdomen, getting more and more uncomfortable until, at last, it synced with the rhythm of her heart – well, the heart of her ethereal body anyway.

She seldom wore her ethereal body when she worked magic in the void unless she had good cause, and she certainly didn't need it for setting the beacons and recharging them. But Tim and Marie were just learning to ride the Ether, and they both still needed a corporeal form and tended to feel a bit disorientated when she had none. Still, they were doing amazingly well considering they had only begun their training shortly after Anderson's disappearance. That Tim was able to enter the Ether at all was astounding. The only other man ever to ride the Ether was Anderson. She wondered if perhaps Tim's abilities were somehow connected to his intimate relationship with Anderson. Of course, it could well be that Tim was another anomaly, as Anderson had been.

Cassandra knew that from the very beginning, long before Tim had any idea, the Elemental Coven had been well aware of just how powerful he had the potential to become, though even now, the man never seemed to view himself as anything special. He always thought of himself as a simple Cumbrian farmer instead of one of the most powerful witches in the most powerful coven Cassandra had ever known. Anything that Marie and Tim were capable of didn't surprise her since almost a year ago, the two of them had subdued Deacon with very little training. That was before she had come into the picture. What they lacked in skill, they both more than made up for in raw talent and enthusiasm.

Most witches avoided ethereal magic at all costs. It was difficult, unpredictable and dangerous. There was always a chance of becoming confused, then lost never to return. But Marie and Tim had both insisted on being trained.

She felt their commitment with a little tug at her ethereal heart. They both loved Anderson. And she knew that he had a very soft spot in his heart for them and had taken them both as lovers, as they had now taken her, for comfort, for strength, and to deepen her bond with the Elemental Coven. She had only spent one night in Tara's bed. Since then, Tara had taken no one for comfort, and would hear nothing on the subject when it was broached by the other coven members.

'That's it. All finished,' Tim said, smiling up at Cassandra and unnecessarily wiping his hands on his trousers. He and Marie shared a meaningful look, and Cassandra waited for it. The two had a bond that was almost telepathic, but she had no need to read their minds with the scheming look they both wore.

'I feel great,' Marie said with a smile that was contagious. 'Don't you, Tim?' She didn't wait for his enthusiastic nod. 'So if we both feel great and our energy levels are good, can we go on and reinforce the third set of beacons?'

Before Cassandra could respond, Tim added, 'We're ready. You said it yourself, we're doing really well, and we both agreed that if we felt OK and if you're OK with it, we'd like to go on to the next set of beacons this time.'

'Are you sure?' Cassandra was careful to keep her voice neutral, to keep the smile that threatened to take over her mouth at bay. They were ready. It would be no hardship for them to reach the third set of beacons and return safely, and their enthusiasm was inspiring.

Marie held her gaze. 'We want Anderson back. Whatever it takes.' She interlaced her fingers with Tim's and gave them a squeeze.

'All right, then.' Cassandra nodded deeper into the Ether in the direction from which she could feel the low, pulsing rhythm of the third set of beacons. 'I want you to let me know when you can feel them,' she said, turning and pressing forward along the path she had magically created in the void. 'Honing your sensitivity is crucial to keeping yourselves safe in the Ether. With no landmarks, the ripples of spell memory are all you have to go on, that and your own internal clock. You can't afford to miss anything.' She had given them the lecture before *ad nauseam*, and yet each time they listened intently, and each time they took her completely at her word. She knew they would already be opening themselves and their senses, feeling for spell memories, for ripples, for flexing, for anything that might give them a sense of the shape of the little section of the void which they now traversed.

Tim and Marie could now do the preparation magic needed to cross the threshold into the Ether easily. And they both could now perform the magic to create the spell clock in their minds to remind them of how long they'd been in the void. But they hadn't yet entered the Ether on their own, though Cassandra knew that would come soon. The couple now spent extended hours in the Elemental Cottage library and took stacks of volumes back to Lacewing Farm with them on a regular basis. And she had noticed that a good number of those volumes were on ethereal magic. Anderson would be proud.

It was as though the thought had suddenly bathed her so strongly in Anderson's presence that she gasped and turned around checking behind her, to each side, heart racing, hope – which she tried to keep in check – soaring.

'Anderson?' both Marie and Tim called out

simultaneously. Cassandra felt them strain too, expecting to see the ghost whose presence they all felt so strongly.

For the tiniest of moments, the Ether felt as though it folded itself around Cassandra in an enthusiastic, yet tender embrace, and the little sob that escaped Marie's throat convinced Cassandra she was feeling it too. Tim, who was not altogether comfortable entering the Ether naked, was suddenly sporting a trouser-tenting erection.

'Come on,' Cassandra shouted, grabbing Marie's hand and nodding for Tim to do the same. 'Hold on and don't let go.' She raced toward the third set of beacons, her feet no longer touching the path that had been magicked only for Marie and Tim's benefit. Her respect for the two, which was already substantial, went up another notch when, in spite of the shock a first flight in the Ether always brought, they kept completely silent, listening, feeling, sending out their senses, doing exactly as she did.

Just as the beacons blipped onto her peripheral senses, the entire void heaved and shuddered, then buckled and twisted as though the torsion would tear it apart. 'Hold on! Hold on!' Cassandra shouted, spinning to throw her arms protectively around Tim and Marie. What appeared to be a communal hug was an effort to keep the two from being torn from her and thrown into the Ether as Anderson had been. She had no intention of losing anyone else in the void.

The feeling of Anderson's presence intensified, quivered, then vanished and the Ether was once again calm as glass. Cassandra felt Tim grunt and convulse, and she knew the experience had made him come. He cursed softly under his breath.

Marie dug her nails into Cassandra's arm just as the third set of beacons burst into flame, exploded, then vanished as though they had never been. The aftershock expanded to fill the space which contained their ethereal bodies, and it was as though a giant hand had given them a mighty shove. Suddenly, they were all three falling at terrifying speed back into their bodies, back to where they lay in the middle of

Tim's lounge floor on a pile of cushions.

Cassandra came to herself shivering and shouting. 'Don't move! Lie still! We've come out of the Ether too fast. Just lie still until you adjust, or you'll be sick enough to regret it.' They were all covered in several blankets and the banked fire still roared in the fireplace. When she went with Marie and Tim, Cassandra was never in the Ether long enough for fires to go out or for bodies to lose terribly much heat, nonetheless they were all shivering. The two obeyed her and lay very still. She scrambled from under the blankets and grabbed her mobile. The same rules didn't apply to her. She was only half-human, and travelling in the Ether had never made her ill. She pressed Tara's number and the coven leader answered immediately with a brusque, 'What is it?' Brusque was only a cover-up for way more concerns than one person should ever have to bear. Cassandra knew that by now, and she had got used to Tara's curt manner.

'Is Deacon still bound?' It was the first question out of her mouth.

'Of course he is,' Tara said. 'We've only just checked the perimeters and strengthened the binding spells a few minutes ago. Why? What happened?'

Cassandra heaved a sigh of relief for that much, though she figured it wasn't him, or he would have made his presence known, and he would have toyed with them before tossing them back into their flesh, which he would only have done if he'd been feeling benevolent. 'We had contact with Anderson, I'm sure,' she began. 'Then there was something else. I don't know what, something that literally shook the whole Ether, left the third rank of beacons in flames and tossed the three of us out like we were so much wadded-up paper.'

'Tim and Marie?' The fear and concern broke through in Tara's voice, as it seldom did. Cassandra had shared Tara's bed. She knew the woman's deepest nightmares. Though she tried not to be invasive, the nightmares of Tara Stone were not easy to avoid for a succubus sleeping next to her. In fact, she doubted if she could have avoided Tara Stone's nightmares if she had been safely tucked away in Wasdale Head.

She glanced over at the couple who were obediently lying very still. 'They're fine. A bit shaken but totally fine.'

After a long moment of silence, Tara asked the question they both wanted an answer to. 'And Anderson?'

Cassandra let out a slow, shaky breath. 'I don't know. One minute I felt him, we all felt him like he was right next to us, and then he was gone.'

There was another long silence, and Cassandra filled the gap. 'I'll be home, we all will be, as soon as Tim and Marie have recovered and eaten.' In her peripheral vision, she could see just the shadow of Lisette, the young ghost from the 1920s who had attached herself to Lacewing Farm and to Tim Meriwether specifically. She motioned the ghost to her, reached out a hand and enfleshed her just as she cut the connection with Tara.

The ghost uttered a surprised gasp, and a shudder ran up her spine. But before she could do more than touch her face in acknowledgment of the flesh that hadn't been there seconds before, Cassandra spoke, nodding to where Tim and Marie lay on the floor, now both fast asleep.

'Lisette, could I impose on you to make something for them to eat? Doesn't have to be elaborate, just food, and they probably won't want to eat it. But make them, and then they'll feel better. I'm sorry. I know it's rude for me to do this to you, but I need your help.'

Lisette was still taking in the parameters of her newly enfleshed body, touching and rediscovering the solid shape of herself, but she nodded enthusiastically. However, as Cassandra turned to go, she grabbed her hand. 'Where are you going?' she asked.

'Back into the Ether to see if I can figure out what happened.' She tried to pull away, but Lisette held her in a firm grip.

'Tara wouldn't like that. Neither would Tim and Marie. I don't like it either.' She nodded to the kitchen. 'There's

35

homemade shortbread that Fiori sent over. Eat some of that, at least, or I won't let you go.'

Cassandra rolled her eyes and bit back a curse, but followed Lisette into the kitchen. 'Next time, I'll enflesh someone a little less cheeky.'

'Next time, I'll ask what you want before I let you enflesh me,' Lisette retorted, though her voice was still warm, and Cassandra could almost hear the self-deprecating smile in her words. 'I'm not the domestic help, you know, and at least Tim and Marie always offer me a good fuck for my efforts.'

'Why are you playing with your cock?' Lucia's voice flooded Kennet's mind, and her presence washed over him causing his penis, which was already heavy in his grip, to surge with the feel of her.

'Men do that sometimes, Lucia. Surely you can't be surprised by my occasional wanking after all this time. Where have you been?' he asked, continuing to stroke the length of himself. 'I woke up and you were gone.'

She ignored his question. 'You have certainly been doing this wanking thing a lot more often since we settled in Cumbria.' He felt her voice almost like a whisper next to his ear. 'Since we settled close to Tara Stone.' Her chuckle felt like silk against his skin, and he had to thumb the head of his cock to keep from coming at the feel of it. He didn't like it when she toyed with him. He didn't like it when she manipulated him sexually. 'She was good this morning, was she not? I have never seen you so aroused, so enthralled. And what a shock when she discovered you were, in fact, not a ghost. You should have seen her face.'

'Where have you been?' he asked again, shoving his boxers down so his arse ground against the tangle of sheets, so he could more easily cup and knead his balls.

'Are you thinking of her? Lucia's voice now felt like a warm breath blowing across his pubic curls. He bit his lip and arched upward into his hands, getting close. Lucia was fascinated with maleness and male sexuality in particular. It was something she hadn't experienced before possessing Kennet.

'You still haven't answered me. Where were you?' His words were breathless, clipped short with the nearness of his release.

Her laugh was light, teasing. 'What? Did you think I had got bored with you and decided to release you and find someone more interesting to possess?'

When he didn't laugh, she continued. 'I had business to take care of in the Ether. Such a dreary place, the Ether.' She sighed, and he felt her move along his skin then up inside him to a place he could never quite pinpoint when she was there, and yet her absence always felt like she had torn him open and his soul had spilled out. He knew that was her doing. It was her way of reminding him that he belonged to her and wherever she had gone, she would return, and he wouldn't be whole until she did.

He felt a chill and his erection softened. 'You didn't –'

'Oh for fuck's sake, of course I did not hurt the ghost. I only shook things up a bit to get the results we need.' She curled tightly around him and he hardened again. 'We are close, my darling, so close to finishing what we began together seven years ago.' He was now certain he felt a female form pressed against him, nipples taut, breasts round and full. 'Tara Stone will not let this incident go, and her response will tell us all we need to know in order to do what we must.' He now felt hips pressed to his groin, thighs opening to provide the sheathing he needed, deep and wet and memorable. It was only as his cock convulsed and he spattered himself and the knot of bedding with his semen that he realised Lucia was causing him to relive sex with Tara Stone. He wanted to hate her for it, but somehow he just couldn't manage it.

Chapter Five

'Are you sure about this?' Sky said. Both she and Fiori flanked Tara at the door to the Room of Reflection. Neither of them made any effort to hide their displeasure.

'I'm sure,' Tara said. 'I'm never in physical danger from Deacon. Not when there are so many more horrible ways he can make me suffer. I figure he'll be delighted at the opportunity to taunt me.'

'That's not funny,' Fiori said.

'It wasn't meant to be.' Tara didn't feel even the slightest bit light-hearted at the moment.

Sky looked down at her watch, which she really didn't need. The spell had already been cast. It was for emphasis mostly, Tara reckoned. 'You have ten minutes. Not a second more. Do you understand?'

Tara nodded absently, already clearing the last of the blocking enchantments as she stepped into the room. They were the spells that had been set so that Deacon's presence would not interfere with any of the magic or other activities in Elemental Cottage or even with the simple serenity that was an essential part of the place's atmosphere. That enchantment worked both ways as there was something disturbing about living in a house that had inadvertently become a prison for a dangerous demon.

As prepared as Tara was for their meeting, the sight of Deacon's life-size image projected above the altar was shocking, even though it was just an image. He sat cross-legged in the middle of the altar. In truth, he could have projected his image anywhere in the room. The fact that he chose to sit right in the middle of the Elemental Coven's altar was an insult he knew full well she would understand. Still, he couldn't help but be slightly wrong-footed that she had allowed him this much freedom from his prison to communicate with her in this powerfully protected space.

She met his gaze as though he were nothing to her. She had learned long ago to remain untouchable to him and never to let him know her pain. She moved methodically around the room opening the lace curtains to allow more sunlight to penetrate the space, to shine through him, her own subtle reminder that he was her prisoner, and he was powerless.

He raised an eyebrow and glanced around the space. 'Where are the others, my dear Tara? I had so hoped to greet each of your lovely coven family in person. It would have been such a tender reunion.'

'This is not a social visit, Deacon,' Tara said.

He offered her a pout that was only a breath away from a chuckle. 'I'm wounded to the core, my darling. I have so few opportunities to entertain these days that I must confess I was looking forward to a little soiree, of sorts.' He looked around the room, then down at his hands inspecting his fingernails. 'Everyone is well, I presume, Fiori, Sky, Marie, Tim, and how's our little succubus settling in? Oh, and I nearly forgot to ask after your ghost. Has he returned yet from his extended stay in the Ether?'

Tara ignored him. 'I'm curious about the Ether, Deacon,' she said, then shrugged modestly. 'As you know, the Ether isn't my forte, and though it's Cassandra's … well, she's young and inexperienced.'

He steepled his fingers beneath his chin and studied her. His form seemed to waver, then grow stronger. 'My dear Tara, surely you know that I am no ethereal magician.' The corner of his mouth quirked slightly. 'No doubt your ghost, when he was with you, told you that. I found myself there quite by accident in my efforts to escape your last attempt to bind me. However, a demon uses what's available, and the Ether is pliable. Even one who is not adept in ethereal magic

39

knows that, my darling. Did not your mother teach you this when you were still on her knee? That in spite of the dangers, any spell performed is exponentially more powerful. If that is so for a mere witch, imagine how much more so it is for a demon.' His face grew suddenly serious. 'Sadly, there's little companionship in the Ether, so naturally I longed to return to my flesh.' He tisk-tisked. 'Such an uncooperative lot, you and your witches.'

She took a deep breath and asked, 'If you chose to, could you find Anderson and bring him back?'

Once again he returned to studying his fingernails. 'If I chose to, perhaps I might be able to.' He offered her a wicked smile. 'But you cannot force me, my dear Tara, and since your Anderson is, after all, a master of ethereal magic, I am certain given enough time he shall prevail.'

She pressed on, ignoring the taunt. 'Could anyone other than a demon manage to powerfully affect the Ether?'

He stiffened ever so slightly and his image became darker, unsettled, like roiling smoke. 'Demons have little need of the Ether, woman. It is the realm of puny human witches with precious little power or imagination to amplify, which of course makes them desperate. He straightened himself and tugged at his waistcoat. 'I myself would not have troubled with the Ether had your debacle of my binding left me any other choice.'

'That's not an answer to my question, Deacon, so I'll ask you again. Could anyone other than a demon manage to powerfully affect the Ether?' She moved closer, and he slid off the altar and came to stand in front of her, nearly nose to nose. Even though it was only his image projected into the room, she felt his closeness like a wave of heat, but she held her ground. She wouldn't be cowed by the bastard in her own home.

'Why?' he asked. 'What has happened that you ask this of me? I may be your prisoner at the moment, Tara Stone, but my incarceration has not rendered me stupid. If you want my help then you must tell me what has happened.'

She held his gaze for a long moment, then heaved a sigh of resignation. 'I don't have to tell you anything, Deacon.' She clasped the pentacle on the dark cord around her neck and stroked the rim of it in a counter-clockwise motion to begin the reversal spell, and his eyes widened.

Then he shrugged and offered her a bored smile as she paused in her working of the spell. 'It matters not to me who is or is not in the Ether, my dear Tara. But you are correct. No one but a demon can do more than the feeble bending and shaping of insignificant spells you witches do. The Ether is too vast for any human mind, or even that of your little succubus to truly penetrate.' His smile looked almost warm and kindly as he moved still closer and looked down on her from his considerable height. 'Now tell me, my dear Tara, what has happened in the Ether that you would summon me from my prison for a conference? Tell me the situation and it may be that we can help each other.'

The words had barely left his lips before there was a harsh buzzing sound in the room. His image flashed bright then vanished, just as the doors to the Room of Reflection burst open and Fiori and Sky rushed in.

'What happened?' Sky asked. 'Did he tell you what you needed to know?'

'Not on purpose,' Tara replied. Her legs were unsteady, and she began to tremble. It was just pride, she knew, but she was thankful she hadn't done so in front of Deacon.

Tara settled at the desk in her study with three books on demons she'd taken from the Elemental library and four very old books of shadows, including two that had belonged to her mother. While she had raided the stacks, Fiori had left a sandwich and a pot of tea for her and built a fire in the fireplace, knowing that doing high magic would have left her chilled. She ate the sandwich without tasting it and burned her tongue on the tea while she flipped through the first of the books on demons.

She had returned from the night's adventure on the fells

and was just out of the shower when Cassandra had called. The whole experience on the fells had shaken her. What had happened was not a mistake she should have made, and now what had happened in the Ether had left her feeling even more unsettled. The stress of having lost Anderson had always been tempered by the fact that he was skilled in ethereal magic and would find his way back if anyone could. But after what had happened today ... Dear Goddess, she dared not even think the thoughts that fought their way into her consciousness.

She tossed aside the book she'd been perusing and carefully opened one of her mother's books of shadows, the older of the two.

Fire draweth a demon as doth no other element. It is the element of a demon's strength, it is the key ingredient to a demon's magic. And all things that have at the heart of their existence heat and fire and flame and the passion and the temperament thereof shall a demon draw upon and revel therein. Though some have speculated such, it hath not been proved that a demon may also draw upon water or air or earth, nor is there recorded in the archives of the elders any such encounter with any demon other than what hath drawn up strength to be made manifest through the element of fire.

Her mother had taught her this when she was still a child, even before Deacon tore their world apart. Tara racked her brain. Had she ever heard of any demon that wasn't a fire demon? Come to think of it, had she ever heard of any other demon besides Deacon? Certainly in her very long life she had never encountered another, for which she was thankful. The thought of more like Deacon wreaking havoc and destroying people's lives made her feel queasy. Could the world even contain another such demon and survive? How could it be that she had spent her whole life doing battle with Deacon and had never really given any thought to the possibility of others like him?

Having said that, if there were others like him, they bore her no ill will that she knew of, and she would definitely know about it if they did. So if it were a demon that Cassandra and Marie and Tim had confronted in the Ether, why was it there? What did it want? And, dear Goddess, grant that it bore Anderson no ill will. She was so caught up in the elegant twists and turns of her mother's script and her own speculation that she hadn't noticed the encroaching chill in the room; she hadn't noticed the flame that danced in the grate had turned an icy shade of blue. And how could she not have noticed his breath raising goose-flesh along the nape of her neck?

'Deacon,' she whispered, feeling her stomach drop. She was careful to keep her words firm and even. 'What are you doing here?'

His breath seemed slightly accelerated, and his chuckle seemed unusually warm in the chill. 'Can I not visit you, my love, for the simple pleasure of your company?' He drew a large warm hand along her shoulder and up her nape where her pulse hammered a sharp staccato she couldn't quite control. Then with his fingers he traced a path upward along the side of her face. The memory of him touching Fiori in just the same way only seconds before her death flashed through Tara's head, and she twisted away from his touch.

He stood behind her, just out of her field of vision, but she felt his breath humid and heavy against the top of her head. 'Do you not yet see and understand, my dearest Tara?' He moved to sit on the edge of her desk, looking down at her with eyes that were dark chasms. 'You and I shall outlive all of the others.' He made an open-armed, expansive gesture around the room. 'Our rage, our anger, our desire for power and revenge shall keep us for ever young and potent long after this ragtag band you've assembled here at Elemental Cottage has perished.'

He took her hand in his and raised it to lips that were impossibly soft and warm against her knuckles. 'Do you think I do not hear the petitions of your nightmares? Do you think I do not understand your very human desire for an end to all of this banality? But of course I shall not destroy you, my beauty. It's your power, your heart, your lust for which I live.

43

Have you not yet reasoned this out, my darling?'

Tara jerked upright in her chair, forcing her way into the Waking World, heart racing, sweat beading between her breasts. There was a soft knock on the door and Sky stuck her head in.

'Cassandra's here with Marie and Tim. Fiori's served lunch.' She stepped inside. 'Tara? Are you all right?'

'Fine.' Tara stood and tugged her cardi tightly around her. 'Fine. Just a bit unsettled by everything that's been going on, that's all. Come on. Let's not keep Fiori waiting. You know how tetchy she gets when we're late to the table.'

Chapter Six

Lunch was a hearty beef stroganoff with homemade Russian rye bread and a salad of beetroot and carrot in pomegranate vinaigrette. Everyone ate ravenously, as was usually the case after magic had been performed. They all listened while Cassandra, Marie and Tim recounted what had happened to them in the Ether.

'I tried to go back in after we were forced out,' Cassandra said between bites, 'but for some reason, I couldn't.' She raised a fork to wave off Tara's anticipated question. 'I was perfectly fine. I had plenty of energy. We'd only gone as far as the third beacons, and we were only reinforcing the spells. I should have been able to get back past the threshold with no problems.'

Tara nodded agreement. 'But what could have kept you out?'

'You're certain it wasn't Deacon?' Tim asked.

'It wasn't him,' Tara said. 'I had the distinct feeling he wasn't any more pleased about what happened than we are.'

'Really?' Marie said. 'That's strange.'

'He seemed rather offended that I would think anyone but a demon could have such a powerful effect on the Ether. Then he seemed almost desperate for me to tell him what had happened. Like suddenly he wanted to be my best friend.'

'But you didn't,' Cassandra said. 'You didn't tell him.'

Tara glared at her. 'What the hell do you think?'

'And you say there was no sense of Anderson after ...' Fiori tried, but couldn't finish the question that plagued all of them.

Cassandra laid down her fork and stared at her plate. 'One minute I felt him as though he were in my arms. Then the whole Ether shook and twisted like it was coming apart. After that the beacons exploded, and the connection was broken. That's all I know.'

'So if we can trust Deacon – and that's a huge if,' Sky said, 'then we have to assume that whoever caused the incident in the Ether was a demon.' That idea silenced them all for a minute, and other than the occasional clink of cutlery and an enthusiastic robin outside the kitchen window, the room was silent.

'Has anyone here ever met a demon other than Deacon?' Marie asked. When no one replied, she said, 'Has anyone ever even heard of another demon besides Deacon? Cassandra, what about your father? Could it have been him?'

'Honestly, I don't know,' Cassandra said. 'The only one who ever mentioned my father to me is Deacon, and we know what a liar he is. There were some things in my grandmother's book of shadows, though.'

'What things?' Tara asked, tapping a fingernail on the edge of her teacup.

'I don't remember the details,' Cassandra said. 'I remember being disappointed that it didn't give me the information I was looking for, you know, about how I … came to be.' A blush crawled up her throat, and she continued. 'When I couldn't make any connection to my own situation, I chalked it up to more myth and lore. Gran was big on myth and lore. Most of it was just stuff about demons always being attracted to and gathering strength from the element of fire. Every fledgling witch knows that. There might have been more, but the book of shadows I have is the only one that survived the fire.'

The kitchen was suddenly silent again. 'What fire?' Sky asked.

'After my grandmother died, before I could go through her belongings, there was a fire in her house. The library was fine, not touched, but there was some malfunction with an electric

46

heater in her study. Her books of shadows were all in there except the one I had. She kept them all in a locked metal safe. They would have been fine if I hadn't taken them out to study them. I had them all sorted by date, lying on her desk.' For a moment, Cassandra sat silently, staring into a past only she could see. At last she blinked, cleared her throat and pushed back her chair. 'Right. I'll go get it.'

She returned shortly with the book, shoved aside her empty plate and opened it on the table. The passage she read was nearly identical to the one Tara had read earlier from her mother's book of shadows. Then Cassandra stopped reading and flipped through several pages, then back again, frowning down at the book.

'What is it?' Tara asked.

'It's some poetry or something. I always thought it was from the *Bible* or the *pseudepigrapha* or some such. Gran said that lots of the passages in the *Bible* and associated texts were really secret spells and stories of our people hidden in an obvious place, but a place where they were guaranteed to be preserved – you know, *Song of Songs*, some of the *Proverbs*. But this, well I thought it might be about the Goddess, but …'

'Read it,' Tara said.

'First, she has this excerpt from *Revelation* Chapter 12.' Cassandra read.

1 And there appeared a great wonder in heaven; a woman clothed with the sun, and the moon under her feet, and upon her head a crown of twelve stars.
2 And she being with child cried, travailing in birth, and pained to be delivered.
3 And there appeared another wonder in heaven; and behold a great red dragon, having seven heads and ten horns, and seven crowns upon his heads.
4 And his tail drew the third part of the stars of heaven, and did cast them to the earth: and the dragon stood before the woman which was ready to be delivered, for to devour her child as soon as it was born.

Cassandra waved her hand absently. 'Gran was always adding bits of scripture. She used it as code that only she and her coven sisters understood. She never taught me. I don't know why. But this bit –' she pointed a slender finger at the text '– I know this is not from the *Bible*. I don't know where it comes from.' She read on.

She who the sun cannot outshine seeks you out in darkness and burns you with her light.

All your gifts are as nothing to her if she possesseth not your soul. And when that gift you freely offer up, she who is robed in flame will give to you the desires of your heart in return.

She shall be with you in your sleeping and your waking, and no secret shall you keep from her, even to the ebb and the flow of the very blood in your veins. And your breath shall she take for her very own until it passes from you and she returns you to dust.

Tara felt suddenly cold. She chafed her arms.

'What is it?' Sky asked.

'I don't know, but I think that woman was in my dreams last night'

Cassandra shivered as though she felt the same chill. 'Wait a minute, do you think Gran was talking about a demon here, a specific demon?'

'Tell us what happened, Tara,' Sky said.

Tara would have rather done just about anything than tell her coven what she'd experienced on the fells, but Anderson was at risk and, for all she knew, three more of her coven could have been seriously injured or worse in the Ether. For all she knew, they could be dealing with a threat as powerful as Deacon. At least Deacon was the devil they knew. She took a deep breath, drank back her tea for courage. Then she told her experience.

When she was finished everyone sat in stunned silence. Perhaps they were embarrassed at too much information. She certainly was. She shifted in her chair and stared down at her hands clasped in her lap.

It was Marie who finally spoke. 'Let me get this straight, you think this demon, if that's what she is, sent this bloke, whoever he is, to fuck you and fool you into thinking he was a ghost, and then she did whatever the hell it was she did in the Ether as well. And she's a she. This demon is female?'

'Do you have a better explanation,' Tara asked.

Marie shook her head, and so did everyone else.

'Wow! She's had a busy morning, whoever she is,' Tim said.

'Did he give you a name?' Cassandra asked. 'This guy you were with?'

'We weren't exactly in conversation mode,' Tara replied.

'The question is why,' Tim said. 'Why would this demon or whatever she is care about your sex life?'

Fiori served up bowls of rhubarb crumble with homemade custard. 'Sounds to me like this woman or demon or whatever she is, did you a favour. You've been acting like a damned nun lately, and abstinence doesn't become you.'

'Mind your own business, Fiori,' Tara said.

'No argument that you needed a good fucking.' Sky dug into her crumble and spoke with her mouth full. 'But what did that have to do with what happened in the Ether? What happened to you was benign, in fact it was a kindness if ever there was one, but did any of you get the feeling that what happened in the Ether was malignant?' She shot each of the three who had been in the void a glance.

'I didn't get a feeling one way or another,' Cassandra said. 'But whatever it was destroyed the third set of beacons completely. I wouldn't exactly call that an act of friendship.'

'And it was with fire,' Tim said. 'Or at least the ethereal version of fire.'

'Also,' Marie added, 'for a second we all felt Anderson very intensely, and then, when whatever happened happened, it was though he had been jerked away from us.'

'Does Anderson have any enemies?' Tim asked.

'None that I know of,' Tara replied. 'And he wouldn't have kept a demon from me, not when he knew what we were already dealing with.'

'Are there any mentions of this woman clothed in fire in your mother's books of shadows?' Cassandra asked.

'No,' Tara said. 'Only the usual teachings about demons taking their power from the element of fire, that and the bits we think could be about Deacon. My mother had her own form of code, and she was inconsiderate enough to die before she taught it me. But there are books of shadows of witches other than my mother in the Elemental library. Under the circumstances, that might be the place to begin.'

'I want to go into the Ether as soon as possible,' Cassandra said. 'I want to look at what remains of the beacons and see if I can get a feel for what happened from any residual energy left there. And –' she took a deep breath '– and I want to see if I can get any sense of Anderson.'

Tara laid a hand on her arm. 'Wait till tomorrow, only because you'll be at full strength then and, if you have to push and shove your way in, you'll be more able.' She held her gaze. 'And I'll be prepared by then to go in with you.'

'We might also make some attempts to find this man you fucked,' Fiori said. 'Do you think you'd recognise him if you saw him? I mean, it was the middle of the night.'

Tara squirmed in her chair. 'I'd recognise his smell, and the feel of him.'

Marie sniggered, then covered her mouth with her hand when Tara gave her a serrated glare.

'I mean the feel of his presence,' said Tara. But she was certain she would also recognise the feel of him if he touched her again. She'd never felt anything like his touch before. Marie offered her a cheeky grin, but had the good grace to keep her mouth shut.

'That's not a lot to go on,' Fiori said. 'You can't just run through the streets of Keswick sniffing men and feeling them up.'

Tara stood, gritting her teeth in what was a very poor

attempt at a smile. 'That being the case, then maybe we should start with the library, since I'm a lot less likely to get arrested for browsing through mouldy spell books, and our chances of success are better.'

'What about dream magic?' Tim asked. 'You said the two of you did dream magic together. Maybe you should try to find him that way.'

Just then the doorbell rang and Sky went to answer it.

'I'll consider dream magic after we've looked through the books of shadows,' Tara said. 'But if this demon is responsible for what happened between me and this man, then she may also be able to keep me from finding him in the dream world.'

'You're assuming he doesn't want to be found.'

Tara recognised the voice before she turned to see the man standing next to Sky at the kitchen door. He was tall with coppery brown hair that glinted in the sunlight coming through the window. His shoulders looked even broader in the light of day. He was dressed in jeans and a brushed denim shirt, and his eyes were a warm olive hazel that held her in the same intense gaze they had only a few hours ago when she could only feel it and not see it. He stepped forward and offered her his hand. 'I thought after what happened on the fells, maybe I should stop by and introduce myself.'

No one spoke, and Tara dared them to even breathe a smirk. But all eyes were on her and the first man – who wasn't a ghost – that she'd had sex with in the better part of a hundred years. And as she took his hand, she knew she was exactly right. She would recognise his touch anywhere. The power of it raced up through her arm and straight to her heart, and the little hitch of his breath and the flutter of his eyelids told her he felt it too. As he stepped closer, she was engulfed in his glorious desert-heat scent of maleness, which she felt in places far removed from the touch of his hand. Her pulse raced, her breath was suddenly rapid and shallow, and the room around her seemed thin and insubstantial. In fact the only thing that felt as though it had any real substance was the man standing in front of her, smiling unselfconsciously, holding her hand in a grip that was warm and tight and somehow almost desperate. She forced her attention back to the words now coming from his parted full lips.

'It's a pleasure to meet you in the daylight, Tara Stone.' His fingers tightened around hers, and his smile made her insides squirm and warm. 'I'm Kennet, Kennet Lucian.'

Chapter Seven

The world spun and faded, and Tara was suddenly falling away from it, like she had done in the dream on the fells. Her vision blurred and she found herself standing in a medieval walled garden that smelled of roses and lavender. The skin along the back of her neck prickled, and the feeling of someone too close, someone who didn't belong there, slithered and knotted its way up her spine. Fighting the overwhelming urge to run away, she turned slowly, cautiously to discover the woman in the flaming robe standing next to her, watching her intently, and somehow, even her stunning beauty didn't quite take away the urge to run.

'Are you all right, love?' she asked. Then she laughed lightly, and Tara felt like tiny silver bells were ringing inside her head. 'He has that effect, our Kennet. Though I have to say, I have never seen such fireworks.' She leaned close, and her full lips curved in a delicious smile that, in spite of her distress, Tara found herself wanting to kiss. 'You should see the effect you have on him. The naughty boy.'

'He said you could help us.' Tara forced the words through her tight throat.

'Did he?' The woman's voice was passive. 'Well, you were dreaming. You, of all people, should know that dream magic is not a precise science.'

'Can you?' Tara said. 'Can you help us destroy Deacon?'

Again the soft bell-tinkle of her laughter. 'Are you so anxious to be rid of one of your most fervent admirers?'

Tara shivered as she thought of the dream of Deacon she'd had in her study, but she ignored the question. 'Can you help us?'

The woman studied her audaciously, and Tara fought hard not to look away from the fire in her eyes. 'Perhaps I can, Tara Stone. Perhaps we can help each other.' A prickly feeling of déjà vu washed over Tara as the woman pulled her into her arms and whispered something close to her ear. But Tara couldn't hear above all the shouting and the ruckus, and someone was calling her name. Why wouldn't they all just shut up? This was important. She needed to hear.

'Get away from her! Get the hell away from her!' Tim was shouting. Then everyone was shouting at once, and she couldn't breathe. As her eyes fluttered open, she realised it was because she was sitting on the kitchen floor clutched tightly to Kennet's chest.

His face was pale and he was stroking her cheek. Just as Tim grabbed him by the shoulders, Kennet back-handed him, nailing him in the jaw with his knuckles. Tim recoiled, cursed and was about to grab him again when Tara forced her way into a sitting position and said, louder than she intended, 'Stop it. Both of you. Stop it now.'

The two froze, as though they were involved in a friendly children's game of statues. 'Are you all right?' Both men asked at the same time.

She nodded, rubbing her temples, which ached as though her head had been in a vice. 'I was with her.'

'You what?' Both men spoke at the same time again, then Kennet said something under his breath that she couldn't quite catch. She figured it was probably just as well. The concern for her on his face was transformed to anger, then back again so quickly that she thought maybe she'd imagined it.

She clambered to her feet with both men trying to help her. Fiori handed her a glass of water, which she downed in a single go. 'I was in a walled garden.' She looked at Kennet. 'She said you had that effect on people. What did she mean?'

His face was suddenly crimson and the muscles along his jaw spasmed. 'She has a sick sense of humour.'

'Did you?' Tim asked. 'Did you do that, or was it her? The demon.'

'It wasn't me,' Kennet said, avoiding Tara's gaze. 'All I did was touch her.'

While he avoided her gaze, Tara studied him unabashedly, hungrily taking in what she hadn't been able to see on the fells. 'We dreamed together. It bloody well was you. She might have helped, but you dreamed with me. Surely you know what happens when that link is properly forged.'

This time he did look at her. The colour drained from his face, and he swallowed hard. For a second he seemed at a loss for words, or perhaps he was just choosing his words carefully, but at last he spoke. 'I also know that the link you're talking about is almost never properly forged, if at all. Two dreamers are very rarely compatible enough to forge that link.'

'What link?' Marie asked.

'There's an old wives' tale among witches,' Kennet said, 'that if two dreamers have lived and loved and dreamed together in another life, or if their paths are parallel and their hearts beat together, they can forge a link when they dream, a link that amplifies their magical abilities.'

'More than amplifies,' Tara added, still studying Kennet. 'And more than just their dream magic. It's called the Dream Knot.' Before anyone could ask, she explained. 'Magic, at least coven magic, is all about forming links and bonds that will amplify and protect, build and encourage,' she said. 'Marie, you and Tim have a bond with each other that enabled you to defeat Deacon. And both of you are linked and bound to each person in this coven through acts of magic and through sex. But each link is different and each link strengthens and amplifies different kinds of magic in different people. The Dream Knot is extremely rare because of the level of vulnerability necessary to forge that link.' Her pulse suddenly raced at the thought of just how vulnerable she had been with Kennet on the fells.

Suddenly Kennet seemed sad. 'As I said, it's very unlikely.'

When everyone was satisfied that Tara was all right and Kennet wasn't a minion of Deacon secretly sent to destroy them all, the Elemental Coven's house rule of hospitality was once again in force. Fiori served Kennet a plate of stroganoff and some bread, and he ate like he'd been practising high magic.

'What were you doing on the fells last night, and why couldn't I tell that you weren't a ghost?' Tara knew she sounded rude, but there was too much at stake, and they had already wasted too much time where Anderson was concerned. She wanted her high priest back now. And if someone was toying with him in the Ether, she wanted it stopped.

'I was walking. I walk a lot at night. It calms me.'

'And you just happened upon me.'

He nodded, mopping the plate clean with the last of his bread. 'I thought there was something wrong with you.'

Tara absolutely refused to blush. These fells at night were her place of solitude, her place to do whatever she needed. He and this demon woman, they were the intruders, and at the moment the whole experience made her furious. 'There was something wrong with me. It was her, giving me … dreams.'

He blushed for both of them. 'She does that. She can be downright intrusive when it suits her purposes. But I promise you, I didn't know about her scheming until after.'

'Is she a demon?' Fiori asked, setting a large bowl of crumble in front of him.

'Yes.' He took a huge bite of his dessert, savoured it, then looked around at everyone. 'She is a demon, and she hates Deacon even more than we do.'

The room erupted with everyone talking at once, a condition that didn't seem to bother Kennet, as he shovelled down more crumble.

'I seriously doubt that's possible,' Tara said.

'And we can assume you hate Deacon too,' Tim added.

Kennet stopped eating and his face darkened. 'More than you can imagine'.

'Not more than I can imagine,' Tara said. He didn't argue, but pushed his crumble aside, seeming to have lost his appetite.

For a second the room was silent; there was uncomfortable shifting in the ranks, no doubt as everyone thought of their own reasons for wanting Deacon gone. Outside on the hawthorn, the robin trilled, oblivious to the drama going on inside. At last Tara spoke into the silence. 'Will she help us? Can we trust her?'

'She may well help you, but you can't trust her. You can trust that she wants an end to Deacon's reign of terror and that she'll do whatever she thinks in necessary to make that happen, though. I'm certain of that much.'

'Tell us,' Tim said, sitting down on a chair across the breakfast bar from Kennet, 'how is it that you know her so well?'

Kennet toyed with his spoon. 'I told you, I hate Deacon. I want him gone, and I hounded her until she gave in.'

Tara laughed. 'You hounded a demon?'

'You've either got balls of steel or you're completely barking,' Tim said.

Kennet didn't smile. 'Probably more of the latter, but I have my reasons.'

Cassandra, who had watched the whole situation unfold in silence, took the seat next to Tim and spoke without preamble. 'I need to know why she messed with us in the Ether, and –'

'Your ghost is all right. She only wanted to get your attention.'

'What, by pushing him away from us, and destroying our search beacons?' Marie said.

He ignored Marie, but studied Cassandra, running his teeth across his lower lip. 'You weren't close. He's farther away than either you or he imagine.'

Tara felt like the man had just punched her in the gut. Cassandra closed her eyes and swallowed back a sob. Marie took her hand and gave it an empathetic squeeze.

Kennet bit his lip again and straightened in the chair. 'Where he is, even moving as quickly as he does, knowing ethereal magic as well as he does, he'll never make it back in your lifetimes – any of you.'

Cassandra stifled a cry and Tim slipped an arm around her.

'We're ghost riders,' Tara said, holding control as tightly as she could. 'We live a very, very long time because of our magic.'

'I know.' Kennet spoke softly.

'Wait a minute,' Cassandra said. 'The first Full Moon after we lost him, he came to us in our dreams, he came to all of us. He couldn't possibly have done that if he were that far away.'

The man's eyes were soft now, his face sympathetic. 'It was her, amplifying the magic. And today it was her again.'

'I won't accept that,' Cassandra said. 'I can't accept that. He'll find his way back. We'll find him.' She pushed back from the breakfast bar, the legs of her chair screeching on the tile as she did so.

In a move that was lightning fast, Kennet reached across the table and grabbed her wrist in a tight grip. Everyone in the room froze. His breath hissed between his teeth at the feel of the succubus's power, but he held her. 'She can help.'

The silence in the room deepened. Tara was certain she could hear the heartbeats of each of her coven family, and Kennet's heartbeat she felt like her own.

'Can she find him? Can she bring him back?' Cassandra breathed.

'I believe that she can.' Kennet's voice was soft, barely audible, but everyone heard it.

'The question is, *will* she?' Tara said. Thoughts of her conversation with Deacon in the Room of Reflection earlier pushed their way into her head. 'You said it yourself, she's not trustworthy, and we certainly can't force her to do our will.'

'It doesn't matter, we have to try,' Cassandra said, pulling her wrist free from Kennet's grip. This time he made no attempt to hold her.

'You have more bargaining power than you might think,' Kennet said, still holding Cassandra's gaze. 'She wouldn't be approaching you if that weren't the case.'

'It would be a start if you would tell us everything you know about her, and how we can contact her.' Tara said. 'We're more than willing to do whatever it takes to get rid of Deacon.'

'And if she can get Anderson back for us, we'd be in her debt.' Marie added.

'Trust me,' he replied. 'You don't really want to be in her debt.' Before anyone could respond to his comment, he continued. 'I'm here to tell you as much as I can about her, because she knows that you have Deacon imprisoned in Elemental Cottage, and she wants to know why.'

A chill rippled through the room that had nothing to do with magic being worked. A fist tightened in Tara's stomach as she recalled the dream she'd shared with Kennet. 'Did she find out because of our dream?'

He shook his head. 'She knew. She's known everything about Deacon from ... who knows how long, but before he was Deacon, back when his name was secret. Well his real name is still secret, isn't it? Deacon is just what remains of the mortal who bargained with him.' A shudder ran up his spine that was as clear to Tara as if he had suddenly collapsed on the kitchen floor in a fit. He caught her gaze and quickly looked away. 'I'll tell you as much as I'm able. That's why I'm here.

Just as it started to drizzle outside, and the anaemic springtime sun was already falling below the peaks of the high fells, they settled into the library with coffee to hear what Kennet had to say. For a long time he didn't speak, only looked down into his coffee cup as though he were contemplating where to begin. At last he sat his cup aside and looked around at everyone.

'It's not really easy to speak about her. She's been with me a long time now, and when she came into my life, things

59

weren't good. I … I sought her out, actually. I'd known about her since I was 14.'

Before anyone could ask, he offered up the information. 'I found my mother's spell book. I don't know how my mother knew the spell that would draw Lucia's attention – that's her name, Lucia,' he added. 'At least that's the name she shares with mortals.'

'Anyway, I shouldn't have been able to work the spell, and I certainly should have been smart enough to know better. But for whatever reason, I was able to do the magic, and the next thing I knew, I was transported to a cave. It was more like the inside of a volcano really. Fire danced all around, and there she was, right in the middle of it, but not burning. She was talking to someone. Really, it was more like a raging argument.

'She was furious. I had it in my mind just to sneak away. Jesus, I was scared silly. I hadn't even expected it to work. And …' He squirmed on the leather sofa and tugged at his collar as though it were choking him. 'Well, I was an adolescent boy and she was like no one I'd ever seen before. So beautiful, even in her rage.' He huffed a laugh that sounded almost like it hurt.

'Whoever it was she was talking to vanished and before I knew it, she had me by the throat.' He shivered. 'She was no longer a beautiful woman. I can't even describe the way she looked. I can't even remember it, really. All that's left of that part of the experience is terror.'

He rubbed his eyes with his index fingers and groaned. Tara felt his discomfort just below her sternum in a tight knot that she wished she could run away from. But she sat. Waiting.

At last he spoke again. 'What she did next, I have no trouble remembering.' His voice was suddenly distant and detached. 'She …' The muscles along his throat tensed, and his lips pressed in a thin line, almost as though they didn't want to let the words escape from his mouth. He took a deep breath and forced them out. 'She possessed me.'

'What?!' Tim practically catapulted off his chair, but Tara motioned him to sit.

Kennet nodded. 'At first I was in her arms, and then suddenly she was inside me, in some part of me that I couldn't quite identify, but at the same time it felt like she was in every single cell of my body.' He wrapped his arms around himself as though he were suddenly cold. Then his gaze came to rest on Cassandra. 'Her touch, her first touch, it felt a little bit like yours, but then you are a succubus, aren't you?'

Tim cursed under his breath. Marie elbowed him. Cassandra sat like a statue, unmoving, barely breathing.

'Then what happened?' Tara asked.

He turned his attention away from Cassandra and was once again staring deep into a past no one else in the room could see. 'Suddenly I felt like I knew everything, like I could see everything, and everything was brighter, more vivid, more real, and I knew how it all worked. I felt ... I felt so powerful, and yet that's such a weak word for it.

'Then as quickly as she was in me, she was out again, and standing next to me, once again the beautiful woman in the robe of flame. And she was suddenly kind, almost tender. Then she said, "You're only a child." She acted like that surprised her. "You're of no use to me. Perhaps if you were older." Then she said, "Go home and tell your mother to guard her spell book a little better in future."' The smile that crossed his face was more like a grimace at the memories he shared.

'Then, I was back on the floor in front of our fireplace. I was sick as a dog for nearly two weeks, high fever, couldn't eat, bad nightmares. I felt like every bone in my body would break and crumble to dust. Then one morning I woke feeling like nothing had ever happened, and I haven't been sick a day in my life since then.' He looked down at his hands now clasped in his lap.

'Later, when I asked my mum about the spell, she said that Lucia could occasionally be called upon in times of need and that if the circumstances moved her – and who really knows what moves a demon – she would aid the petitioner with justice and revenge, though often at a very high price. Then my mum locked her spell book away and told me I was never to mention Lucia's name to anyone and that I was never, under any circumstances, to return to her. I kept my word for a long time. But then I needed her, and I went to her without question.'

A hush blanketed the room. The only sound was the crackle of the fire in the fireplace. It felt as though a heavy spell had fallen on all of them, as though no one would ever move or speak again.

Then Kennet's breached the silence. 'There is one more thing. It was Deacon who was with Lucia that day when I was 14. I didn't know that at the time. I mean, I didn't know who he was. But he … he never forgave me for my intrusion.'

There was a collective murmur among the coven followed once again by more stunned silence.

Tara shivered and chafed her arms. 'She wanted you to tell us all this.'

'That's right,' Kennet said. 'Lucia can't exactly come knocking on your door. But me, I'm flesh and blood. I can pay you a visit. You'll be more comfortable with me. And certainly with your experience of Deacon, you have no love for demons.'

Tara ran a hand through her hair and huffed out a tight breath. 'You may have just offered us the trump card against Deacon – so tell me, why don't I feel better about it? Why am I not dancing a celebration jig?'

'Probably because you feel deceived after what happened to us up on the fells this morning.'

Everyone in the coven remained silent, and in the way only a well-trained coven could do, they afforded the couple as much privacy as possible without leaving the room.

'I didn't know what you thought.' He spoke almost like they were alone in the room together, and Tara could almost believe it with the intimate tone in his voice. 'I didn't realise you thought I was a ghost or I would have told you otherwise. I don't know how you could have made that mistake.' He surprised her by taking her hand and laying it on his chest next to the steady thump-thump of his heart. 'Do I feel like a ghost now?'

'No, of course you don't.' She pulled away a little too quickly and struggled not to blush. 'Did she do that? Because that's not a mistake ghost riders make.'

'Probably. Especially since you were dreaming about her before.'

'Why? Why did she do that to me?' she asked, wrapping her arms around herself.

He seemed disappointed. 'Was it that unpleasant?'

She found it suddenly difficult to meet his gaze, and felt the presence of the rest of the coven like a weight. 'You know that it wasn't, but that doesn't answer my question.'

He straightened in his seat and cleared his throat as though he had only just become aware of everyone else in the room. 'She wants you happy and strong, and I suppose she was aware that you wouldn't make love to me if you knew that I wasn't a ghost.'

'Tara's a ghost rider,' Sky said. 'She needs to have sex to be healthy and strong, The demon was right about that. Happy, however ... well, that's another matter.'

'Sky, no one has asked for your opinion.' Tara sounded a lot snappier than she'd meant to.

Sky simply shrugged. 'No one has to ask. It's freely given.'

'Lucia wants everyone at their best for the coming battle. We've all fought Deacon before, and we all know that we'll need every ounce of strength we have.'

'We're not at full strength without Anderson,' Tim said. He sat between Marie and Cassandra on the leather sofa, opposite Kennet with his arms folded sceptically across his chest. Everyone nodded agreement.

'And we're certainly not happy,' Cassandra added.

Again everyone nodded.

'All I can say is that Lucia knows this,' Kennet said. 'I'm not privy to her plan, but she knows.'

'And we're supposed to just trust you when everything you've done so far is untrustworthy,' Tara said.

Kennet took her hand and raised it to his lips in an act that made a ripple of surprise pass through the whole coven 'Then dream with me, Tara. Dream with me and let me prove to you that I'm trustworthy, that what we want is the same thing.'

'How can I know that Lucia won't interfere? Nothing that's happened since she came into my dreams is as it appears. How am I going to know if it's real or if she's just manipulating us in the Dream World?'

'Tara, the dream we had together had nothing to do with Lucia,' Kennet said. 'It was real, and you know it.'

She pulled her hand away. 'I need to think about it.'

'I want Anderson back.' Cassandra said, her voice a low warning.

'You think I don't?' Tara snapped. 'The whole world has turned upside down in less than 24 hours. Way less. I'm sorry, but I need to think.' She clambered to her feet and left the library, heading for the greenhouse.'

Chapter Eight

'If it's any consolation, I don't trust him either.'

Tara wasn't surprised to hear Cassandra's voice behind her. She didn't look up from her efforts with the thyme seedlings she was planting on for Fiori's kitchen and for Sky's apothecary. The greenhouse was awash in the dry-heat scent of the Mediterranean.

'He's offered us everything we want, an end to all of our suffering. He's all but promised Anderson back in our arms. Everything. All tied up in a shiny ribbon,' Tara said, continuing to work.

Cassandra came to her side and took over preparing the pots for the seedlings. Tara was still amazed at the woman's natural feel for gardening when she had never touched the earth until she came to Elemental Cottage. Somehow it felt like the young succubus had always been a part of the Elemental Coven, and Tara felt the ache of her loss of Anderson as deeply as she felt her own.

'If something sounds too good to be true, it usually is,' Cassandra said. 'And who in their right mind would make a deal with a demon?'

'Probably not the question to ask, Cassandra,' Tara said. 'You know we all would, in a heartbeat, if it would get us what we want so desperately.'

'Will you dream with him?' Cassandra asked, as she handed Tara the last pot.

'I don't see that I have much choice, do I?'

'Is it really that much of a hardship?'

They both turned to find Kennet standing in the door of

the greenhouse.

Tara laid aside her dibber and gently touched Cassandra's hand, feeling the welcome buzz of her power. 'Go and tell the others to prepare the Dream Cave.'

Once she was gone, she turned her attention back to her seedlings.

Kennet moved inside and pulled the door to. 'I understand you not trusting me,' he said. 'I'd feel the same way, I'm sure. But Tara, I'm not the enemy. I need you to believe that.' He rested a hand on her shoulder, and she stiffened.

Carefully he removed it and turned his attention to stroking the leaves of the thyme plants. 'You're afraid,' he said, his voice barely more than a whisper.

'Aren't you?' She continued to fuss over the seedlings, mostly just to stave off the panic of his nearness.

'Terrified.' His answer surprised her.

She turned to face him and as she looked up into his eyes, it suddenly felt like she had looked into the sun.

'But not for the same reasons you are,' he said. He crooked a finger under her chin so she couldn't look away. 'Why do you make love only with ghosts?'

Everything in her wanted to turn and flee before it was too late, but she stood her ground and held his gaze. 'It hasn't ended well for the living when I've had sex with them.'

'Are you afraid it won't end well for me?'

She didn't answer. She was afraid of what might happen if she tried to speak. There were too many memories too close to the surface, memories she had taken lifetimes to bury deep, and this man had dug them all up in only a few hours.

He took both of her hands, ignoring the compost on her fingers, then brushed a kiss gently across her lips, making her want like she hadn't allowed herself to want in a very long time. Then he pulled away and brushed the pad of his thumb along her lower lip. 'I'm already dead, Tara. Physically I may not be a ghost, but I'm already dead. Everything that I lived for was taken from me seven years ago.'

She pushed him away. 'Seven years? Only seven years?

You're not dead yet, Kennet. You haven't even begun to die. You haven't had nearly enough years to really beg for death, long for death, pray that it'll come in the night and set you free.' She reached for the staging table for support. Her knees were weak, her insides felt like snow on the wind. 'But then you realise that you'll be no freer of him dead than you are alive. So no, you're not dead, Kennet. Don't even wish for it, and if you think your pet demon will protect you, then you don't know demons.'

This time he grabbed her by the front of her shirt and pulled her to him with such force that she gasped out loud. He took her mouth with stunning anger, like nothing she'd ever felt before, and she returned his assault with her own rage, meeting his tongue thrust for angry thrust, bruising his lips with the force of her mouth and teeth, biting and aching, as he bit back. Then he pulled away breathless. 'She's not my pet demon, Tara and, trust me, I fucking know demons.'

Then they were kissing again as though they would tear each other apart, as though they would rip the very breath from each other in angry, scorched shreds. His hands moved to her hips, and he hoisted her onto the staging table, shoving aside the gypsy skirt until she could feel the rough wood against the silk of her panties. He fingered aside the crotch and she tried to squirm away from him. 'I don't fuck the living,' she gasped against his mouth, then she bore down as his thick middle finger found its way between her labia and thrust upward. She pulled him to her even as she tried to push him away with her words.

'Yes you do, as of this morning you do. You need it, I need it, and it's time you stopped letting Deacon call the shots.'

She felt his last words like a slap and like an aphrodisiac at the same time, and everything in her felt wet with need. 'Do it, goddamnit,' she growled. 'If you're gonna do it, do it and don't make me wait!' She grabbed for his fly with an awkward grip from a bad angle that caused him to flinch and push her hand aside. 'Damn it, get them off,' she gasped, 'I can't wait!'

With trembling hands he practically ripped the zipper out of his fly, then shoved his jeans and boxers down around his hips and his erection bounced free from its exquisite nest of copper-brown curls. The view was brief and she told herself, in a sliver of a thought that was left to her, that sometime she'd like to linger and explore, though in her heart she didn't really believe she'd ever be afforded that luxury, so she'd take what he'd give her.

Once again he tore at her panties until they were stretched over one buttock and she could feel the cool air of the greenhouse against her gape, then while she held herself open, he cupped his hands under her arse and lifted her from the table, down onto his heft. With a grunt and a slight thrust, he pressed up into her, and she yielded like soft butter, then gripped like a fist. Then she grabbed him by the hair and pulled his face back to hers, and their tongue-dance matched the rhythm of the thrust and glide. Grunts became feral cries, throats became raw, and vision blurred in searing heat that had nothing to do with Lucia.

'Great Goddess,' he gasped. 'If I'm not dead, I'm dying now, and it's your fault.'

She bit his neck hard and he flinched and surged inside her tight grip. 'You asked for it, and I don't believe in making people beg.'

'I can't think of a better way to go,' he grunted.

In truth, she wasn't entirely sure she wasn't dying right along with him, but it didn't really matter. Dead or alive, it was pretty much the same to her.

'Fuck,' he breathed between barely parted lips. 'I can't hold back any longer, woman. I have to come now.' And as his cock convulsed inside her, and his groin raked upward against her clit, she came in great sobs that made her throat ache, that made her body feel as though some animal, curled deep at her centre, had awakened ravenous and needy with an emptiness to fill that was bigger than the void. And strangely enough, Kennet Lucian felt like he might begin to touch the emptiness.

For a long time, he held her there, both of them gasping for breath, her arms and legs wrapped around him, his large hands cupping her bottom. 'Tara,' he whispered against her ear. 'Please trust me.'

She ran a hand through his hair and nipped his ear with her teeth. 'Then prove to me that I can.'

He had just settled her onto the floor, and they were straightening and tidying when Cassandra knocked on the door and stepped inside. 'We can't get to the cave, Tara. There's flooding. It was only then that Tara noticed it was pouring with rain.

The Room of Reflection was made ready. It wasn't ideal. Tara much preferred the cave for dream magic. She had occasionally used the spare suite with the big four-poster bed, but with Kennet, that felt too much like lovers meeting for pleasure, and this wasn't about pleasure. She didn't want her strange mix of feelings for him, nor the fact that he was her first living lover in a very long time to interfere with the magic, to interfere with her discernment. She really needed to be clear-headed, and she couldn't guarantee that with a romp in the big bed, so the Room of Reflection would have to do.

The enchantments to keep Deacon's presence from distracting them during the ritual were reinforced, everyone had eaten again, and the circle had been cast. Tim, Cassandra and Marie had settled onto the cushions provided for them on the floor. Their role was to raise the sexual energy. Tim was already lying on his back with Marie mounted on top of him. While one hand caressed her breast, his other hand cupped and kneaded Cassandra's bottom where she sat straddling his face, shifting her hips against the laving of his tongue.

Fiori and Sky, who would witness, caressed and fondled each other on the opposite side of the cushions nearest the altar where Tara and Kennet would dream together. Once the energy that was needed had been raised in the circle, Tara took Kennet's hand and led him to the dream bed, pulling him down next to her. The magic was thick and heavy, and Tara already felt the weight of it in a way she had never felt it with Anderson. But then Anderson's speciality was ethereal magic, not dream magic, and because she refused to have sex with the living, she had never raised dream magic with Tim. It was wrong of her. She knew it. Tim was a powerful witch, gifted in dream magic, but she couldn't bear the thought of something happening to the young farmer because of her.

And now she was with Kennet, who clearly had his own battle scars from Deacon, and who hopefully would help them rid the world of him once and for all. Dear Goddess, she hoped he was right, she hoped Deacon wouldn't turn his wrath on the man because he had pleasured her. Clearly Deacon already had it in for Kennet, and certainly him having sex with her wouldn't improve his standing with the demon. There was nothing to be done for it. She was committed now, and she forced herself to focus on the magic building in the room.

The heaviness of the magic would mean that she would sleep soon, so would Kennet. So would everyone except for Sky and Fiori, who would witness from the Waking World. And once everyone else slept, she and Kennet would enter the Dream World together. Expertly, as though he knew, he caressed each part of her that was most sensitive to the magic. His tongue snaked up over the soles of her feet, his lips suckling each toe, his teeth grazing her sensitive instep causing her to writhe and … for fuck's sake, did she just giggle?

'Bless these feet as they traverse the Dream World.'

Was she hearing his thoughts?

'Bless these knees, and the humility of the woman who has walked in the service of others.'

Dear Goddess, he was offering her blessing and anointing for the journey. It was basic fundamental magic, not a sexual thing, and yet by the time his breath tightened her clitoris and his kiss against the Keystone opened her by blessing the creative power of her womanhood, she found herself in a place she had never been before, a place raw with emotion and

70

ravenous with need.

He gently cupped her breasts, then kissed her sternum. 'Bless the heart so tender that it has broken a thousand times for those it loves.'

By the time she felt his penis pressing between her folds, by the time he rose above her so she could see his shining eyes, her face was wet.

'Bless these eyes, and let them see joy once again and know no more tears of sorrow.' He kissed away her tears, then kissed her eyelids and smiled down at her, and she had never felt more exposed. 'Enter the dream with me, Tara, and let us discover the truth.' He cupped her hips and she lifted her legs around his waist, an act which opened her just enough for him to push into her tight wet depths, and they both shuddered from the feel of it. Then he began to thrust, and she thrust up to meet him, once, twice, thrice, and they were chasing the dream.

'The enemy of my enemy is my friend,' she heard Kennet say, Kennet from his hospital bed, Kennet dying, Kennet wanting to live only for revenge, and the pain he bore, he hid it behind a wall of flames.

'Why?' Tara asked. 'Why hide it?'

'I couldn't protect those I loved,' he said. 'They're dead because of me. I don't want you to see my shame.'

'Shall I show you what I've lost?' she said. 'Those I couldn't protect, those who are dead because of me? Shall I show you my shame?'

'I know your loss,' he replied. 'Lucia told me. And in it, there's no shame.'

The world took shape around them and they were suddenly walking hand in hand. They were coming down into the Ennerdale Valley off Black Sail Pass. She could see the Black Sail Youth Hostel far below them.

'Then why have you brought me here if you wish to keep secrets?'

'My sister, and my wife.' His voice was suddenly distant. 'Deacon killed them.'

'Why?'

71

'I told you, it was because I saw him with Lucia.' His voice was suddenly void of all emotions. 'I interrupted them. It was more than an argument. He would have destroyed her if I hadn't interrupted. She told me that later, much later. Up until then, I had dreams, nightmares really, about Deacon and Lucia, and they were always battling each other. I never imagined he'd seek me out, I never imagined I'd done anything worthy of his vengeance, not until he killed them. Then he made certain I knew, while he tortured them and made me watch, he made certain I understood why.'

Suddenly they were in the morgue. 'You really were dead,' she said as they watched the doctors in their confusion. 'And you made a pact with her?'

'Something like that. She promised me revenge.'

'And she did this out of the kindness of her heart?'

His voice sounded suddenly bitter. 'She has no heart.'

Then they were falling back into their bodies again. 'Not yet! I'm not finished. I need to know more.' Tara said.

But it was too late. She woke in her body on the floor in the middle of the Room of Reflection. Around her everyone slept. Though Kennet was still nestled in her arms, his penis still fully erect inside her, his fetch had left his body and stood by the altar next to Lucia. As Tara wondered groggily if she were still in a dream, she heard Lucia speak.

'Did you know, my darling boy, that the scrying mirror prison was my doing?' She waved her hand dismissively. 'Oh, the mirror was only a trinket from a wealthy man I once knew, but the creation of a prison from the Ether using the mirror as its door was very ancient magic lost to humans long ago. Synchronicity, I think they call it nowadays, when somehow against all odds things end up exactly as they were meant to be. And so it is with the prison. Is it not astounding that it should be Tara Stone and her ghost who discovered how to use it for exactly the task it was created?' She smiled down at the mirror in its wrap of black silk. 'Of course, they did not know about the mirror in the beginning. They only ever entered from the Ether side. Never mind that. All things happen as they should, do they not, my dear heart?' But Kennet's fetch seemed uninterested in Lucia's craftsmanship.

'Don't make me do this,' he said. 'You don't even know this'll work.'

The demon flashed bright and the room was suddenly flooded with blinding light. 'Did you think I could offer you a guarantee, Kennet Lucian? Deacon is the liar who offers what he may not be able to perform as though it were universal truth. I have never lied to you. If we are to fulfil our task, if we are to end Deacon's miserable existence for ever, then this is the risk we must take. You knew this from the beginning.'

Tara struggled to rise, struggled to find her voice to question the demon, but she couldn't move; she couldn't speak. She could only lie dumbly and listen. Then she was falling again, farther and farther away from the scene in the Room of Reflection, and she landed with a little gasp in the middle of her own bed. For a long time she drifted in darkness, then her awareness returned to the Dream World. Again she could feel Kennet's arms enfolding her, and still his penis nestled inside her, thick and heavy with need. One enormous hand cupped and stroked her breast. She felt chilled, and no matter how closely she nestled to Kennet's body, she felt no less chilled. The chill expanded in her chest into an icy knot of fear that exploded into full-blown arousal so quickly that it took her breath away. She opened her eyes and found herself looking up into Deacon's face. Her legs were wrapped around him and he filled her fuller than she had ever been, and the sheer lust with which he consumed her was bottomless. He smiled down at her. 'Did you not know, my darling Tara? But how could you not have foreseen? No other lust can fill you as mine can. Surely in the deepest depth of your heart you've always known this to be true, just as I have. You've secretly longed to share my lust, just as I have yours.' He raised a hand and they were back in the Room of Reflection. He motioned around the circle where everyone else slept. 'Once they are all gone, once they no longer divide your attention, my love, then we can be together as it was ordained from the beginning.'

'Tara, Tara my love. Wake up.' A familiar voice rose out of the icy terrifying arousal, and strong arms embraced her. 'Wake up, my darling. It is only a dream.'

She woke with a strangled cry that felt like glass in her dry throat. She was drenched in cold sweat and trembling like she would shake apart. But it wasn't Kennet's embrace that she woke to. It was Anderson's.

Chapter Nine

By the time Kennet got back to the house every part of his body ached. When he placed the scrying mirror on the table, which had been prepared with protection spells similar to those at Elemental Cottage, he felt as though his insides were being flayed and burned. He stumbled to the couch and sat with his head in his hands, not sure if he were going to pass out or throw up.

'You need to eat.' Lucia knelt in front of him and ran a cool hand over his forehead, a hand that he knew was only in his imagination, only what she projected for him to see, to feel. 'You have just performed powerful magic.'

'I can't,' he breathed between clenched teeth. 'I won't be able to hold anything down.'

'Yes you will. It's just the magic. You know it has that effect sometimes. Now eat.' She nodded to a bowl of nuts on the end table next to where he sat. 'Do it. Our work is not finished yet, and you will need your strength for what lies ahead.'

At first taste, his stomach roiled and clenched, then relaxed and he found himself shoving the nut mix into his mouth as fast as he could swallow. Though he felt somewhat stronger, he felt no better – the pain in his joints and muscles felt like a bad case of the flu and the torturous knots in his insides felt no less painful. 'Why are you doing this to me?' he asked. 'I've done what you told me to. I brought you the scrying mirror. I betrayed her.' The thought of what he had done to Tara hurt worse than anything Lucia had ever done to him.

He felt her embrace like a long-lost lover seeking to comfort, and he heard her voice like a whisper in his ear. 'My dearest Kennet, none of what you feel is my doing. I am not so cruel. You have done all that I have asked, and with way more finesse and elegance that I would have expected of a mortal. But then you have always been extraordinary among mortals.'

'Then what?' he said, trembling so hard he could barely hold the bottle of water she urged him to take.

'Did you not hear your words, my dear boy? You feel that you have betrayed her, and you feel that way because you have done exactly what I warned you not to, you have opened your heart to her. Did I not warn you that Tara Stone was formidable in ways you could not easily imagine? It is not just that she is a powerful witch, though she most certainly is. It is the depth of her, the unfathomable depth of her and the steadfastness of her heart.' She moved inside him, even though her image still wavered on the couch next to him. Then she made a space for warmth, for comfort, for well-being, all perks of her possession of him, all things that made the horror of his loss and the mourning of it more bearable. But suddenly it seemed like putting a plaster on a severed limb.

He curled up on the couch in a foetal position and pulled the wool blanket he slept under up over him. 'Do you know what she's lost? Do you know how deeply she loves?' he asked.

'My darling, of course I know. Did I not warn you that if you looked into her heart, even for a moment, it would be your undoing? When I offered you her body on the fells, it was to be for your pleasure, for her pleasure. There was to be no dreaming. There was to be no bonding. You knew this, and yet you let it happen. Did you not understand the pain you would bring upon yourself? Could you not see?'

For a second he recalled his first view of Tara Stone on the fells, and then the feel of her arms, the feel of her body, the feel of her heart. 'Yes,' I did see,' he breathed. And strangely even in his physical pain, he felt better, holding on to the memory. And then he felt a whole lot worse. 'I saw, and then I betrayed her anyway.'

'Oh my sweet Kennet,' Lucia whispered, intensifying her efforts to ease his suffering. 'You have not betrayed her at all, and she will see this soon. You have done only what must be done to ultimately destroy Deacon. And this is the gift that you shall give to each other, the gift that we shall all give to each other. Please do not worry so, and do not wound yourself for doing what you must. She will come to understand.' He felt her on the couch next to him, cradling him in a spoon position, gently stroking his chest right over where his heart felt like it were some sort of dying beast. 'Rest now, my darling. You are exhausted. Sleep here in my arms. Let me comfort you, and when you wake and are rested again, we will do what must be done together.'

Do what must be done, he thought. Release the monster into the world, turn him loose in hopes that what was written in dusty aging spell books was more than just some witch's idea of a joke after too much strong cider.

'Kennet,' Lucia whispered inside his head. 'I will offer you comfort in any form I am able, as I always have, but –' her voice became soft, almost to the point of inaudible, to the point where all he could really hear was the warning. 'Never, ever forget how badly I can hurt you.'

Tara clung to Anderson, sobbing like a child, even when Cassandra pushed in, and he opened his arms to her and smothered her in kisses. Even when the others crowded around, she clung to him, and he patiently endured it, as he always had, all these years. 'Please tell me I'm not still dreaming,' she breathed against his neck. 'Please, dear Goddess, let this be real.'

'Indeed it is real, my darling, or at least I believe it to be real. I am in the flesh and having the very breath squeezed from me by more affection than I have felt in all these four long months.'

'How?' Tim asked, sitting cross-legged on the cushions

next to Anderson, who was also naked. 'Kennet told us you were so far away we'd all be dead by the time you found your way home.'

'Indeed, the woman who came to me in the void told me the same, and then she folded her arms around me and I slept. And when I came to myself, I was in Tara's arms in the midst of what I can only assume was dream magic. But where is your high priest, my love? Have you replaced me so easily? Well, I am not surprised, since I have never really been suited to dream magic.'

'Where is Kennet?' Marie said, standing to look around. As she turned to face the altar, she gave a startled cry and grabbed Tim's hand hard. 'Where's the scrying mirror? Where's it at? Where the hell's Deacon?'

'Kennet took it,' Tara said, as certain as if she had seen him walk out the door with the mirror. 'Dear Goddess, Kennet took it. He intends to release Deacon.' The dream on the fells came back to her like a riptide washing over her and pulling her under.

'Why would anyone want to do such a thing?' Anderson asked.

'Apparently Lucia believes that only if Deacon is released can he be defeated for good and destroyed,' Tara said.

'And you didn't see fit to tell us this earlier,' Fiori said.

Tara ran a hand through her hair and fought back the rising panic. 'I only just now remembered it. I wouldn't have kept something like this from you, believe me.'

'Well he hasn't released him yet,' Cassandra said, 'or we'd feel his presence.'

'Then we've got to find Kennet,' Marie said. 'He can't have gone far. Tara, you're connected with him, surely we can find him?'

Her connection to Kennet was responsible for all that had happened, Tara thought. It was that connection that had brought this whole thing on because she had allowed her lust, her attraction to the man, to cloud her vision.

'Stop it, Tara,' Sky said. 'None of this is your fault, and

we need you to be clear headed now. We're all being manipulated by the man, who's more than likely being manipulated by the demon, so just stop with the blame shit.'

Though Tara pretended to ignore the lecture, she knew Sky was right. She squared her shoulders and pulled a robe around her to stave off the chill that had nothing to do with being naked. 'Cassandra's right. We have to find him.'

'Nobody does anything until we eat,' Fiori said.

By the time they had all dressed and piled into the kitchen, Fiori had a fry-up well underway. As they ate, they filled Anderson in on all that had happened. Unable to control himself, he pulled Cassandra into his lap and toyed with her hair while he listened.

'You haven't eaten enough.' Fiori nodded to Cassandra. 'If we have to fight Deacon, he'll target you, you know that, and love won't win the day where demons are concerned.' Anderson gave her a squeeze and offered her a piece of toast with marmalade.

When Anderson had been brought up to speed, Tara asked, 'Did you actually meet Lucia in the Ether? Maybe you can tell us something we don't know.'

'I felt her presence many times, though I did not know what it was that I felt. I knew it was nothing I had ever felt before. And in the latter days, I was suspicious that my plans of escaping the Ether were being thwarted, though I did not know why.' He paused to feed Cassandra another bite of toast. 'In truth I do not understand why, if the power had always been hers, she did not return me home sooner. But who can know the mind of a demon?

'However, just before she sent me home, she did appear to me, a woman robed in fire, and I knew instantly that she was by no means mortal. She told me that it was her desire to rid the world of Deacon. She told me that she would need my help, that she would need the help of all the Elemental Coven, and that she had need of us at full strength. And now we must find this minion of hers, this Kennet.'

In spite of herself, Tara bristled at the use of the name

"minion" for Kennet, even though he had clearly betrayed them, even though that was clearly what he was.

'No one here's fit for another run-in with dream magic tonight,' Tara said.

'Maybe we don't need dream magic.' Cassandra spoke around a mouthful of eggs. 'Isn't there some way to access, online, recent property sales or, more likely, places close by that lease properties? I'd be willing to bet our Kennet is not far from Elemental Cottage and that he's in a low-rent place that's been let recently.'

'That's a start,' Tara said. 'And I'll put out some basic search spells. I mean, I am connected to him in the Dream World. Perhaps the bond will bleed through to the Waking World.'

'If what happened when he first showed up is any indication,' Tim said, 'I wouldn't be surprised – unless his demon pal is blocking the signal.'

'I've been thinking,' Cassandra said. 'Is it possible that we misinterpreted the books of shadows? They all say, "Thrice bound and once released." We all assumed that meant that once Deacon was thrice bound, we'd be free from him. Clearly that hasn't happened. Maybe Kennet and this Lucia are right. Maybe it's the once released part of the spell that'll defeat him.'

'I suppose it's possible,' Tara said. 'Anyway, whether that's the case or not, if Kennet believes it, then our help may very well be needed if the scrying mirror prison is opened.'

The wave of pain took Tara by surprise, and she cried out and doubled over in the chair, holding her belly. Instantly, Tim was kneeling on the floor in front of her. 'He's in pain,' Tara gasped. 'Kennet is. Jesus! What the fuck is going on?'

'You're certain?' Tim said, taking her pulse and feeling her forehead.

'Of course I'm certain! Whatever's happening, he's in real danger, and it still has nothing to do with Deacon. Deacon is still safely tucked away in his prison.'

'It's just a guess,' Marie said, 'but there's a semi-detached up the road from Lacewing Cottage that's just been let. He was doing high magic. Did he even have a vehicle when he showed up here, Sky?'

Sky shook her head. 'I didn't think to look.'

'He wouldn't have been in any kind of condition to drive after performing high magic, and though it's possible he might have had an accomplice or called a cab, it's not very likely,' Tara said, as the wave of pain eased off a little.

'Deacon could have made anybody do whatever he wanted them to do and not even remember it,' Marie said. 'It's likely this Lucia could do the same.'

Tara practically fell off the chair when the next wave of pain hit. When she could speak again, she gritted her teeth and said, 'Let's give Lucia the benefit of the doubt and check this place out. Quickly, if you don't mind.'

'She dreamed about Deacon,' Kennet said. His head now rested in Lucia's lap, and she stroked his hair tenderly. 'It was a horrible dream. She was filled with despair and terror. I wanted to take her in my arms and tell her none of it was true. I wanted to tell her he's a liar and that we wouldn't let him hurt her again. And then you came, and I had to leave her.'

'Do not trouble yourself, my darling,' Lucia said. 'I have returned her ghost to her, so she is not without comfort. The Elemental Coven is whole again, and all shall be well.'

'Will it?' He sat up, and his head spun. Somewhere far away Tara was in pain, his pain. How could that be? And it wasn't really that far away, was it? He could go to her. He could maybe convince her to forgive him.

'Of course all shall be well, darling. We can make it better for her. That has always been what I have wanted. What you have wanted. You are feeling better now, are you not? And now we have work to do, work that will make it better for everyone. At last, my dear boy, you will have your revenge.'

He stood and walked to the table where the scrying mirror lay, only a thin piece of black silk separating the horror within from the world without – the world that seemed so peaceful. Even being close to it without all of the spells and enchantments of Elemental Cottage made his head ache, made him feel nausea, just noticeable enough to be uncomfortable, coiled in the pit of his stomach. He wished he had never touched it. He wished he had never known anything about it.

'But you do.' She spoke inside his head again. 'You do know about it, and you know that it is not natural, it is only a temporary solution for a scourge that has defiled the world for way too long.'

'And you think you can make it right by forcing me to betray her,' he said. The words were out before he had a chance to think about them, and indeed it had always been the plan for him to betray Tara Stone. He'd always known that it would happen like this. He'd always believed that it was for her own good. A part of him still believed that, but now he knew her. Now he had loved her and dreamed with her. Now he didn't like that he hadn't just come forth and told her what he believed, that he hadn't tried to reason with her, to be honest with her.

'She would not have listened,' Lucia said. Usually she didn't read his thoughts, or if she did she kept her own counsel. He knew it was a sign of how impatient she'd become now that they were this close. 'She would not have believed you. You know this as well as I do, Kennet. She does not trust you.'

'And with good reason,' he said.

Her patience snapped, and he felt it like a whip at the base of his spine. 'Oh, for fuck's sake, Kennet, stop navel gazing and just do it. Only when you have done it can we do what we have to do, what we must do. The magic is ready. You are shielded by me, as you have been these past seven years. He cannot hurt you when you release him.'

'And them? Can he hurt them? Can he hurt her?'

'I cannot promise that no one will be hurt, Kennet. You know this. I cannot just zap Deacon out of existence the moment he is set free. Do you not think I would have done it long ago if it were that simple? It will take time. But at last the end is in sight. Though I cannot promise no one will get hurt, I can promise he will not harm her.'

'Of course not.' He closed his eyes, but he could still see the afterimage of the scrying mirror. 'That's how he does the most damage.'

'What must happen, must happen.' Her words now felt as though they were scraping bone inside him with her rising impatience. 'You have always known this, since you first came to me so desperate for my help. So now, Kennet my love, do what must be done, and we can begin the end.'

He stepped back from the table, and the relief of it was almost unbearable. How could such a thing cause such darkness in his soul? If he could just talk to Tara, just explain to her ...

'She will not understand,' Lucia wrapped herself around him like a garment that was too tight, and he squirmed with rising claustrophobia. 'Now, my darling, do what must be done. Please do not make this more difficult than it need be.'

He took another step backward and the grip that sheathed him tightened, then released so quickly that it felt as though it had removed the very skin from his flesh. Hot abrasive pain seared his brain and he fell to his knees, trying to hold in his mind a vision of Tara.

The pain intensified, as though his flesh were being peeled away from the bone. 'Please do not make me do this, darling,' Lucia said. 'I do not want to hurt you. I can force you to do my bidding, just as Deacon would do. I would prefer not to. I would prefer not to hurt your lovely body, which has given me so much pleasure in the last seven years, but I will have my way, and you cannot stop me.'

Dear Goddess. If only he had met Tara before. If only. Her face swam before his eyes. Would that he really were linked to her in a Dream Knot. To be so joined to such a woman would be more of an honour than any man could possibly imagine. But he was already dead. He was already dead.'

'Yes, my love. You are already dead. There can be no

83

bond, no Dream Knot with the dead. You belong to me. Not to her, though I will happily share you once you have done what I have asked of you, what you agreed to do. It was your bargain, not mine, remember? And I did not lie to you about what the cost would be, about what would be required of you.'

'Please,' he breathed, 'Just let me talk to her. I can make her understand. I know I can.'

She stroked his face tenderly, and it was as though her touch bore shards of glass. 'Do what I ask, Kennet Lucian. Then you may speak to her. Then you may explain, then you may lie in her arms until hell freezes over for all I care, but not before.'

'Then just kill me,' he said. 'I won't do what you ask. I won't betray her.'

'Not in a thousand years will I kill you, Kennet Lucian. I thought I made that very clear to you. Not in a thousand years will I simply let death be your way out of our bargain, and I can easily guarantee you that many years to suffer, though I would prefer not to.'

Tara in his arms on the fells. Tara touching him. Tara dreaming with him. Tara making angry love with him in the greenhouse. Tara. How could she fill his world so completely in such a short time? How could she be worth so much pain? Centimetre by centimetre Lucia took away every fragment of who he was and replaced it with pain, infinite pain that rose slowly, almost tenderly. It rose from silent suffering and crescendoed to exquisite heights and anguished depths of despair he could never have imagined, even in the pit of mourning his own loss. And yet he held. This was the beginning. How long was a thousand years? Ultimately it didn't matter as long as he could remember her face, as long as he could see Tara's face at the point of their shared pleasure, at the point of their joined ecstasy, at the point of their dreaming together. He could no longer remember Patrice's face, nor Annie's face, but Tara's face, every detail of it, every nuance of it, he knew better than his own, and he didn't know why that should be.

Lucia was saying something in her endlessly patient, deceptively gentle voice, but he could no longer hear her. The vision of Tara grew clearer by the minute. She was closer than his breath. How could that be? They could not have made the Dream Knot, not when Lucia possessed him. It wasn't possible, but Tara knew, and she knew where he was. Dear Goddess let her hurry. If only she could get here on time, then Lucia would see, and they could all talk this out and they could all work together.

Somewhere in the back of his mind, Lucia cursed out loud. 'Very well,' he heard her say. 'It sickens me to be like Deacon in any way, but this must be done.'

And as quickly as it came, the pain was gone, but the relief was short lived. The pain was replaced by something much worse. The pain was replaced by the knowledge that he would do exactly what Lucia told him to do, and no matter how hard he fought it, he now no longer had any say in the matter. She didn't toy with his mind. She couldn't be bothered with such subtleties. They were unnecessary. Tara was coming, and she wouldn't be alone. Lucia would wait no longer. The deed must be done and it must be done now. She didn't take over his mind, only the driver's seat, as she called it. And that was even worse because even as he watched with horror while he walked to the table and unwrapped the silk, while Lucia spoke the enchantments to open the bonds of the scrying mirror prison that held Deacon, he could do nothing but what she willed him to do.

At last the true horror of what he'd had to ask of her seven years ago came upon him. She needed nothing more than his body. She needed flesh to do her bidding. And the fact that the flesh offered her had more than a decent command of magic was all the better. He watched helplessly as she finished the spells, and there remained just one little task. His to do. He hated her with an intensity of hate he had not known since the death of Patrice and Annie. 'It will pass, my dear Kennet. It will pass,' she said with a voice one would use to discipline a child. 'You shall not hate me when Deacon is destroyed.'

Inside his head, he could see her beautiful smile. She taunted him with her most exquisite form. For the first time he wished that while she forced him to do this horrible thing, she would do so with her true visage.

She laughed softly. 'I hate no one but Deacon badly enough to unleash that part of me upon them, my darling boy.' Then she nodded toward the mirror on the table, and he knew exactly what to do. They had talked about it so many times. His hands moved without his willing them. He could not will them otherwise, no matter how hard he tried, and he knew that he was near the point of exhaustion from trying. That, coupled with the pain, had left him little choice but to yield. Too late he realised that for the last seven years of his life he'd had little choice. And ultimately it was his own fault. She nodded once again, and her smile was so tender that if he didn't hate her so much, he'd love her. Even as he cried out in anguish, he did exactly what he had known from the beginning he would do. Lucia willed his hands, and he lifted aside the shattered amulet that belonged to Marie Warren, the final lock that held Deacon in his little piece of the Ether.

And the spell was broken.

The world flashed bright in anger and rage that filled the whole universe. Just as Lucia relinquished him, the door burst open and Tara caught him in her arms as he crumpled to his knees. She settled on the floor, easing him down into her arms, holding him, speaking words he couldn't quite make out, words that seemed unbelievably gentle considering what he had just done. He had betrayed Tara. Dear Goddess, he had betrayed her. It was the last thought that filled his head before the pain returned, and he slipped into darkness.

An instant later, on a hill where the property of Lacewing Farm met Elemental Cottage, the earth split, lightning cracked, and the dry stone wall that had stood for hundreds of years along the boundary crumbled and fell as the demon dragged his incorruptible flesh from the place where it had rested for the past year.

Chapter Ten

The knock on Cassandra's door was soft and unnecessary. It asked permission that had already been granted. Afraid that her voice would betray her, she opened it, and Anderson took her into his arms. For a long time they stood on the threshold. He held her there, folded against his chest, against the hammering of his heart, against the flesh that he didn't need, but that he wore with such exquisite finesse. Her own heart felt as though it would burst its boundaries to be even closer to him.

'Oh how I have missed you, my darling Cassandra,' he spoke against the top of her head. At last he released her enough that she could lead him inside and shut the door.

Then she took his hand and guided him to sit on the sofa near the large window that looked out over the fells. 'How's Tara?' she asked.

'She is much better than our demon thief is at the moment. Though I think his ill health weighs on her heart almost as much as what he has done –' he corrected himself '– what he was forced to do.'

She laid her head on his chest. 'Do you think it's possible? That they share the Dream Knot, Kennet and Tara?'

'I have never heard of such a thing happening beyond the banter and tales of old women, but I have no other explanation as to how she could have found him, how she could have known his struggles with the demon, Lucia. He has suffered much at her hand.'

'And no one's heard from Deacon?'

'Indeed not, though I am sure each of us feels his freedom like a noose around our necks.'

'Anderson, I –'

He stopped her words with a kiss, and she heard the hitch of his breath at the feel of her magic, magic that delighted him long before it did her, magic that no longer frightened her, thanks to her time and training in the Elemental Coven. At last he pulled away and spoke. 'Forgive me, my darling. I am only too aware that these are difficult times and that we all hope this Lucia is acting wisely in the release of Deacon. As for myself, I am not optimistic. However, I believe that if any shall prevail, it shall be this coven, as we have always done, as you did so bravely four months ago in the Ether, my love.'

'Anderson, it was the most horrible thing I've ever had to do – and then losing you. I didn't want to keep it from you. I wanted to tell you everything. I thought I would never get the chance to tell you that I love you.'

He kissed her again, his breath coming almost in a sob as he pulled away. 'There are no words in life or beyond that I would more wish to hear from you, my dearest woman. Oh, how I have dreamed of hearing those words from your lips these past long months, of having the opportunity to declare my love for you. But surely, my darling, my ardent feelings can come as no surprise to you.' He held her in his dark gaze. 'And surely you know that my reasons for coming to you at this hour are purely selfish. Had my homecoming been under happier circumstances, I would have taken you right there on the floor in the Room of Reflection, and none present would have begrudged me that pleasure. Indeed, since my return to the World of Flesh, I have longed for nothing so much as to love you physically, while revelling in the boundless joy of what our hearts share. We have not yet had that pleasure, my darling, and I can scarce contain my desire to offer all of myself to you while taking all of you unto me.'

His mouth quirked in a self-deprecating smile and he added, 'I have had only the pleasure of my own hand all these four long months, and that only when my need became unbearable because of my lustful thoughts of you.' He shifted on the sofa in such a way that his heavy erection was clearly visible against his trousers. 'I am in such need, my darling Cassandra, as can scarcely be expressed, and it is a need no one else can satisfy but you.'

In spite of the racing of her pulse and the tightening of her sex with its own powerful need, she raised an eyebrow and folded her arms across her chest. 'I'm a succubus, Anderson. Of course no one else can satisfy your need like I can.'

He moved closer to her and slowly, with infinite patience considering how long he'd been away, opened the buttons of her blouse and pushed it off her shoulders until her bare breasts were freed into his hands, nipples already tensing to his touch. Then he pushed her back on the sofa and moved up tight against her until he could lay his head between her breasts. 'It is this that satisfies me as no other can, Cassandra. It is this heart beating in the breast of the woman I love, and I am beside myself with joy that I have returned to tell you in person what time so cruelly denied me when last we were together.' He kissed each of her nipples in turn, lingering to fondle them until they were distended and heavy above the rise of her areolae, until she felt each tug of his lips, each press of his tongue far away from her breasts, down between her legs. She was reminded again just how much like magic Anderson's lovemaking was. No one was as suited for her to partake of as he was, and no one could give back with such depth, such intense pleasure.

With one hand he undid his fly. He was always amazing at finessing awkward clothing in times of need. Then he shifted enough that his trousers slid down over his hips and she could feel the silky smoothness of his cock, hard and moistened at the tip, as it gouged against the inside of her thigh where his efforts had rucked up her skirt, and her legs fell open to provide him a path to her pussy, which was as free from underwear as her breasts – a little piece of advice from Sky that had served her well. A woman should either wear pretty underwear or no underwear at all. Since Cassandra found most pretty underwear uncomfortable, she was inclined toward the latter and, as Anderson's hand moved to caress her tight curls, then slipped down over her clit to part her labia, the acceleration of his breath, the surging of his penis told her that he might just agree with Sky.

'Oh, my dear, your womanhood is softer than the finest silk.' He stroked two thick fingers up between her parted lips. 'And when your lovely womanly lips yield and open to my caressing, it is as though I have touched paradise, and I want only to enter and never to leave.'

'Can't think of anything I'd like better,' she breathed, grinding her arse against the plush cushion of the sofa. She pulled her knees upward to open herself a little more, to offer him the access they both needed, and he pushed into her slowly, sucking a deep breath as he did so. As he positioned himself, she lifted her legs around him and he thrust deep. His eyelids fluttered, his lips parted and the shudder that went through the hard muscles of his body caused her to grip and press upward into his embrace. 'Will you take from me, my love?' His breath was warm and soft against her face. 'I have so missed the feel of your magic. The memory of your hunger, your lust, has kept me safe from despair, and since I have been restored to you, my manhood has grown impatient with months of waiting.'

'Are you strong enough?' she breathed. 'You've been in the Ether.'

'Do not you worry, my dearest heart.' He shifted to position her on top of him, knowing that was the position from which a succubus could take most deeply. 'The demon has magicked me home well-rested and heavy beneath the weight of my own lust. You may take freely.'

She didn't close her eyes. She couldn't bear to for fear that the man beneath her was still only a dream. She had had so many heart-wrenching dreams these past months, only to wake and find her arms empty – even her very soul felt the emptiness. She opened his shirt, way more awkwardly that he had done hers, then rested her hands on the rise and fall of his pectoral muscles, her thumbs raking his tight dark nipples to lovely stiff peaks.

He groaned at her touch, then returned the favour, kneading the fullness of her breasts almost but not quite to the point of pain. He shuddered as her power moved over him, surrounded him, engulfed him and she began to take from him. He moved his hands down to her hips, as though he were holding on for the ride, and in truth, she supposed that he was.

She was open and receptive to pull his libido into her in ravenous, sumptuous shiftings and tuggings of her cunt. The sounds coming from his throat were unintelligible, deep and animal. The world fell away, as it always did, and she walked with him in the Ether, feeling his disciplined thoughts struggle to push back despair, struggle to focus, always on home, always on those he loved, and always it was the vision of her at the vanguard of all he thought, all he felt, all he needed.

'Do not fret.' His voice came from a long way off. 'Oh, do not weep, my darling Cassandra. I am home now, here in your arms, and if this is all that is afforded us, it is enough, dear Goddess, it is enough'

Beyond the Ether, she could see his fears, his doubts. He didn't trust the demon or her Kennet. He feared for those he loved. Most of all he feared for her.

'I'm all right, Anderson. I'm all right.' She wasn't sure if she spoke out loud or if the words passed to him through her magic, magic that built on his memories, his dreams, his hopes, and fed back into the part of her that was not human, the part of her that understood only lust and libido and life force. And yet the very human part of her spoke, her heart, and her body full of the man she loved way beyond anything the succubus alone could understand. 'You're back, the coven is whole again, and Deacon won't defeat us, Lucia or no.'

She pulled him into her to the very point at which she could feel his strength just beginning to wane, then she clenched, and let go, and they both spiralled into orgasm, him arching upward as though his spine would break, her falling forward onto his chest, drowning in the depths of lust and magic and release, feeling the flood of him inside her in shudder after shudder.

'My beloved –' he spoke in breathless gasps '– I think that perhaps I shall stay here, my manhood nestled so perfectly inside you, for at least the next four months. Yes, that shall alleviate a tiny bit of my lust. Only a tiny bit, however.'

Sky knocked softly and stepped inside the darkened room where Tara sat next to the unconscious Kennet. She came to the coven leader's side without a word and handed her a cup of tea, automatically examining the aura of the injured man. 'She did a real number on him.'

Tara nodded, and took the cup Sky offered.

'You need rest too,' Sky said. 'The past 24 hours haven't exactly been a waltz in the park for you.'

'You can see it, can't you?' Tara said, ignoring Sky's suggestion. 'The hole in his aura?'

'Of course I see it. You could drive a lorry through it. I don't know how the man's still alive. I'm beginning to understand how you mistook him for a ghost. But this is not something I would have missed when he came to the door earlier today. I swear, his aura looked completely whole – a little strange, but then that's not unusual for a powerful witch.'

Tara sat the teacup on the night stand untouched. 'Why didn't he just tell me? Surely he knows that we're not without substantial power, and maybe we could have helped, maybe we could have brought this whole thing to an end without suffering.'

Sky huffed. 'That would be a first, wouldn't it?'

Kennet moaned and cried out, then thrashed on the bed, but he calmed when Tara laid a hand against his forehead. 'What the hell has she done to him?' she said, pushing the damp hair away from his face.

'Hold it right there,' Sky said, her gaze locked on the man in the bed. 'Don't move.'

'What? What is it?' Tara asked. Just then Kennet grabbed her wrist in a grip that belied his weakened condition, and Tara offered a startled little cry at the buzz that passed through her.

'Don't let go of him. Now look at his aura.'

Through the peripheral half-gaze that allowed a witch to see the aura of another, Tara examined Kennet, who once again seemed to be sleeping peacefully. 'Great Goddess,' she breathed. 'That's impossible.'

The hole in his aura was gone, and what had been only a dim band of light close to his body pulsated and expanded to a depth of several centimetres around the slow rise and fall of his chest. Then, from where his hand gripped her wrist, it expanded to encompass Tara.'

'Bloody hell.' Sky's voice was barely more than a whisper. 'Can you see it? Can you see what happens to your own aura when you touch him?'

'I can feel it,' Tara said, 'but I can't see anything.'

Sky blinked hard. 'I can barely look at it, it's so bright. It's like your aura has expanded to protect him, and his aura is … well, it's whole again. No, it's more like the two of you are sharing the same aura. I know your aura, like I know everyone's in the coven, but this… Well, this is not like anything I've ever seen before. It's like you're suddenly, well, like the two of you are suddenly one.'

Tara shivered in spite of the feeling that was quickly becoming pleasure the longer she touched Kennet. 'I don't understand how this can be.' Her voice was breathless, almost the bedroom voice of arousal. Carefully she took her hand away and sat back on the chair. The buzz dissipated, and the hole in Kennet's aura reappeared, but he remained peaceful.

For a long time, the two women watched the sleeping man in silence, then Sky spoke again. 'The protection spells have been strengthened at the perimeters and all precautions have been taken to enhance dream magic and allow Lucia in, just as you asked. Are you sure that's a good idea?'

'No,' Tara said, 'but we need to know what's going on, and she's the only one who can really tell us. Either her plan didn't work to rid the world of Deacon, or her release of him was only step one. In that case, she'll be contacting us soon, I have no doubt.' She heaved a sigh and settled back into her chair. 'If she wanted to hurt us she would have done it by now.'

'I don't know,' Sky said. 'She certainly chose her time with him.' She nodded to Kennet. 'She may well be toying with us too.'

'Could be, but he made a pact of some sort with her, then defied her. Demons tend to get really nasty when they're defied. We've made no such pact with her. We owe her nothing.'

'She returned Anderson to us,' Sky said.

Tara felt a bloom of warmth at her centre, and in spite of the horrendous circumstances in which they once again found themselves, she couldn't fight back the smile when she thought about her high priest safely back in the arms of his coven family. 'He's with Cassandra?' She noticed Sky was also smiling.

'Of course. As soon as he was sure you were all right, he was off to her arms.'

'Good. I hope everyone in this house is fucking like rabbits. We'll need all the strength we can raise, Lucia or not.'

Chapter Eleven

Alice wasn't sure what woke her up from a sound sleep, but she was wide awake the instant her eyes opened, and a sudden burst of adrenaline, as though she had come up from a nightmare, put her on high alert. But there had been no nightmare, none that she could remember. There hadn't been for several weeks now.

She threw off the duvet and slipped into her robe. For the past four months, she'd been unable to sleep through the night, but she'd finally got past the nightmares. The new psychologist, whom Tara Stone had recommended, really seemed to be helping. One of the Elementals had stayed with her round the clock in the early days, but it had been a while since she had needed someone to hold her while she sobbed after the worst of the nightmares. It had been a while since she'd awakened in a cold sweat, dreaming that Deacon had returned for her.

But tonight felt different. She chafed her arms and walked the perimeter, as Tara called it. She walked from room to room checking the dark corners where the ambient light couldn't penetrate, all the while chanting a protection spell, like it was a mantra, chanting it over and over until the words became only so much white noise that comforted her against too much silence. On the good days, she chanted the spell silently. On the bad days, she chanted it out loud.

Tonight, for no reason she could put her finger on, she repeated the spell out loud. She chanted it in the bathroom, where Deacon had appeared to her in the mirror. She chanted it in the kitchen, in the lounge, in the conservatory which led to the garden. Her boots sat muddied and drying after the day's walk up Walla Crag. The weather had been soggy and windy, but it didn't matter. In walking she felt more at peace somehow. Even Deacon hadn't changed that.

For a long time she stood in the cool room watching the rain hitting the glass – it made a sizzling sound, like eggs frying in hot oil. The light from the all-night porch lamp Tim Meriwether had installed for her just before she'd moved back home cast a soft glow across the weeping birch tree that had been one of the reasons she'd bought this bungalow. Birch trees were a symbol of new beginnings. She had really believed all that meant something back before Deacon turned her world upside down.

The bare tree now hung heavy with early catkins that danced manically in the wind, making the shadows of the long thin branches look a little less like skeletal fingers reaching out for her. It wouldn't be long until the tree would be covered with leaves and then it would look much less disturbing in the nights when she wandered about the place unsettled.

She stared into the garden repeating the spell mantra until it came and went with her breath, until each beat of it matched the rapping of her pulse in her throat. Slowly the skeletal dancing of the tree faded from her view like an optical illusion, then the play of light and shadow reflected in the windows like a mirror, and her own robed image came to the forefront. Once her eyes were focused on the shape of her body, it was no longer possible for her not to see herself. As her focus shifted from the shadow dance of the garden to the world reflected back at her through the conservatory window, it was also impossible for her not to see the room behind her taking shape; the drop-leaf table, the bookshelf full to overflowing, the antique American rocking chair she had found at a shop in Grasmere.

And Deacon.

The scream never left her throat. He moved faster than the pounding of her heart until the solid press of his body engulfed her from behind, and she was overwhelmed by the size of him as a thick hand settled to her mouth.

'Forgive me for startling you so, my darling Alice. I simply longed to stand and gaze upon you. You are indeed an exquisite sight to behold.' The heat of his breath stirred the hairs on the back of her neck. 'Oh my dear, how could I ever have believed you were not comely to look upon?'

His hand moved inside the robe to cup her breast, and the press of his erection low against her spine suddenly became impossible not to feel. He shifted until she could feel the hard, anxious shape of him as though they were both naked.

'Yes, my love, now I have flesh with which to pleasure you, and you will no longer have need of rendezvous in pubs and dark alleys.' His hand slid down inside the waistband of her pyjama bottoms and he tut-tutted. 'My, my, you are such a dirty girl, aren't you? I think you can hardly wait for the feel of my cock in your pouty little cunt. Goodness me, I've seen bitches on heat not needing to be mounted as badly as you do.'

To her horror, she realised he was right. She was suddenly more aroused than she could ever remember being in her whole life. She felt as though she would surely die if he didn't fuck her. And yet her whole body was paralysed with the utter terror of his presence in her house again. Only this time her nightmare was made flesh.

He moaned softly and nuzzled her neck as she writhed against him. 'My dear, I can make you tremble like those catkins on that tree and make you flood your gaping twat until you knees collapse beneath you, and I can do it all right here where we stand without so much as touching your sex.' He kissed her neck and tugged her nipple between the rough pads of his thumb and forefinger. 'But would you not rather I pleasure you in the comfort of your own bed, for I promise you, once I have begun, you will never want me to stop. Ever.

'Oh, and look at you, my little one, you are trembling so hard you can barely stand, so great is your need, so great is your fear. And fear and lust together are such a delicious combination. You shall see. But do not you worry, once I have pleasured you, once I have made your hole shiver and convulse with delight, you'll hold your fear to you with such ecstasy, and you'll lie open and begging beneath me, and I won't deny you.'

He turned her to him and lifted her into his arms as though she weighed no more than a fledging bird. 'In fact, my darling, once I have coaxed the first release from your needy aching cunt, you'll forget about everything else but me and how I make you feel.'

As he laid her down on her bed something in the back of her mind recalled the empty place where he had held her captive, the horrible things he had made her do, and how she had done them all willingly because of him.

'Please don't.' Her voice was barely more than a whimper. She wished that she could be strong like Tara. She wished that she could fight him back like Cassandra could, but all she could do was beg. 'Please don't.' The words were a breathless sob. 'This is not what I want. Please don't make me do this.'

'My dear Alice, do not tease me so. Do you think that I don't know your lust? Of course I do. I know your lust better than anyone, better than you know it yourself. Did I not prove that to you when last I companioned you? And was your sex not well satisfied?'

He sat on the bed not touching her, and yet his very nearness made her feel like she would go insane if he didn't touch her, if he didn't make her come. He bent and brushed a chaste kiss across her lips. 'Do you not know how much better your cunt will be pleasured now that I have the flesh to do it myself? All that you felt before will be as nothing compared to what I can give you.' He undid the belt of her robe and pushed it aside, then slowly, almost torturously, undid her pyjama top. By the time he pushed it off her shoulders and cupped her breasts she was crying and writhing and whimpering. In her fevered head she wanted him, while all that was sane and good and decent in her cried out for him to leave her alone.

He bent and kissed each nipple, then rested the heavy

splay of his hand low across her belly. 'I won't do to you what you do not desire, my love. As any gentleman, I will wait for you to ask.' His smile was almost tender, and yet his gaze felt like fire. 'But you will ask, my love. Do not you worry, you will ask, and when you do, you will want me with every fibre of your being.' Again he offered a tender smile. 'And I, my love, would never deny you.'

In the dream, Cassandra stood in her gran's garden next to her mother. It was a dream she'd had often enough. Though she couldn't remember her mother, she'd seen enough pictures of her while growing up in her grandmother's house, and the visits in the Dream World were not that uncommon. Her mother's belly was big, and Cassandra knew it was she who lay settled in the womb, soon to be born.

'What shall I do?' her mother said. 'She won't be fit to live in the world with mortals. What shall I do?'

'I'll be all right, Mummy,' Cassandra said. 'I've found a wonderful coven. They've trained me to use my powers so I won't hurt anyone. Oh, Mummy, please don't worry so.'

But, as was always the case in her dream, her mother could never hear her. Instead, she continued to pace awkwardly as women do who are close to their due date. 'You didn't tell me it would be like this. I thought she would be normal. I thought she would just be a powerful witch, one my mother could be proud of, not like me. Not like me.' Her mother's eyes filled with tears, which she dashed away irritatedly with the back of her hand. 'And don't give me that rubbish about how powerful I am. You know that's not true. You know I only let you do this because I'm weak.'

'Mummy, what are you talking about? You're not weak. It wasn't your fault. How could you have known?' Cassandra said, pacing next to her mother, trying to get her mother to listen to her, as she always did.

'It wasn't supposed to happen – yes, I know it wasn't supposed to happen, but it did, didn't it?' She rested her hands on her belly. 'I didn't tell you I'd carry your child. That wasn't our agreement. I won't give birth to this.'

Even as her mother's words shredded her heart as they always did, all of Cassandra's pleadings fell on deaf ears. She never saw who her mother was talking to, she never understood her mother's despair, and the agony of knowing she was the cause of it made the dream nearly unbearable, even as it happened over and over again.

Cassandra felt a great sense of relief as the scene beneath the oak tree in Gran's garden suddenly washed out and flashed bright like an over-exposed photo, and the world went silent. But the sense of relief was short-lived. She found herself staring into the bright eyes of Lucia. She knew in an instant it was Lucia. She felt it in her blood, in her marrow.

'What do you want?' Cassandra asked.

'Help for Alice.' The woman's voice was sweet and rich, and urgent, and gone as quickly as it had come, as was the bright dream.

'Cassandra, darling? What is it?'

When she came to herself, she was sitting upright in the middle of the four-poster bed, and Anderson was sitting next to her.

'Alice.' Cassandra said. 'She's in danger. Lucia just came to me and told me.'

'Please, my darling Alice, you suffer so needlessly – only yield to your lust, and I will make love to you, and you will feel so much better.'

'Cassandra,' she whispered softly, trying desperately to focus on the succubus, the one who had rescued her from Deacon the first time.

'My darling, the succubus is too busy fucking her ghost to answer your feeble plea. Yes, he has been returned to her by some foul magic, and Elemental Cottage is all aglow with homecomings. Did you not know? Of course you didn't. They would hardly consider telling you their good news. I doubt they even remember who you are, truth be told. Yes, my darling, the succubus is busy, as is everyone else at Elemental

Cottage. They have no time for you. But I do, my lovely. I have all the time in the world for you. Oh, how hot and desperate your little cunt must be right now, Alice, and so needless your suffering. Only but let me mount you my darling, only but let me fill you with pleasure and all of your doubts, all of your suffering will be as though it had never happened. Would you like that, my darling? Of course you would. This,' he said guiding her trembling hand to rest on his erection, 'is only for you, my love, only for you. Oh how it will please you. Yes, that's it, my love, you are so close now, so close to taking what you want. Yes, that's it, touch it, feel it in your hand, and imagine how it will pleasure you in your dirty little cunt. Oh so very close. The words are only a breath away.'

Alice's fingers trembled and tightened a fraction on Deacon's erection, and even as she took breath into her lungs, she still couldn't allow herself to think about what she would now do. In the space of a breath, the choice was still hers, and she was, for a moment longer, her own person.

So powerful was the fever that had come upon her, Alice was never sure what happened next, but the room flashed bright and there was a woman shining like the sun, and her robe looked like dancing flames. What happened then, what she saw, what she heard, was more like a dream.

I had forgotten just how sickeningly petty you are, Deacon,' Lucia said.

Deacon chuckled without looking up at her, his hand still caressing the delirious Alice. 'And yet you released me, my darling Lucia. I may only assume you were bored without me to entertain you.'

'You may assume what you want, but leave the little witchling alone. She has done nothing to you, and I have already alerted the Elemental Coven to her distress. They will be here soon.'

'I have no desire for a happy reunion with my dear friends at Elemental Cottage just yet,' he said, 'though it was rather

101

rude of you to ruin my homecoming party with Alice. I have had four months to plan it. It would have been exquisite. And really, I loathe living in the world of mortals without someone to be my helpmeet. It can get so tedious and banal, don't you think?'

When she didn't answer, he stood and came to her side. 'Where's your pet, the one whose body you now invade?'

'That is not your business, Deacon.'

He circled her once, then again. 'Why have you released me, Lucia? I cannot believe that it was an act of kindness.'

'I would have thought the answer would be obvious, Deacon. I have released you so that I may destroy you. Surely that can come as no real surprise.'

He shrugged as though he had been told nothing more significant than the time of day. 'Indeed. I had hardly expected you to release me for my companionship, not when you have such a luscious pet to pleasure you and companion you, and no doubt he's much more pliable than I.'

It was Cassandra who burst through the door first. All of the Elementals had keys to Alice's bungalow. She had insisted after she returned home, and they hadn't argued. Deacon brushed a kiss across Lucia's knuckles and disappeared instantly, but Lucia remained. For a second the succubus and the demon stared at each other. Then Alice moaned on the bed, and Cassandra rushed to her side. Instantly she threw her arms around Cassandra and sobbed.

'She is unharmed,' Lucia said, as she watched. 'Only frightened. Deacon has that effect on mortals.'

'Yes, he does. And you set him free,' Cassandra said, without looking at Lucia. Then she bundled Alice in the duvet. Anderson materialised at her side and lifted the woman into his arms. 'The Land Rover's outside,' Cassandra told him. And as he carried Alice through the door, Cassandra turned to face Lucia, who offered her a soft smile.

'I see that your ghost has been restored to you, and none the worse for wear.'

'Yes, he has. Thank you.' Cassandra moved toward the

door then stopped to face her once more. 'Oh, and what you did to Kennet, don't you think that was just a little over the top? But then again, you did release a nasty demon back into the world, so I'm guessing over the top is your strong point.' Then she turned and left without looking back.

Chapter Twelve

'You stupid, stupid boy. Do you not know I did not want to hurt you? And what you forced me to do was so much worse. I feel ill just thinking about it. Why did you have to make it so hard? You knew this had to happen. You knew it from the beginning.'

Tara half-surfaced from dozing in the chair to find Lucia pacing back and forth in front of the bed talking softly to the sleeping Kennet. Instantly she was awake and on full alert.

'Hello, Tara Stone,' Lucia said, smiling as though she had just encountered a long-lost friend. 'It is a pleasure to see you again.' When she saw Tara's look of surprise, she raised a golden eyebrow and offered half a smile. 'You have all but invited me to tea, Tara Stone. My presence should not come as a shock to you.' Then she shook her head in a tumble of golden hair. 'Oh, do not worry. It is as you planned. I alone have come. Deacon cannot penetrate your defences. He is not as close to anyone in the coven as I am to Kennet. Though Deacon is quite close to you, my dear. However, I think that bond is much more troubled than the bond Kennet and I share.'

Tara's insides twisted at the hint that she might be close to Deacon, especially after her recent dreams, but she ignored the comment and addressed Lucia's relationship with Kennet. 'You nearly killed him, then you forced him to release Deacon. That sounds pretty troubled to me.'

'I am terribly sorry I had to do both. I shall regret the whole unsavoury incident for a very long time, but circumstances demanded it, and I daresay my regrets shall be mitigated when Deacon is well and truly destroyed and

104

nothing more than a fading memory.'

'In the meantime Deacon's harassing Alice. You know she's not strong enough to withstand a prolonged attack by him. She's only barely recovered from the last time.'

'Then it is good that I was there, is it not?'

'Now that you've released him, what?' Tara asked, the hairs on the back of her neck prickling each time Lucia touched Kennet. 'Are you just going to leave us to it? Because I'm not really pleased about that plan. We had Deacon under control, then you come in and –'

'This is the only way to defeat him for good,' Lucia interrupted. She nodded down to Kennet. 'He knows this, and he got squeamish when it came to doing what had to be done. This is what happened.'

'Fine, if that's the case, I'll be chuffed to bits to get rid of the bastard once and for all.' She nodded to the door. 'We're about to have a coven meeting, see what we can learn from Alice, regroup and do damage control. If you have the ultimate plan of action for us, then by all means join us.'

The image of Lucia bloomed, then wavered as though she were giving Tara's invitation some thought. Then she smiled and shook her head. 'I do not enjoy group activities, but Kennet may speak for me.'

Tara nodded to the unconscious man in the bed. 'Any suggestions on how he might pull that off?'

'Oh for fuck's sake!' Lucia's image bloomed bright enough that Tara had to shield her eyes, then it settled back again to a gossamer tremor. 'After the stunt he pulled, he deserves to have to suffer until his miserable frail body can heal itself, but I suppose what happened should not have surprised me when the man is in love. I did warn him, and if you are wise, you will give him no encouragement that he cannot act upon. I do not mind if you fuck him, in fact it would do you both good. It is absurd for practitioners of sex magic to abstain from the very act that empowers them. But remember, it is intercourse, nothing more.'

Love? Tara could do nothing but gape in response, but

before the full impact of what Lucia had said could sink in, the demon leaned down and kissed Kennet on the mouth, lingering just a second too long for a chaste kiss. And, as she did so, the room flashed bright and Kennet's aura expanded then contracted around him until it was barely visible, and finally it settled, healthy and strong, around his body. But the hole was still there.

Then Lucia turned back to Tara. 'By the way, your succubus has quite the smart mouth. Though I suppose I am in part to blame for it. It might get her in trouble one of these days if she encounters someone less benevolent that I am.' Then, she was gone, and Kennet sat upright in his bed.

For a moment, he was confused, then he saw Tara and offered her a sleepy smile. 'I dreamed I was here in Elemental Cottage with you.' He looked around. 'Nice guest room.'

'It's my room,' she replied.

The smile vanished from his face and he lay back on the bed, his arm thrown over his face. 'Your bed,' he whispered. 'Dear Goddess, I'm in your bed after what I did.'

'Well it's not like you were much fun in my bed. You actually haven't done anything but sleep since we got you here. Not very entertaining at all,' she said, feeling a lot closer to tears than she wanted to be. That pissed her off.

'I'm surprised you didn't make me sleep with the dogs.'

'We don't have any dogs.'

He sat up on the edge of the bed, oblivious to the fact that he was naked. 'Aren't you angry?'

'Damn right I'm angry. You should have told us. Don't you think we'd happily consider anything to rid the world of Deacon?'

A look of pain crossed his face, and for a second she thought Lucia had changed her mind and he was suffering again, but instead he squared his shoulders and spoke. 'This is what I've been planning with Lucia for seven years. You were only an abstract, a thought, a part of the plan to destroy Deacon.' He looked down at his hands resting on his knees. 'Then I met you.'

There was a knock on the door and Sky poked her head in and raised an eyebrow when she saw Kennet. 'Everyone's downstairs. Is he going to join us?'

Both women looked at him.

'Could I have a quick shower first?' he asked. 'And maybe some clothes.'

'Keep the crowds calm for ten minutes,' Tara said.

A hush settled over the library when Kennet joined them, his arm wrapped around Tara's. He really didn't need her support, but he would take what he could get, and that she was even speaking to him at all, let alone nursing him back to health in her own bed, made him happier than he had felt in a very long time. Until he remembered why the meeting had been called in the first place.

When they had all settled and Fiori had served tea and banana walnut bread, Tim spoke first. 'Marie and I visited the grave.' He shuddered. 'No surprise it's empty and the stone wall on either side has collapsed for several hundred metres. He couldn't have been too long out of the ground when he headed your way, Alice.'

'I don't know how long he was there before Cassandra and Anderson got to me,' Alice said. 'Keeping track of time wasn't the first thing on my mind.' The woman with short brown hair sat wrapped in a McKenzie tartan and looking much worse for the wear than Kennet did. His heart ached for her if she'd had to face Deacon alone. And his conscience stung powerfully knowing that it was his fault.

'I'll send someone for your things, Alice. You're not to go back, do you understand? We can't protect you there without shorting ourselves here.' Tara studied her for a moment, then shook her head. 'I mean it. This time I'll tie you to the bedpost, lock the door and throw away the key if I have to. I don't fancy rescuing you from the Ether again.'

Alice blushed, but made no effort to protest.

'Lucia paid us a visit a little while ago,' Tara said. She raised a hand to silence the mumbling of surprise, then continued. 'She decided to heal the damage she's done so Kennet could represent her, since she doesn't like crowds. Also, she said that our succubus has a smart mouth.' There was sniggering, but Tara held Cassandra's gaze. 'We all know that you have a smart mouth, Cassandra, and we love you anyway, but Lucia's a demon. She might not be as tolerant as we are, so if there are future encounters, keep your mouth shut. Are we clear?'

Cassandra nodded and settled in closer to a dark-haired man with a very closely trimmed beard, who Kennet guessed must be the ghost returned from the Ether.

Then Tara took what was clearly a very old book of shadows from the end table next to where she sat on the leather sofa, opened it and read.

Thrice bound and once released. The spell shall reverse what was not meant to be, so shall it be done.
Thrice bound and once released. Banish the demon, the smoke and the flame, as above so below.
Thrice bound and once released. The reflection of reflection. His seed passed to dust as though he'd never been. So completes the circle, so begins again.

There was shifting in the seats and Kennet could tell that everyone was now looking at him.

Tara spoke. 'Kennet and Lucia believe that the emphasis of this passage is not on the thrice bound, but instead on the once released. Clearly when we bound Deacon the third time, nothing happened beyond the fact that we ended up with a nasty demon prisoner in Elemental Cottage. Not a pleasant experience for anyone.'

'The once released isn't proven to be much more helpful,' the American woman said. Then she nodded to Alice. 'Now that Deacon's free, we have to try and figure who he'll target next in his efforts to get even with the coven and Tara. Not very helpful at all, Kennet.'

Once again all attention was on him. Lucia wasn't in

residence at the moment, and he was really miffed that she'd left him to wing it through the plan she'd never actually got around to telling him. Clearly she was still pissed off at him. Strange that he felt less empty when Tara was around. He barely noticed Lucia's absence. But he knew if he took one false step, she'd be there to slap him back. 'Semantically it only makes sense this way,' he said. 'Thrice bound and once released. The actions all speak of each other, think about it. If the passage were talking about binding Deacon three times in order to be free of him, it would read differently. Thrice bound and once released speaks of what has to happen in order for the spell to be reversed. It doesn't refer to the release we'll have from Deacon once he's been bound three times.'

'That makes sense,' the dark-haired ghost said. 'But as our Marie has already indicated, the releasing of Deacon has, based on the evidence so far, not destroyed the demon.'

'Maybe the passage is talking about what has to happen in order to make Deacon vulnerable to destruction,' Fiori said. 'The second line about banishing the demon, the smoke and the flame, well, that could be talking about Lucia, I suppose, and maybe about how she'll have a part in it.'

Sky spoke up. 'With a demon's fondness for fire, it could just as easily be talking about Deacon. Or I suppose it could mean he can be destroyed with fire.'

'The last part,' Marie said, 'the part about the reflection of reflection. His seed passed to dust as though he'd never been. That sounds in a lot of ways like what Tim and I already did. But if that was the original way that the demon's power entered Deacon, and if the circle is to be completed, maybe that's worth revisiting.'

Tara tugged at her lip with her teeth and shook her head. 'Well at least we're thinking outside the box. Surely there must be something else you can give us, Kennet.'

'I've already told you, even the first time I saw Lucia, she was fighting with Deacon, and at the time she was losing the battle. My interruption gave her a reprieve,' Kennet said. 'She has reason to hate him, and she'd never release him if she didn't have a plan to destroy him.'

Tim burst out laughing. 'So that's it. That's all you can give us. Lucia's pissed off at Deacon, therefore we should trust her. Shit!'

It happened so fast that Kennet felt like he had been hit in the gut as Lucia returned to him, took up residence and filled him. Everything seemed brighter and clearer as he spoke. 'Do you want to be rid of Deacon or do you just want to piss around like children in a school yard? I've lived with the presence of a demon for seven years. I know what she's capable of. Believe me I know.' He turned his attention to Anderson. 'You're back with your coven and with your lover because of her. All she's done has been in an effort to prove her goodwill, but certainly you wouldn't have let her release Deacon, even if I'd asked. Even if my logic had been flawless.'

'You tried to stop her.' Tara said, quietly. 'And she nearly killed you for it.' Before he could respond she continued. 'We're the bait, aren't we?'

She caught him off guard, and even with Lucia in residence, he found himself suddenly speechless. The bait. Lucia had always used euphemisms for what the role of the Elemental Coven would be in her plan, and anyway it had never mattered before he'd actually met Tara. The bait. Lucia had said that, no matter what happened, Deacon would always be drawn to Tara Stone and those she loved. No matter what happened, he would be close to her, hoping to take from her anything, everything that gave her joy, made her happy, brought her pleasure. He remembered thinking it was genius to go to the place where Deacon was sure to be drawn. He remembered thinking that he was glad Deacon held such a grudge against someone, someone who could hold his interest, distract him, while he and Lucia destroyed him. The very thought now made him feel ill. He drew his attention back to Tara, who held his gaze with accusing eyes.

'We're the bait, aren't we?' she repeated. 'Lucia knows

he'll keep coming back and coming back until he's robbed me of all that's mine, until he's decimated the Elemental Coven. And all she has to do is keep trying and, with any luck, eventually she'll get it right before he can destroy the whole coven. Isn't that it? Isn't that the plan?'

Lucia's silence inside him, the way she settled in when the truth was on the table made him reel with the weight of it. He felt as though he might be sick. He felt as though all the oxygen had gone out of the room, as though he would never be able to breathe again. 'Tara.' His voice was little more than a whisper. 'Believe me, when I approached Lucia, I didn't know who you were, I didn't understand –'

'And yet you trusted her.'

He could swear he felt the room tremble with her anger, and the cups in their saucers trembled, and the light in the chandelier dimmed.

'Yes.' His own words felt like stones, breaking him to bits as they forced their way out into the open to be heard by everyone, to be heard by Tara. 'At the time, it didn't matter.' Goddess, how he wished that weren't true! How he wished he could lie to her, say what she wanted to hear, make her believe better of him, better than he deserved. But she would know. There was not the tiniest bit of doubt in him. She would know.

All eyes were on him and he felt more naked that he could ever remember feeling, more miserable. But there were no words, and it didn't seem to bother Lucia at all.

Tara closed her eyes for a moment and took a deep breath. Then she opened them, and her gaze was hard and colder than the wind that blew off the high fells in the dead of winter. 'Get out.'

The room erupted in chaos. He didn't hear what was being said. He didn't care. He only cared that he had, once again, betrayed her, even without intending to. He reached out and touched her arm. 'Tara please, Listen to me. I need to –'

She jerked away from him. 'I said get out. Now.'

As Sky escorted him to the door, he could barely believe

everything that had happened in 24 hours, and now he was going to lose the only thing in his life that had mattered in the past seven years. How could it be that this, this woman could matter so much in such a short time? How could it be that she could make him so miserable with so little effort?

Lucia moved inside him, positioning herself as she always did when he needed comfort, and up until now it had always worked. Yes, she had been harsh with him, but she had also been gentle, she had also given him comfort in his darkest times, times that were surely darker than these. But at the moment it didn't feel like any times could be darker. At the moment it didn't feel like he could ever be comforted again.

'Do not worry, my darling,' she said, inside his head. 'She does not mean it. She will come to her senses soon enough, I promise. Oh please do not mope. I promise all shall be well. You shall see.'

For the first time in all the years he'd been with Lucia, he wished he had just accepted his fate and died in the hospital rather than throwing sanity aside and seeking out the demon. And yet, even before the thought had time to form clearly, he realised he'd do it again if it would give him a chance to be with Tara Stone, only for a little while.

Lucia could always take the tiniest grain of hope and make it seem huge and, at the moment, he needed all the hope he could get.

'Come, let us go home, darling. You have had a very rough day, and you need to eat, then I shall make you feel better.'

For the first time in seven years, he seriously doubted that.

Chapter Thirteen

Tara stood like a statue, not moving, while the storm broke around her.

'We've never cast anyone out,' Sky said. 'What the hell's the matter with you?'

'I certainly wouldn't be here if you did,' Tim said.

'Has everyone just forgotten that the man released Deacon, who nearly cost us Anderson?' Marie paced, gesticulating wildly, as she had a tendency to do when she was angry.

'He hardly had a choice, did he?' Sky said. 'Let's not forget it was Lucia who brought Anderson back to us, if we're pointing fingers here.'

Tara heard it all, somewhere far removed from herself. And when she could listen no more she turned on her heel, and stomped into the kitchen. At the door, she slipped into her boots and waterproof jacket, which hung on the peg. Then she headed out the back gate across the fields. It was a longer walk to the fells from here, and it was drizzling, but it didn't matter. A long walk in any weather beat the suffocation threatening to burst her chest. She felt as though her heart had been ripped from her. How the hell would she be able to protect those she loved? And this! This she had no say in. This was nothing to do with her.

She hadn't gone far before the drizzle became a wind-driven horizontal assault, stinging like tiny needles in her face as she pressed into it. Deacon, she could deal with – hadn't she kept ahead of him all these years? But a demon who only wanted to use her as bait, and a man who was so hell-bent on avenging something that had happened seven years ago that he didn't care who got hurt in the process – what the hell was she supposed to do with that?

As the weather worsened, she found herself heading toward the Dream Cave. The route was flooded. They couldn't have got to it with a vehicle, but she was on foot. The path had turned into a full-blown stream, which filled her boots and drenched her legs nearly up to her knees with icy water, but she barely felt it. By the time she made her way into the dry comforting interior of the cave, she was well and truly soaked.

Feeling leaden and raw, she plopped down on the stone ledge where the witnesses always witnessed the dream. She buried her face in her hands. Her world had collapsed yet again. Would she ever fucking get used to it? Would she ever be able to make it stop happening? And this time it was all beyond her control, taken completely out of her hands. Up until now there had always been an element of control, even when she felt helpless. It was always her and the coven against Deacon, and Deacon, she understood. His agenda was never a secret one.

For a long time she sat in silence, just breathing, just listening to her own heartbeat. But years of recognising Deacon's presence as the portent of bad things to come meant she felt his nearness instantly. It started with a shiver down her spine, somewhere between terror and lust. But she recognised it, and she spoke without looking up.

'If I could, Deacon, I'd destroy you now, this minute. And if all that was needed was my rage, you would have been destroyed long ago.'

She felt him settle around her like a cold mist, and then he took physical form and sat down beside her.

'If all that you had was your rage, Tara Stone, then you easily could have destroyed me long ago. But you are still mortal, my love, and like all mortals you cannot refine your feelings to the level of purity necessary for destruction such as you wish upon me.'

His voice sounded so sad that she had to look up to see that she had not imagined the lines drawn on his face, a face that was strikingly handsome, though it was long since she had noticed his looks. The sum of his actions had rendered him hideous in her eyes almost since she could remember. But his moods were always powerfully etched on his face. Even in the dim light of the Dream Cave it was not hard to make out his demeanour. But then he was a demon. What he projected would be seen as he wished it to be seen. He'd be certain of that.

'Mortal feelings are mongrel at best,' he said. 'They're never pure, never sharply defined, never single-minded. My darling, you don't even understand your own feelings, you can't speak them clearly even when they're writ larger than life, clear for everyone else to see. That's no fault of your own. That's simply the neuroses of your humanity making purity of purpose impossible.'

She had no strength to argue with him. It was an exercise in futility, and she knew she should walk away. He sat next to her as though they were old friends, as though she had invited him around for tea, and she knew full well that there was nothing she could do about it. She also knew that he wouldn't harm her. In that there was comfort. Not that he would do her no harm, but that while he was here in her company, he was not harming those she loved.

For a long time the two sat side by side in silence. It would have been considered companionable silence by anyone watching from the outside who didn't know their circumstances. Then he spoke again. 'You are not your rage, Tara Stone. If you were only so, then I would have tired of you long ago. But I'm no more capable of forgetting about you than you are me. The complexity of your feelings, the intrepid loyalty of your heart, the anger, the lust, the tenderness that you so often push away, all of those facets draw me to you like a lodestone. All of those facets of you compel me to do what I must to intensify and refine the enticing muddied, neurotic, mongrel mix that makes you so exquisite, that makes me unable to stay away from you.'

'I'll do whatever I have to do to protect my own,' she replied, looking back to the entrance of the cave where the rain had stopped.

He laughed softly. 'My darling woman, I have never doubted that you would for even a second. And that is a part of your exquisiteness.' He nodded to the cave entrance. 'Kennet, the one possessed by the she demon – surely you'll relent and welcome him back into the Elemental fold. His suffering to protect you from me has been touching to behold, and indeed the inner workings of the man are no less muddied that are yours.'

She felt the bottom drop out of her stomach. Her pulse beat like wings against her ears. And suddenly everything made perfect sense. She possessed him! Lucia possessed him! Kennet was, in some strange way, possessed by Lucia.

'Did you not know that, my dear woman?' He smiled as though he were reliving a fond memory. 'Indeed, he offered himself to her in order to exact revenge on me. The lad would not take no for an answer, as I understand it. I was, and am, flattered to have been the cause of such a bold, yet foolish act.' He shrugged. 'Lucia has always enjoyed taking up residence in the flesh of mortals, a situation I find to be much more awkward, much less elegant than my own method of walking among the living. But then such a choice is all up to personal tastes, I suppose.

'When you and I had our lovely little chat earlier in your Room of Reflection, I suspected that Lucia might be the cause of the strange goings on in the Ether. And indeed, she shall make my existence, and yours I daresay, much more interesting. I think that we shall all find the times ahead exhilarating.' He heaved a happy sigh as though he had just been chatting with his best mate. 'I must go, my darling. I have plans to make, as I'm sure you understand. I've enjoyed our little rendezvous. We must do it again. We have so very much to talk about.' As quickly as he appeared, Deacon vanished, but she felt the lingering brush of his disembodied

116

embrace before he left the cave completely.

'That will be Tara Stone,' Lucia said, concerning the relentless hammering on the front door. 'Even more quickly than I anticipated. You see, my dear Kennet, I told you she would come around. She is just a little hot tempered, but then neither of us is unaccustomed to a fiery temper, are we?'

When he opened the door, she stood before him drenched to the skin. She stood unmoving until he motioned her inside. He didn't know quite what to say, and he didn't trust his voice. Besides, he was still more than a little bit wounded that she'd kicked him out of Elemental Cottage.

Inside, she only stood dripping on the rug in front of the door, staring at him.

'Can I take your coat? You'll catch your death,' he finally managed.

When she still only stood staring at him, he slid the open anorak off her shoulders and hung it on the peg by the door. She let him.

Inside him Lucia was talking non-stop. 'Get her warm, she looks like she is in shock, find out what happened. No! Get her warm first. Make her some tea. Maybe she needs to eat.'

Fucking hell, he thought, she was behaving like an overprotective mother. He felt her bristle with resentment at his insinuation.

He settled Tara onto the sofa and unfolded the blanket from the end, draping it gently over her shoulders. 'Can I get you some tea? You really should get out of those wet clothes. I've got a clean tracksuit. I know it's way too big for you, but at least it's dry. Really, you need to get dry and warm.'

Lucia was now smirking. Mentally he gave her the finger.

When Tara still only stared at him, he took her hand, and he felt Lucia flinch. Tara mirrored the flinch and pulled her hand away. 'It's true. You let her possess you.'

Inside he felt Lucia tense, but there was nothing she could do.

There was no real need for him to respond. It wasn't a

question. He braced himself, expecting the worse. She continued. 'That explains so many things. That explains why I thought you were a ghost. That explains the hole in your aura.' She ran a hand through her wet hair and blew out a breath. 'Jesus, this is way more than some nebulous pact, Kennet. You let her possess you.'

He stiffened. 'I didn't let her. I hounded her. She didn't want to do it. I wouldn't leave her alone. I knew she wanted what I wanted – Deacon destroyed – and I knew if anyone could make that happen, she could. I couldn't do it alone. Hell, I wasn't likely to even survive my injuries – injuries he left me with after he tortured and killed my family. Either way I was a dead man, and I didn't care.' He felt almost like Lucia was pressing up tight against the back of his eyes, on the edge of her seat so to speak, wanting Tara to understand almost as much as he did. Then he added, 'You'd have done the same thing in my shoes.'

She stared at him as though he had two heads. He supposed, in a way, he did have. Then she nodded. 'I bloody well would have if I'd known it were even an option.'

He blinked and gave several fish gasps at the answer he so hadn't expected. Inside him Lucia shifted with interest at the thought. Though he was certain, if anything, Tara Stone would have been even more poorly behaved than he was. No doubt Lucia considered that.

Tara continued. 'So far as I know none of my people ever came in contact with Lucia, though I have a suspicion perhaps Cassandra's grandmother might have.'

'Cassandra's grandmother was Elizabeth Dalton, wasn't she? My mother's mother was in her coven before the family relocated. There could be some connection. You would have done what I did?' He had to ask again just to double-check he hadn't imagined it.

She nodded. 'In a heartbeat, at least a dozen times. More like a hundred.' Her answer tore at him. How had she endured it? He wasn't sure that even if he had survived his injuries he could have endured without Lucia. There was no denying she made it better. She healed him in more ways than just physically.

'You're shivering,' he said. 'Please let me get you some dry clothes.'

She shook her head. 'I have to get back. I left in a huff, then when I found out … about you, I went back for the Land Rover and no one knows what the hell's going on. I need to get back.' A blush crawled up her throat and onto her cheeks. Goddess, she had a beautiful throat. 'I have a bad temper sometimes, and sometimes the coven suffers for it. And none of this is their fault.' Her eyes were suddenly dark with the pain of worry, pain he'd brought on her, he knew, and his stomach ached for it. 'This is not a good time for me to get pissy,' she said.

He reached out and took her hand and, to his surprise, she didn't pull away. 'Can I go back with you? I've caused this, and I'd like to help end it. I mean, that was the plan all along.'

She eyed him suspiciously. 'Are you bringing her with you this time? Because we could really use both of you.'

He nodded. 'Don't worry. She's never very far.'

It didn't take him long to pack a few things. He only had a few things to pack. Once he was buckled into the Land Rover next to her, she spoke again. 'You say she wasn't with you when we made love.'

'No,' he said cautiously. 'I reckon that's why you though I was a ghost.'

She sat mulling over what he'd said, still not starting the engine. 'What does it feel like, having her there inside you?'

He laughed nervously. 'It's not something I've ever talked about with anyone before. I was dead for 15 minutes. I was never quite sure if that was when I worked the spell to find her or if that was, you know, when the changeover took place, and she possessed me.' He looked down at his hands folded in his lap. 'After that, I woke up feeling full … not in a bad way, but like there had been all this empty space inside me I'd not realised was there until she moved in. Then everything was clearer, brighter. I don't know. It's hard to explain. Things are easier for me. I'm never ill, and I heal really fast. Well, instantly if she wants me to. Slowly if she wants to make me suffer. That doesn't often happen.' He saw her grimace, and he added quickly, 'I knew all of this when I badgered her into possessing me. She didn't try to soft-pedal. She tried to get me to bugger off, but I wasn't having it.'

'Sounds like you're making excuses for her.'

'No. I'm not. I'm telling you the truth. And what she did, what I did when I released Deacon ... well, she's never, ever forced me to do anything before. Ever.'

'Lovely.' She started the engine.

After she had pulled out on the road, he said, 'she wants you to like her.' He felt stupid the second he'd said it. Lucia gave him the internal equivalent to an elbow in the ribs

'Why would she care? She's a demon.'

'Maybe because she needs you. I don't know. I want you to like her.' He caught his breath. 'I want you to like me.' There was another demonic elbow to the ribs.

'Then give me a reason.' She downshifted hard and didn't speak again until they pulled into the drive in front of Elemental Cottage.

When she turned off the ignition, he asked, 'How did you know?'

She sat very still for a minute looking out into the pouring rain. 'Deacon told me.'

Chapter Fourteen

'He's quite lovely, your little pet,' Deacon said. 'I'm rather surprised you ever let him out of your sight. They're so poorly behaved, mortals, when you give them their head.'

'Do go away, Deacon, I do not desire your company at present.' Lucia stood on the ridge between Maiden Moore and High Spy looking down into the Borrowdale Valley.

'Ah, but you must be bored, Lucia. After all, Kennet sleeps, a mortal weakness of which our kind does not partake.' He shook his head sadly. 'And, if I am not mistaken, your Kennet sleeps alone. Inconvenient for both of you. I was so sure Tara would take him to her bed. The two are so good together, don't you think? She certainly hardens his cock. Oh, forgive me, my dear. How rude of me to make such an observation. It was not my intention to make you jealous, though I certainly can't blame you. Would that he were mine, I would have him up my arse with abandon. But then it is more difficult when you exist in the flesh only when you possess his lovely body, is it not?' His laugh was thick and indulgent. 'Oh my dear, I cannot tell you how often I have entertained myself in the days of my confinement with thoughts of one so very feminine as you residing in the flesh of such a virile young male. No lovely breasts, no tight wet cunt, just this flesh –' he stroked his own cock through his trousers as if to demonstrate '– which can stiffen at the most inopportune moments.' He continued to stroke absently.

'Why are you disturbing me?' she asked again, watching him stroke himself as disinterestedly as she might watch an ant crossing the pavement.

'My dear, I have come to see how your plans for my destruction are progressing. Oh, you and your pet shall have such fun scheming my demise with Tara Stone and her lackeys. I shiver with delight at the very thought. I'm almost sorry I can't join the party.' He moved closer. 'He fascinates me so, your pet. And even more importantly, he fascinates Tara Stone. He's your weakness, my darling Lucia. Surely you can see that. And I see that he's also Tara Stone's weakness, though I doubt she knows it yet.'

'He is my strength, Deacon, do not doubt that for a moment. And he will be her strength as well.'

'And yet when you're finished with him, he shall die.' He smiled brightly. 'Fascinating, these mortals, how willing they are to sacrifice life and limb for the love of flesh and bone and for their diminished visions of revenge. But he certainly has been willing to sacrifice more than most.' He raised a hand. 'Oh, please don't misinterpret my meaning, dear Lucia. I admire him deeply, that he has adjusted so very well to living a life that's only half-human. And truly he's had to adjust. On the other hand, our poor dear succubus has struggled her whole life to divorce herself from that part of her which makes her such a unique treasure in a world that's so mundane. She's done all so she might pass as more ordinary, more fit to live among mortals.' He raised an eyebrow. 'What is it, my darling? You seem very sensitive where the succubus is concerned.' He stopped stroking his cock and moved to stand next to her – so close that his flesh nearly skimmed the edge of her visage. 'Did you perhaps fuck the dear thing's father? Are you perhaps jealous that his seed would only grow in a human womb?'

'Don't be absurd, Deacon. I have no desire for the travails of mortal women.'

'And yet it was the succubus whom you called upon to come to the rescue of dear Alice. I find that rather strange.'

'Not strange at all. A succubus is a creature at home in the world of dreams. It was easy for me to contact her, and I knew she would be with her ghost, who could be there instantly.'

'Oh please, my dear woman, do not take me for a fool. You've had dream contact with several of those who reside at Elemental Cottage, including Tara Stone herself, and any of her ghosts could have come to wipe poor suffering Alice's nose in less than a heartbeat. And yet, you approached the succubus, who, if I'm not mistaken, has no fondness for you in her heart even after you rescued her dear Anderson from the void.'

He paced the fell in front of her, looking out over Derwentwater. Then he turned to face her, eyes bright with humour. 'She is rather a delightful creature, our Cassandra, is she not? And it was she who put me in that horrid mirror prison.' He shivered. 'Mind you, it was more luck than skill, but still, I do owe her for that little four-month holiday at Tara Stone's expense.' He rubbed his hands together. 'And she would be such a delightful helpmeet. Why, the two of us together, our strength would be unimaginable.'

Lucia's power flared, and it was as though the whole fell was on fire. Her countenance changed from loveliness to the substance of which the very worst of nightmares are formed, and even Deacon cringed at the sight of her. 'Stay away from the succubus!' Her voice roared like the sound of fire raging through a forest. 'And from all that is mine.'

Deacon didn't see the blow coming but, in bodily form as he was, he couldn't deflect it. There was another bright flash, and the aftershock hit him full on, sending him reeling from his body into the most remote part of the Dream World. It sent him into the realm of night terrors and monsters, into the place he had only ever traversed once before – and that had been when the young succubus had dragged him there. She had done so in order to force her release, nearly losing her own life for her efforts. He was not certain whose nightmare he now walked, but it was not that of Cassandra Larkin, though there were echoes of the horrors she had shown him. The place was darker than suited him. There seemed to be a strange absence of fire, and fire often populated nightmares.

Of course, he was in a cave, the realm of the unconscious mind, deep beneath the surface of human awareness.

At first the chant sounded like nothing more than dry bones rubbing together in a graveyard, a sound few would know as he knew. He cocked his head and listened, and the sound became words, rhythmic and repeating like a poem, like a spell ...

Thrice bound and once released. Thrice bound and once released. Thrice bound and once released.

It matched the rhythm of the heart he no longer had. It clawed at his lungs and throat like the breath he no longer needed, and it made him feel something he had long forgotten, something more unpleasant than anything in all of his experiences – fear, panic, terror.

With a shudder that felt as though it would rip him apart, he was instantly back in his body on the fells, gasping for breath, shivering and wet in the rain, and the rage he felt was more powerful than any he had felt since his own death.

Cassandra woke from another dream of her mother. They were always so disheartening. In them her mother never saw her as anything but a monster; in them her mother never loved her enough to try and see her for who she was. There had been nothing even remotely resembling unconditional love in her life until her grandmother had found her in the orphanage. But then, she reminded herself, her mother had died soon after she was born, and these were only neurotic dreams. Her mother might have grown to love her in time. And anyway, she shifted in Anderson's arms and felt him move against her, anyway now her life was filled with unconditional love, love she'd never imagined she'd have.

As she swung her legs over the edge of the bed, Anderson stirred next to her and reached to stroke her back. 'What is it, my love, another dream?'

She nodded, then she stood and began to dress. 'I need some fresh air. I'm going for a little walk.'

'Then I shall come with you. You know you cannot leave

the grounds alone.'

'Damn it,' she said. 'Deacon's free and now we're all prisoners thanks to Lucia.'

'I am sorry, my love, but Tara is right in desiring none of us to leave the protection of Elemental property alone.'

'Of course she's right. I'm not complaining about the choices Tara's made. Tara had the situation all sorted if that bitch would have just left things alone.' She offered him an apologetic smile. 'I'm sorry, Anderson. I didn't mean to complain. You go back to sleep. I'll just go to the greenhouse. Sky mentioned stocks are running low for the apothecary. There's plenty to do there.'

'My darling, I am not in need of further sleep, as you know, and though you delight in the labours of the greenhouse, I confess I do not understand why. I shall give you time alone with your thoughts and, with your kind permission, I shall entertain. myself in your absence by enjoying a good book in the library, an act which I have sorely missed these past four months.' He moved to stand behind her still naked and warm from sleep, his erection a reminder of what she could have if she would only return to the bed with him. 'Though I would happily hold you to me for ever if there were only my own selfish feelings to be considered.'

She leaned back against him and let him nuzzle her neck, the coarse hair of his beard tickling her soft nape. 'I promise I won't be long, and when I return ...' her hand snaked between them to caress his cock, and he groaned against the side of her throat. 'When I return, I'll have some of this.'

'And I shall see that you get a full portion, my love, a very full portion indeed.'

Cassandra had just set to work transplanting the coriander seedlings when she realised she needed more compost from the garden shed. As she stepped out into the rain-washed air she caught movement out of the corner of her eye and looked up to see Alice running down the lane away from Elemental

Cottage.

'Alice!' She slammed the greenhouse door behind her and raced for the garden gate, shoving it open with a hard thrust of her palm. 'Alice wait!' But the woman glanced over her shoulder and only ran faster. Cassandra sprinted after her, breathlessly calling her name, but the harder she sprinted, the faster Alice ran. How was that even possible? Then Cassandra remembered Deacon's marionette act with the poor woman four months ago above the Honister Slate Mine, and the thought both sickened and terrified her. She had to reach Alice before she got to the crossroads where the protection spells of Elemental Cottage came to an end. With a burst of speed that nearly split her lungs, she lunged for her just as the woman vanished into thin air, and Cassandra plunged headlong through the crossroad and over the boundary. The second she realised that there had been no Alice, that it had all been an illusion, was a second too late. Her body crumpled at the side of the lane, and her fetch was yanked from her with such force that it would have taken her breath away had she had any left to take. It all happened so fast. There hadn't even been time to cry out for help.

She didn't know how long she floated in peaceful silence just barely aware of the boundaries of her own consciousness. At some point, she realised she was dreaming. And then she woke lying on the familiar four-poster bed. A chill ran down the spine she knew she didn't really have. Strange that the bed should be under the oak tree in her gran's back garden. Her hands were tied above her to the headboard, wrists crossed, and her ankles were tied with soft silken ropes so that her legs were splayed, exposing her vulva. She was naked. Then the age-old dream began. Her pregnant mother sobbed and wailed to some unseen person about the monster growing in her belly, about how she would never have agreed if she had known it would be like this.

Cassandra struggled to rouse herself from the hated dream, not wanting her mother to see her naked and so exposed, but it was no use.

'Welcome, my darling Cassandra.' Deacon settled on the edge of the bed next to her, watching the scene playing itself out in front of the bed. 'I have so longed to partake of your lovely company since I was released from my accommodation at Elemental Cottage. You and I have much catching up to do.' He folded his arms across his chest and listened raptly as her mother ranted about the monster growing in her belly, then he shrugged. 'I wouldn't pay the bitch much attention, my darling. People often label those of us they don't understand. They call us monsters and aberrations. But it's our exquisite natures they can't comprehend in their small-mindedness. He whispered next to her ear. 'Your grandmother thought you were a monster too. Did you know that? Oh, she kept it from you. Why, I think she even kept it from herself. It's hardly the thoughts one wants to have about one's own granddaughter, is it? Then there was the guilt she felt at sending her daughter away in her hour of need.'

The dream shimmered and shifted, and Cassandra's grandmother now paced next to her daughter. 'You stupid girl! You're not fit for magic, not fit for the Ether, so now you go and get yourself knocked up by a demon. At last, you've found your gift, Celia. Whoring, I believe they call it. And now you bring home your mistake, your monster for me to raise?'

'That didn't happen,' Cassandra said, trying desperately to block out the scene playing itself in front of her eyes. 'That never happened. My grandmother loved me. She rescued me from the orphanage where my mother left me.'

Deacon tut-tutted and stroked her face as he would an ill-informed child. 'My darling why do you think you were in an orphanage in the first place?' He nodded to the dream, which continued in all its 3D, surround-sound, gory detail.

'I'll have no whore in my house, Celia. You're no daughter of mine, and that, that bastard growing in your belly – do us all a favour and don't let it see the light of day. Get out. Now!'

'That's not true. That never happened!' Cassandra whispered, fighting to remain calm, fighting tears she didn't want to shed in front of him.

'But my dearest girl, how would you know? You were but a babe in the womb. You were not privy to such venom, such hatred, were you?' He stroked her hair gently. 'Of course, later your grandmother felt guilty, after your mother's death. And if you were that creature she was certain that you would be – well, what an opportunity for her to study you, experiment on you, test your boundaries. Think of it; up until you came into the world, my lovely, no one even knew such exquisite creatures as yourself existed. And I daresay you may very well be the first, the only.' He leaned very close until she could feel the heat of his breath against her ear. 'But then I'm only speculating, aren't I? After all, it is your dream.'

As the argument raged between Cassandra's mother and grandmother, there was a knock on a non-existent door.

'Oh, look who's come to see you, my lovely,' Deacon said, standing and moving away from the bed.

At the foot of the four-poster stood a man with pale blond hair. His face was young, still not in need of a regular shaving, and his eyes were cool blue.

'I believe his name's Danny, isn't it? Your first boyfriend, and oh what a hard-on he had for you that day. If I have my facts right you were both 19, late-bloomers in this filthy modern world of youth and lust, but oh my, did you give him an experience he would never forget.' He covered his mouth jovially, as though he'd just made a silly blunder. 'Oh gracious, that's right. He did forget, didn't he? Your grandmother had a spell especially for such occasions.'

Cassandra squirmed and jerked at her restraints, but Deacon only chuckled.

'Yes, my dear, I have visited this nightmare, and it particularly delights me.' With a thick finger, he motioned the young man to the bed.

His bright blue eyes were locked on Cassandra as he fumbled his way out of his clothes. 'I can't believe we're doing this, Cass. I'm so glad. I've wanted us to … you know … take our relationship to the next level.' He took off his white underpants last, releasing the weight of his erection with a blush before he crawled awkwardly, almost shyly, in between her bound legs.

'Please don't,' she whispered. 'Please don't, Danny. I can't control myself. I'll hurt you.'

But Danny couldn't hear her any more than her mother and her grandmother could. 'We're old enough, Cass. We know what we want, and we love each other. It'll be good. We'll make it good.' She watched helplessly as he struggled into a condom. The poor lad had no idea that safe sex was not something he could ever have with her.

She cursed. 'Goddamn it, Deacon. It's a dream! It's not real. That was a long time ago. I didn't know.'

Suddenly Deacon lay on the bed next to her. He settled onto his side and reclined on one elbow, observing. 'Of course it's a dream, my darling. It's your dream, so enjoy it.'

She caught her breath as the inexperienced Danny pushed up into her, just as he had the day it happened, the horrible day she discovered that her mother was right, she really was a monster. Then Danny was thrusting, thrusting, endlessly thrusting, making grunting sounds and little moans. And she was thrusting back, the predator in her awakened for the first time and oh so ravenous, meeting him move for move, frenzied shove for frenzied push. His inexperienced hands fondled her tender breasts, tugging at her nipples, kneading her fullness in clumsy fistfuls. And it was somehow exquisite. His sloppy efforts at a tongue kiss were sweet with newness. She was delighted with him, everything about him, every awkward coltish movement made her vulva blossom with heat that felt like it could never be quenched.

'You're so tight,' he whispered, just like he had back then. 'I never felt anything so good.'

And it happened, just exactly as it had happened on that day, the flush of heat on his face suddenly darkened, and his body tightened with the growing closeness of his ejaculation, an ejaculation that never came. Then he lost all colour and his skin paled and sheened with sweat.

'Danny! Danny, you have to get off now. Danny, I'll hurt you, you have to stop.' Even though she knew it was a dream, even though her mind told her that what was happening was a lie, she couldn't stop herself. Suddenly the bonds were gone, and it was she who couldn't pull away, she who ate at his very life force, rolling to top him in his weakened condition, riding the tidal wave of everything that had been his life, everything that he had ever hoped for, everything he loved, everything he feared, every single breath of it until there was nothing left. She felt it happen. She felt his life force pass into her, the very dregs of it, the very last drop, and the orgasm that blazed through her felt like it would blow the world apart, felt like she had been filled with the power to do just that and more. The exhilaration of it was stunning, elegant in its simplicity and, from the darkest parts of her unconscious, the urge to do it again reared its terrifying head.

It was only as Danny's last breath filled her that she heard her gran say to her mother, 'You see? I told you she was a monster. She'll never stop. She'll always hunger, and she'll kill again and again and again. I warned you. You should have ended her miserable existence before she drew breath.'

'May I come in?' Kennet knocked on the partially opened door of Tara's study. It was early. The rest of the house slept. Tara hunched over her laptop with a cup of coffee steaming next to her.

'Door's open.' She nodded to the cafetiere on the coffee table. 'Help yourself if you want. You'll have to grab a mug from the kitchen.' She continued to peruse whatever site it was that she had up.

'Did you sleep?' he asked.

She shrugged vaguely. 'You?'

'Not as well as I'd hoped.'

'Sorry to hear that. I can have Sky put you in a different room if you'd like.' She still didn't look at him.

'I prefer the room I had the first time I was here,' he said, sounding a lot bolder than he actually felt. It wasn't what he'd intended to say, but he couldn't accuse Lucia. She wasn't in residence at the moment. She got bored when he slept and usually took that time to wander, he didn't know where.

If Tara were offended by his boldness, she didn't show it. 'Are we alone, or do we have company?' she asked.

It took him a second to realise she was talking about Lucia. 'Does it really matter?' Goddess, he wished she'd look at him. He couldn't judge her mood, couldn't interpret the nuances of her response with her back to him, and he really needed to know if he were truly forgiven or if she planned to make him suffer. At the moment, whether that was her plan or not, he was suffering anyway.

She forced a soft laugh. 'I suppose not. I've had threesomes before.'

His insides fluttered. 'You want to make love, then? Now?'

At last, she turned the chair to face him and looked up at him. 'Isn't that what you came for?' Her hair was slightly mussed, as though she had just come in from the wind, and she wore a turquoise skirt and a loose black pullover that draped and flowed against the swell of her clearly braless breasts. How could he not want her?

He ran a hand through his still damp hair, fresh out of the shower, which he'd hurried through with thoughts of finding her, being with her. 'Actually, I thought we could talk.'

She reached for the belt loops on his jeans and pulled him to stand in front of her, between her open thighs, spread wide beneath the skirt. 'You wanted to tell me again that you're sorry about what happened. I got that. You've already said it.' She ran her hand over the bulge that, in spite of his good intentions, pressed anxiously against his fly. 'You wanted to tell me that really it's not all that bad and Lucia will win the day. You've already said that too.' She undid the button then inched down the zipper. 'Then you wanted to tell me that Lucia doesn't mind if you fuck me. I also figured that out

131

after the last two times when she didn't fry me to a crisp. Plus, she gave me her permission while you were unconscious in my bed.' She shoved his jeans down over his hips and smiled knowingly up at him when his hard-on tented the front of his boxers. Then she tugged them down, grabbed his arse cheeks and pulled him to her, leaning forward in an amazing hands-off act that managed to land his cock right in her mouth.

'Oh God!' he gasped. For a mortifying second, he thought he might come right then and there with the intense tug and pull of her tight mouth and the velvety warmth of her tongue pressing and circling on the underside of his cock. 'Tara, please don't. I can't …' He sucked air between his teeth and fought for control, curling his fingers in her hair, only half-trying to push her away.

'You feel like a ghost,' she said when she came up for air.

He dropped to his knees in front of her and pushed up her skirt. 'I'm not, though, Tara. I'm not a ghost. Being possessed by her doesn't make me any less alive than you are.'

'It's different, though, isn't it? She can hurt you.'

He raised up and kissed her hard, tasting coffee against her tongue, which darted in and out in a game of tag with his. Then he spoke breathlessly against her lips. 'She can't hurt me nearly as badly as you can.'

'Don't say that, *please* don't say that.' She tried to pull away, but he held her trapped in the chair until she relaxed. 'That's not my intention,' she whispered.

'I know,' he said, holding her gaze. 'I know.' He ran his hands up the outsides of her thighs to her hips, hooked his fingers in her panties and tugged. She lifted her bottom enough for him to shimmy them off. Then he pulled her down in the chair and pushed her legs apart still further. She gasped and lifted her bare feet onto his shoulders, splaying herself before him, and he suddenly felt weak with want, intoxicated by the damp warm earth smell of her there, open and expectant before him. He slid a finger up from her perineum, coaxing the heavy dark folds of her to open lazily and revealing the slippery yielding path of her lust, the path that they protected and shielded. The sight of her so vulnerable, so aroused made his bare cock tense and ache, made the weight between his legs feel almost unbearable.

They both caught their breath in a nervous wave of laughter as the chair rolled back until it hit the edge of her desk, where it could roll no further. Holding his gaze, she gripped the chair arms and lifted her butt until he could see all of her from the tight clench of her anus to the urgent budding of her clit, which he rubbed and circled with his thumb, as she rode the two fingers he slid up into her, the two fingers that probed and stroked the tight grip of her. Her feet found purchase on the tense muscles of his upper back as he watched her pussy quiver and grip. The close-up view of the rise and fall and fold and shudder of her femaleness was exquisite, beautiful, undulating with need that pulsated through her body and up into his own.

He cupped her buttocks in his hands and pulled her to his face, placing a kiss against her clit as though he were blessing the Keystone, as though they were about to do dream magic. And he felt her muscles tremble from her own need. 'I want you, Tara Stone, you can't know how much I want you.'

She curled her fingers in his hair and pulled him to her. 'Yes I can,' she whispered.

He buried his face in the sweet, damp valley of her, and the little cry that escaped her throat vibrated down against his lips and his tongue. He lapped the deepening trough of her, until his face was wet with her as she flooded herself and the chair with a heady mix of her juices and the watering of his mouth at the buttercream taste of her.

The chair trembled and squeaked beneath her straining and bearing down as their efforts grew more demanding, as he nibbled her labia and suckled her clit.

He pulled away and looked up at her face. Her eyes were closed, her lips were pressed tight in concentration. 'Tara,' he whispered. 'I want to be inside you.'

She practically fell out of the chair on top of him as he

positioned his cock, then she settled onto him, sheathing him in the deep tight heat of her. And he was lost in her, lost like he'd never find his way back, lost like he didn't care, lost like the only one who could ever find him again was her. How could that be? How could he feel her – so much of her – like he did?

At some point, the point just before he tumbled over the edge and took her with him, he realised he was calling her name, over and over again. Tara, Tara. Her dark hair danced around her face, her strong sleek muscles tensed with her approaching orgasm. Tara, Tara, Tara, and the droplets of moisture falling onto his t-shirt were tears, Tara Stone's tears. How was that even possible? How could she have allowed herself to be so vulnerable for him?

At last, when the shudders of pleasure passed, and she lay on top of him still wrapped in his arms, her legs drawn up to his ribs, she spoke. 'I can't let Deacon take anything else, Kennet. He's already taken so much. I won't give any more.'

As he stroked her hair and pulled her still closer, the weight of her responsibility, the weight of her worry was heavier than he could ever have imagined, and the weight of her loss took his breath away. 'We won't let him take anything else, Tara. Not ever again.'

Without warning, Lucia entered him with such an impact that he felt like his diaphragm would explode. Tara gave a startled yelp and stumbled to her feet as he rolled into a foetal position. 'Oh dear Goddess,' he breathed. 'Deacon has Cassandra.'

At that second Anderson shoved the door open, ignoring the awkward position in which he'd found the couple. In his arms, he held the unconscious body of Cassandra. 'I heard her cry out for Alice, but Alice was in the library with me. When I found her, she was lying in the grass just beyond the crossroads.'

Both Tara and Kennet were instantly at his side as he laid her down on the sofa, and pulled the McKenzie tartan up over her.

'She's not in the Ether,' Kennet said, passing on Lucia's words. 'He has her in the Dream World.'

On the sofa, Cassandra thrashed and cried out, her eyes moving rapidly below closed lids.'

'Jesus,' Tara said. 'He's trapped her in a nightmare.'

Anderson cursed and, with a sweep of his hand, knocked the cafetiere and milk jug off onto the floor with a crash, filling the room with the strong scent of coffee. 'I will destroy him! I will make him regret every second he has plagued humanity if he harms one hair on her head!'

'Anderson. Anderson!' Tara took him in her arms and held him, feeling his rage tremble through her, a terrifying thing she had never felt from him in all the years she had known him.

'I should have suspected this,' Kennet said. 'When last I talked to Deacon he was quite interested in the succubus and –'

Cat-fast and at least as deadly, Anderson grabbed Kennet by the throat and forced him against the wall, his dark eyes fire bright, his superfluous breath coming in great gasps. 'Then you shall share his fate if any harm comes to her. Do not think I am unskilled in dealing out death, nor at disposing of a body so none will ever find it – none will even miss it.'

'Anderson! Anderson, get off him!' Tara shoved the ghost with all her strength just as Tim burst into the door at the sound of the commotion and helped her pull him off Kennet, who grabbed at his throat. 'Anderson,' Tara said, taking him in her arms. 'It's Lucia, Lucia's speaking. Not Kennet. Anderson! We'll get her back.'

'Then we must go to the Dream World now.' Anderson took Tara by the arms. 'We must go now and get her back. Each minute we wait she is in torment.'

'I'll go,' Kennet said, between coughs as he recovered his breath, his hand still on his throat.

'Have you not done enough?' Anderson growled.

Tara laid a hand on his arm. 'Anderson, this time, Kennet's right. He's a strong practitioner of dream magic, the strongest

I've ever known. You said it yourself, you do dream magic only because I insist. But, Kennet, he's our best bet to get her back swiftly and safely.'

'And whether you like it or not,' Kennet said, 'Lucia has the best chance of dealing with Deacon.'

'When they are on such lovely speaking terms,' Anderson said, 'I would not be surprised if he were to invite her for tea.'

The room flashed bright. The overhead light bulb exploded with a loud pop and the curtains at the bay window were tossed about as though they were caught in a storm at sea. 'I promise you it was not teatime, Ghost! He came to me unbidden.' The voice was Kennet's, but clearly the words were not his. 'He came only to taunt me, I'm sure. In my rage, I sent him into the Dream World, into the realm of night terrors. Beyond that I do not know what happened to him, nor did I imagine he would attack Cassandra or I promise you I would have done much worse to him. Perhaps you would care to save your temper and use it where it might do some good?'

The shudder that passed through the room at the coven's first encounter of Lucia's power in possession of Kennet was visceral. Guided by Lucia, daring Anderson to touch him again, Kennet walked to Cassandra, laid a hand on her forehead, and she calmed. 'That's just a stopgap, but it'll ease her suffering for a while.'

'I will not let you go without me,' Anderson said. 'It is my fault that she is at the mercy of Deacon. I should not have let her out of my sight. It is clear to me why he would desire her above all others.'

'It's not your fault,' Kennet said, this time clearly speaking for himself. 'And there's no reason why you can't come. Enforcements are a good thing.'

'How will we find her?' Anderson asked.

'Lucia knows her nightmares. Lucia will find her,' Kennet replied.

'Wait a minute,' Marie said, 'how the hell does Lucia know her nightmares?'

'Please, Marie,' Anderson said. 'It is a question to be

136

discussed once we have restored my beloved. Now we must to the Room of Reflection.'

In all the commotion Sky and Fiori had materialised and Alice pushed her way into the room.

'Anderson, I don't think we need the Room of Reflection, or any added magic,' Tara said, holding Kennet's gaze. 'We just finished making love when you arrived with Cassandra. The Keystone has been blessed, and the two of us have already established a rapport in the Dream World.'

A makeshift circle was swiftly cast. Anderson sat on the sofa with Cassandra's head resting in his lap, and Kennet pulled Tara back onto the floor and into his arms. She gasped at the feel of him with Lucia in residence. He was right, with Lucia he felt full, larger than life, like the Kennet she knew, only much more so. His first kiss sent electric shivers up her spine, and she balked at the intensity of his touch, fearing she would drown in the depth of it and lose her way back to herself. But then he steadied her with a hand on her face, holding her gaze. 'Look at me, Tara,' he whispered. 'Only at me, and Lucia will fade to the background.'

The smell of sex was still on them, the moisture of their love anointing the gateway, which was still open and yielding, and with a kiss and a sigh, they crossed into the Dream World, with Anderson not far behind. As they approached the place of nightmares, Lucia led the way, walking next to Kennet, as she could only do in the realm of Dreams.

Chapter Fifteen

Cassandra lay in a foetal position, staring into the lifeless eyes of Danny. She wanted to look away but she couldn't. She couldn't move. She had tried and tried. She had raged in her head, battled with her mind, told herself over and over again that this was a dream, and yet she could do nothing but lie next to a corpse. Night had settled. It was dark around her, but still she could see Danny's lifeless form as clearly as if it were day, pale and drawn, unseeing eyes staring accusingly at her.

'Oh, my darling, that was magnificent.' Deacon appeared at the foot of the bed clapping slowly. 'I must confess I have always wondered what it would be like to be drained of life while fucking a succubus. Surely it must be the most exquisite way to die.' He offered her a sad look lacking in sincerity. 'Since I technically have no life of which to be drained, I am forced to be only an observer of the deed but oh, my lovely, you were truly a delight. And the power!' He gave her a smile as though they had just shared a private joke. 'Come now, Cassandra, admit it, you have never felt anything so exhilarating as the power that comes from draining the life force of another. And as it feeds and nourishes and strengthens your own, do you not feel as though the whole world – nay, the whole universe – has filled you, is coursing through your veins? Are you not expanded as you have never imagined possible, expanded beyond the mortal pettiness that binds those who walk sightless and powerless among the living? Was it not an experience that even your very deepest fantasies could not have conjured?' He moved closer to her practically vibrating with delight. 'Are you not already longing to do it again, hungering to taste once again that last succulent drop of life force as you fuck another out of existence? Oh, I have heard that there is nothing sweeter, nothing more ecstatic than that last precious breath, that last delicate spark. Will you not, now that you've experienced it, long for that each time you open your cunt, each time another arouses your desire, your hunger? Oh, come now, my darling, we're old friends here. There's no need to lie. I do know that you have such fantasies. And really, my love, how could you not, when it's your birthright?'

He absently shoved Danny's corpse off the bed and onto the ground with a sickening thud, then he sat down next to her and pulled her into his lap, holding her as one would a sleeping child. She didn't struggle. She still couldn't move. 'Not even your ghost can give you that kind of pleasure, can he, my dear Cassandra?' He pulled her close and sniffed between her breasts. 'I can smell the scent of earth on you, my love, and oh, the succubus scent of you is always sex most purely refined. Sadly I cannot smell your ghost on you, even after he has pleasured you repeatedly in his feeble lifeless way.'

Her insides raged at Deacon's words, but she could neither speak, nor move. She could do nothing but endure his fondling and listen to the vileness that came from his mouth. 'Oh, I would not deny that the ghost has stamina, and that he is brave – stupidly so, I think. But do you really believe you shall not tire of him with time? Do you really believe that when you cannot take to the dregs with such a raging lust as yours, that you will not despise him, hate him for his weakness? And he? Will he not surely recoil from you with disgust when he knows the depth of your hunger, the dark heart of your depravity?' He slid his hand between her legs and stroked her, and she trembled. She was ashamed that it felt good, but it did. 'Yes, my darling, you delight me in every way, and indeed, I doubt there is another in existence so deliciously suited to satisfy my lusts as you, my beauty.'

There was a shimmer and a shifting around the bed and

suddenly they were lying side by side. Deacon wore only thin undertrousers and his body glowed with unnatural light. The beauty of him was both stunning and terrifying. He lay on his side, stroking her flank and her belly and the hard peaks of her breasts. 'I had heard that nothing delights such as sex with a succubus, and that for mortals who succumb to such delights, their last memory is of pleasure they scarce can endure.' He laughed. 'In fact, they cannot endure it. I must say I was not sure I believed it until I witnessed your little demonstration with Danny just now.' He kissed her ear. 'And you, so squeamish as you are, cannot allow yourself the full pleasure and power your gift will afford you because you care too much for the mortals. Oh my darling, how my heart breaks to know this.' He stroked her cheek tenderly, then dropped a kiss on her lips, the sweetness of which was almost unbearable. 'But I, my love, am not mortal, and I will be able to endure your lust, though I daresay you shall find my libido an equal match to your own. Tell me, my lovely, are you not dying to discover what will happen when you truly are able to set your lust free with no restrictions, with no precautions for the one who fills your cunt – nay, even without the boundary of death itself to stop you? You have never known such pleasure, have you?' He circled a finger around first one areola and then another.

'That one,' he said, nodding to the body on the ground, 'died happily in the throes of his passion for you. What more could any mere mortal ask? And yet for you, my love, it was not enough, was it?' He whispered close to her ear. 'It will never be enough. You are a succubus, a monster of insatiable lust. No mortal, no ghost, no powerful witch can ever fill that fathomless void within you. But oh, how you have fantasised about it, about having that void filled. I have traversed your dreams enough to know, Cassandra Larkin.' He bent and kissed each of her nipples. 'I can give you that, my love. I can give you what no one, living or dead, can offer you. Surely that must tempt you? Surely you must long to sate your lust after all these years of denying yourself.' He kneed her legs open and lay on top of her. She could feel the insistence of his hard-on from beneath the thin layer of fabric, and she suddenly realised she was free to move. And now it was a struggle not to move against him, not to fan the flames of her need any higher than they already were, not to give in to what Deacon could offer her. No one knew where she was and, even if they did, who could rescue her from her own dreams? She closed her eyes and thought of Anderson. There had to be a way out. There had to be a way back to him.

She focused all of her thoughts on Anderson, on being in his arms, on being lost in his love and, as Deacon shoved aside his underwear and freed his cock against the inside of her thigh, she felt the monster inside her stretch and move and hunger in her pit of emptiness. She braced herself. She didn't know if she could do it or not, but she prepared to do the only thing she had the power to do, to take from him, to take from a demon. She knew she had weakened him at least a little when she had forced him into the prison, but then she had been well nourished with Anderson's power, with Anderson's essence, which he had forced her to take. The memory of the experience made her shudder. Still, there was nothing else she could do. The monster inside thrashed and yearned and anticipated. Perhaps it was time to set it free.

Just as she prepared to release the succubus, as Tara had taught her to do, the dream exploded in a flash. For a fraction of a second, she saw Lucia, Kennet and Tara. A fraction of a second later, Anderson scooped her into his arms, and she remembered nothing else.

It was only as it all happened that Kennet questioned the foolhardiness of his plan, but as Tara screamed for him and reached out for him, as Lucia yanked her out of Cassandra's nightmare, he knew in his gut, no matter if he survived or not, that he'd made the right decision. For the briefest of seconds he felt Tara's concern for him flood him in warmth that he would have loved more than anything to dwell in, but, more important still, Lucia dragged her away to safety.

The succubus was safely restored to her lover; there would be no horrible death today, or worse yet no prolonged suffering at Deacon's hand. Well, that might not be entirely true, but then his life had been forfeit long ago. He would endure what he had to.

For the first time, Kennet noticed his surroundings. There was an oak tree with a four-poster bed beneath it. Otherwise the dream was as empty as the Ether, but a whole lot darker. He seemed to be the only person in the dream. But just seconds before, Cassandra had been in the middle of the big bed with Deacon preparing to mount her. Even in its shapelessness, the dream shell gave Kennet the shivers. It took him a moment to realise it wasn't the dream that made him shiver, it was the fact that he wasn't alone.

Deacon's laugh was cheerful, light-hearted as though he had just heard a great joke. 'I am astounded, my good man,' he said. 'Your handler has actually kept her bargain. I would have never believed it of the sneaky bitch, but then here you are, and as you can see, the succubus I was about to fuck is gone, no doubt wide awake now and safe in the arms of her ghost. Though I must say I was looking forward to fucking a succubus – you know, from one bloke to another – just to see if it's all it's cracked up to be.' He raised a dismissive hand. 'Oh well, I'm sure there'll be other opportunities. What? Oh you still don't understand, do you my boy? You are the ransom.' He laughed a hearty belly-laugh. 'That's right, you are the price for the succubus's release. Your dear Lucia sold you up the river after seven years of loyal service. Didn't see that one coming, did you?'

'Lucia would never bargain with you,' Kennet said. 'She hates you even more than I do.'

'Ordinarily I would be inclined to agree with you,' Deacon said, 'but you see, I have just become privy to the most intriguing piece of information.' He moved close to Kennet, so close that Kennet could hear the slow even intake of his breath, could see the rise and fall of his chest. Then he embraced Kennet and whispered against his ear, 'Your demon bitch has a special fondness for the succubus. Can you imagine the power a demon like Lucia could have if she were to possess a succubus? I'm all a-tingle just thinking about it. And if she does possess our dear Cassandra, then she will be that much closer to destroying me. Or at least that's how she sees it, and who can say? Maybe she's right. It'll certainly make the game more interesting and ... what is that phrase? Oh yes, it will be a double whammy for Tara Stone. She'll not only lose her succubus, but she'll lose you.' He tightened his embrace. 'You who still smell of her cunt. And no one's cunt smells lovelier than Tara Stone's. She doesn't know how sweet she smells when she's near me. I think she truly believes she can hide her lust from me. Yes, I do plan to fuck her senseless after I've destroyed her silly little coven. Perhaps if you're still alive, I'll let you watch.' He shivered with delight. 'But that's a pleasure for another time. I'm nothing if not patient. In the meantime, I think that she shall not be pleased with my plans for you, which delights me all the more.' He reached down and stroked Kennet's crotch. 'And I promise you, your existence as my possession will be so much more interesting than it has been with that stupid cunt Lucia. What I have planned for your cock will be so very exciting. Suffice to say, Kennet Deaconson, for you must certainly now wear the name of your new master, I will be in far more places than simply your head,'

Tara found herself walking the path of the old railway line into Keswick between Chestnut Hill and the swimming pool. At the base of her spine she felt an uncomfortable cold ache, perhaps from being thrust out of Cassandra's dream so quickly. It was the middle of the day and the path was crowded; women with prams, families on bicycles, runners, elderly people walking dogs. And she was completely naked. Of course no one noticed. 'Damn you, Kennet,' she cursed. 'This isn't funny. He won't hurt me. You he won't be so careful with!' No one seemed to notice or even hear her shouting or cursing, nor did they notice her instantly disappearing from the dreamscape. She woke with a start back on the floor of her study. The cold ache had grown to feel as though someone had bathed her lower back in ice. She quickly forgot about it at the sight of Anderson holding Cassandra in his arms. She was awake. The rest of the coven gathered around the couple, making sure she was all right. Tara's relief was short lived at the sight of the unconscious Kennet lying on the floor next to her.

Anderson and a somewhat shaky Cassandra were instantly at her side. 'He pushed me off into some dream of walking naked on the old railway path. I don't know where he's at. I've got to go back.'

On the floor next to her Kennet cried out and began to thrash.

'Oh dear Goddess,' Cassandra breathed. 'We have to do something. He's in the throes of the nightmare, and I'm too weak to go in.'

'You will not even think about such a thing, my darling,' Anderson said.

'I'm going.' Tara gazed up at Anderson. 'Just keep Cassandra close and safe.'

'How can you go back?' Marie said. 'How will you know where to find him?'

'I don't know. I just will.' She reached for Tim. 'I need your help to get back in.'

The surprise on the man's face that Tara had actually asked him to help with dream magic passed quickly, and he took her into his arms. With the heightened energy and magic already in the room, it didn't take long for her to cross the threshold again. Alarmingly, there was no evidence of Kennet's energy in the maze of nightmares. The depth of her connection to him, and the fact that they had only just had sex, should have made his energy signal shine like a bright red beacon to her. And yet there was no evidence he'd even been in the Dream World – ever.

She hadn't gone far when she honed in on Lucia's energy. Perhaps the demon's energy was masking Kennet's, though that had never been the case before. Besides, if the two had reunited, they would have returned immediately to the safety of Elemental Cottage. She shivered at the thought. She knew only too well that Deacon would love nothing more than to get his hands on Kennet, who was now vulnerable, and all because Lucia had tricked her into making love with him, tricked her into thinking he was a ghost. Damn Lucia, she thought. She'd messed up everything. Everything!

She found Lucia wandering the unconscious path that was like a motorway running endlessly between millions and millions of dreamscapes. 'I cannot find him,' she said to Tara.

'What the hell do you mean you can't find him?' Tara felt panic rise like bile. 'Deacon'll hurt him. Deacon'll hurt him badly, surely you know that. I thought you were connected to him. Isn't there some … I don't know, some sort of strange umbilical cord connecting the demon to the possessee? You have to find him. You have to find a way.'

'Deacon is somehow blocking that connection,' Lucia said. 'This is the Dream World. Deacon can manipulate it because he is awake, just as I am. Only demons can perform such an act in the Dream World while they are still awake.'

'I don't care! We have to find Kennet. He's already having nightmares in the Waking World. We need to find him now.'

'I am telling you I cannot find him,' Lucia said. She held Tara's gaze with her ember-bright eyes and the fire-dance of her robe flared. 'I am not mortal. The connection between Kennet and me is not a natural one. It is forced. If Kennet were less powerful than he is, my possession of him would have killed him or made him crazy very early on. But he has adapted somehow and grown stronger. Deacon has only taken advantage of the unnaturalness of our joining and, in the Dream World, broken that bond.' She laid a fiery hand on Tara's arm. 'But your bond with him is a bond of flesh and blood, a joining most intimate, and you have walked the Dreamscape with him. It may be that you can find him, I do not know. His scent is still on you – nay, the joined scent of your lovemaking, two practitioners of sex magic, two who traverse the Dream World. That is strength beyond strength.'

Tara stretched her senses out into the Dreamscape but felt nothing other than the white noise of a million different dreams going on at once. 'I can't,' she said, shaking her head. 'I can't feel him. Deacon's shielding him from me as well.'

And suddenly her attention was drawn back to the cold ache very low in her spine. As she focused on it, the ache became lust that thrummed down between her legs, over her perineum and trembled up into her vulva. In an instant, she understood, and with understanding came horror. She couldn't find Kennet's essence in the Dreamscape. Deacon had masked it thoroughly. But he had made his own signature powerful enough that not only could she not miss it, but she would know exactly from whom it emanated.

'I know how to find him,' she said. But she didn't tell Lucia how. Instead she turned and raced into the deepest darkness of the dreamscape, paying no attention to the night terrors and agonised nightmares going on all around her. As the darkness grew thicker, she closed her eyes and felt her way as the icy tremor in her stomach tightened still further.

At last Lucia stopped.

'What is it? What's wrong?' Tara asked breathlessly.

'I can go no further.'

'I don't understand. Why not?'

'I do not understand either, Lucia said. 'But the way is blocked to me. I can go no further. I cannot help you, Tara. I am sorry.'

Tara's insides now felt like icy winter had spread from her spine up into her chest. 'Fine. Wait here. If I can reverse the spell to clear the way, come as soon as you can.' She didn't wait for Lucia's response. She knew that if she came up from the dream too soon, she wouldn't be able to go back a third time, at least not for several hours, and that might be too late.

'I had not planned it so, but I have heard the unconscious has much more control over our choices than we could ever easily imagine, Kennet, my lad. Do you think that is so? Are you not

146

struck by the similarities between dreams and reality?

Kennet had been stripped to the waist and tied to one of the posts at the foot of the bed, his hands bound behind his back with the post pressed to his spine. 'As I recall, I bound you just such the night of your wife and your sister's tragic deaths.' He smiled at his reminiscence. 'You were a captive audience, were you not, my dear man? Oh, how you raged. I finally had to silence you just to hear myself think. You were terribly unruly.' He rubbed his hands together. 'But now there is only you and me, and you may rage all you wish – after all, this is a nightmare. It certainly is an appropriate place for raging, wouldn't you agree?' He brought the very tip of a large curved bladed knife to rest just below Kennet's sternum. 'I think that I shall begin your new life as my helpmeet by punishing you once more.' He traced the tip of the knife down to Kennet's navel, not breaking the skin, but leaving a pressure mark. 'You do understand, do you not, that I would have rid the world of that crazy bitch, Lucia, once and for all if you hadn't interrupted with your childish spell from your cunt of a mother's spell book. I took the loss of my prize very badly, boy, very badly indeed. In fact, I've never properly recovered psychologically.' He laughed raucously at the look of confusion on Kennet's face. 'I thought perhaps to couch my anger in modern terms, terms that you would understand. The truth is, I hold grudges for a very long time, Kennet, much longer than your pitiful seven years of suffering. And my revenge is exquisite, indeed, is it not, Tara Stone?'

Kennet felt his heart leap in his chest and cold fear constrict his throat. Damn it! Why could the woman not just stay safe? He could do nothing to protect her here, didn't she know that? He was able to turn his head just enough to see Tara standing in the garden near the oak tree, watching.

'Tara,' he gasped. 'What the hell are you doing here? I sent you away. I sent you away where it's safe.'

She boldly approached him and kissed him hard on the mouth. 'And I told you he won't hurt me – not physically anyway.'

147

'Of course I won't harm you, my darling woman. I want nothing on this earth so much as your continued safety and good health.' Deacon smiled magnanimously. 'I see that you had no trouble following my little trail of breadcrumbs, my love. I didn't want you to miss the fun.' He flipped the knife from side to side in his hand so the blade caught the flash of the sun that wasn't real. 'I contemplated a scenario in which you would take this one's life before I could torture it out of him, just as you did our dear Fiori's. Do you remember that, my darling? You robbed me of my prize, and yet it was you who suffered for it. I certainly did not.'

'Jesus,' Kennet cursed. He knew the story of Fiori's death. Lucia had told him, but he had never before felt the full horror of the choice Tara had been forced to make.

'Oh yes indeedie, my lad. Our Tara is no stranger to dealing out death. In fact she does it rather efficiently, as I recall. And I'm sure it will comfort you greatly to know that if she deems my pleasure with you is beyond the endurance of your fragile mortal mind, she'll take your life herself. Oh, but do not you worry, your death at her hand will be swift. Is that not true, my darling woman?'

'There'll be no deaths today, Deacon,' Tara said as calmly as if she were discussing the weather.

The demon chuckled. 'Perhaps not, my dear Tara, but you know you cannot stay in the Dream World for ever. This one, though, I can keep as long as I desire. How his mind holds up … well, that shall be interesting to see. He has lived as the possession of a demon for seven years and seems no worse the wear from it. Therefore it is safe to assume that I shall have a good long time to entertain your lover before his mind is gone. And though I have led you here to me today, my darling, you know I could just as easily have masked my signature and you would have never found this one.' He ran the tip of the blade just along the low ride of Kennet's jeans, and Kennet sucked a tight breath as the knife pierced the skin just enough to raise a thin red ribbon of blood from rib to rib, parallel to the waistband. 'But I would have made certain that

148

you saw his suffering, my darling, in his poor dream-ravaged body as he withered into insanity and eventual death in the Waking World. And when you –'

'I told you, I will never allow you to take what is mine from me again, Deacon. You're a petty, insignificant coward, who means less than nothing to me, and I will suffer your insolence no longer.'

'Oh I think that you shall, my darling. I think you shall suffer whatever I demand of you.' Almost quicker than Kennet's eyes could follow, Deacon grabbed Tara by the shoulders and pulled her to him, with such force that she cried out, barely managing a startled gasp before he took her mouth with a devouring kiss. For an electric moment, she struggled against him, then all sounds of shock and surprise were swallowed up in a lethal growl deep in her chest. And to Kennet's surprise, she curled her fingers in the demon's hair and returned the kiss with the violence and rage of many lifetimes, the power of which left Kennet breathless and stunned.

And it was Deacon's turn to cry out with a groan that could have been agony or ecstasy – Kennet couldn't tell. Nor could Kennet tell if he were struggling to get closer to Tara Stone or struggling to escape her.

The knife dropped from Deacon's hand with a clatter. A shiver ran up his spine and the moan that he breathed into her mouth was anger and anguish, fury and lust. When she pulled away, she bit him hard on the left cheek, hard enough to make him flinch. Then she moved to Kennet, the rage in her shaking the whole dreamscape like an earthquake. 'I take back what's mine, Deacon.' Kennet was suddenly free, and she pulled him to her. 'And when next we meet, be warned, I'll be bringing the battle to you, and you will not survive it. You will not survive it!' She wrapped both arms around Kennet and, he wasn't certain whether Deacon were laughing or raging as the dreamscape vanished. Then he woke back in the study with Tara wound protectively around him. He woke calling her name as he surfaced back into the Waking World, and before he was fully conscious, he felt Lucia enter him in an embrace that felt nearly ecstatic as she settled in.

Chapter Sixteen

Kennet invaded Tara's privacy. He figured it was a risky thing to do, but he couldn't wait any longer. When they'd come back from the Dream World, she'd pulled away from him so quickly that it felt like she'd ripped him in half. She stumbled to her feet, barely able to stand from the strain of the magic she'd just worked, but she wouldn't let him touch her. She'd checked to make sure the succubus was OK. Then she spoke without looking at anyone. 'We'll talk about this over lunch.'

'You need to eat,' Fiori had called after her. 'I'll bring up a sandwich.' Tara had made no response, and when he tried to go after her, Tim stopped him with a very firm hand. 'Trust me,' the farmer said, 'you don't want to do that just yet. Give her a little while.'

No one else could ignore Fiori's demand that they eat. He was cajoled into wolfing down breakfast before he could go to Tara, and Fiori wouldn't let him leave until he'd had seconds. From inside him, Lucia nodded her hearty approval, although she was still angry at him for the risk he'd taken. He was sure the breakfast was delicious, but he barely tasted it. As for the conversation around him, the solicitous concern of the other coven witches, he barely heard it. He could think of nothing else but Tara. The only one at the table who was less sociable the he was Cassandra. Anderson kept coaxing her to eat her breakfast.

'You shouldn't do this,' Lucia spoke inside his head as he ascended the stairs. 'She was wise to leave as she did. She did it for you. Don't negate what she's done. It'll only make matters worse when the time comes.'

'Are you going to force me not to?'

He immediately wished he hadn't said it. For a second he wasn't sure, but he thought he felt something like pain from Lucia. But he really wasn't thinking of her at the moment. She said no more, however she didn't leave him as she often did when he needed a little privacy.

She was right. He knew it, but he couldn't stop himself.

Tara's suite was unlocked. He knocked softly, then stepped cautiously inside, pulling the door to behind him. There was a half-eaten sandwich on the night stand and a cup of tea that had not been touched. He could hear the shower running in her bathroom.

'What do you want, Kennet?' she called out even before he could knock on the open bathroom door. It still unnerved him how sensitive they now were to each other. For the past seven years of his life no one but Lucia had penetrated his defences and yet, for some unbelievable reason, since they had dreamed together, to Tara he was as permeable as water. He knew it worried both Tara and Lucia. It worried him too, but he couldn't help himself. He had to talk to her. More than that. At the moment, he felt a deep need just to be with her.

He stepped inside the bathroom to find her in a cloud of steam with her back to him. Through the clear safety glass of the shower, the dance of water vapour around her body revealed and concealed and revealed again the lovely sweep of her long spine and the tightly rounded muscles of her buttocks, and he wanted her with a visceral ache he had never known before Tara Stone. The mist cleared a little, and he saw that she was leaning against the dark blue tiles, her head resting on her forearms while the water coursed over her back and shoulders, and his desire was suddenly spiked with pain, pain that was as much hers as his.

'We need to talk.' He forced the words up through his tight throat.

'I don't want to talk. Go away.'

He was halfway out of his clothes before he was fully

aware of what he was doing. 'I'm not going away, Tara.' He shoved open the shower door and stepped inside, eliciting a little gasp from her as he slid his arms around her from behind, pulling her close. 'If you want me to go away, you can always kick me out.'

She went rigid. Even beneath the pelting hot water, her body felt cold, and he could feel her trembling.

He pulled her still closer against his heat, heat to which Lucia contributed.

'This is why I only fuck ghosts,' she said, her voice tightly controlled. 'This is what he does when I care too much, when I let someone matter.'

'Anderson's a ghost,' he said, stroking the tight muscles of her belly with an open palm. 'Deacon took him. Your discrimination makes no sense, and you know it.' He nuzzled her neck and spoke against the soft shell of her ear. 'I won't let you push me away, Tara, so stop trying. Stop worrying about what might be and enjoy what we have right now. Besides, you told Deacon the next time you see him you'd bring the battle to him. You said he wouldn't survive, and I believed you. Hell, I think he believed you too. He looked a little pale when you pulled me out of there.'

He felt her laugh deep in her belly, felt it against his palm, and he could hardly believe how good it was when she laughed. She relaxed into his arms and leaned back against him.

'I'm angry at you, Kennet Lucian,' she said, raising an arm around his neck, caressing his wet hair. 'If Deacon hadn't left me a trail, I wouldn't have been able to find you and that doesn't bear thinking about. That he did leave me a trail, that he let me take you without a fight doesn't bear thinking about either. He's up to something.'

'I was afraid for you,' Kennet said, sliding his hand up to cup the fullness of her breasts in turn.

She shifted back against him until his penis swelled and stretched and nuzzled at her bottom. 'I told you he won't hurt me. Physically I'm safe as houses with him. I'm no fun for him if I'm dead or injured. I've been the bastard's entertainment and obsession for years. He needs me alive and healthy. He needs me to be horrified at his atrocities. He gets off that way, the sick fuck.'

He pulled her so tightly against him that he heard the grunt of her breath forced from her, and he would have pulled her still closer if he'd been able. 'Then let's finish him, Tara. Let's be done with the motherfucker and have him gone for good.'

Her shifting and undulating against him suddenly stopped, and though she was no longer rigid, she stood still; the only movement was her accelerated breathing expanding and contracting her ribs against his body. And then it all shifted. He let out a startled little gasp at the feel of her closer than his own body, at the feel of her moving against Lucia.

'So it's a threesome this time, is it?' Tara said.

As she turned to face him, his cock surged at the thought of Lucia and Tara making love to him together. Tara's eyes locked on his, as though she could see inside him, as though she could see the place where Lucia's own arousal spilled over into his chest, into his groin. Then she cupped his balls in her hand, kneading them just between pleasure and pain, and he was suddenly aware that their lovemaking would have to be in a place in between. It couldn't be otherwise with Lucia present. Lucia was naked inside him, and the shower stall felt like it was bathed in sunrise.

'Love the light show,' Tara gasped as he lapped at the rivulet of water running down between her breasts. Then he nursed on each nipple, thumbing and licking and sucking each to ecstatic dark pink points. She groaned and leaned back against the wet tiles, pulling him to her with a gentle but firm pressure of the hand that cupped him. Her other hand snaked down over his butt to the vulnerable clench of his arsehole. She slid a wet middle finger knuckle-deep into his tight grip and began to stroke and thrust. For a second he thought he would come just from the skilled press and probe and thrust of her finger. Inside him, Lucia shivered with the delight of

154

maleness she felt as full-on as he did, even while his internal view of her was of femaleness, pussy swollen and shimmering.

Tara nipped his throat and spoke in a breathless rush. 'She feels what you feel?' She wriggled a second finger into the stretch of him and the pained pleasure had him biting his lip and pressing a thumb to the head of his cock.

'Yep. She does,' he managed with some effort. 'And what you feel, as well.' He forced her legs open with his knee and shifted, careful not to dislodge her delightful efforts in his backside. Then he pushed in close, sliding a palm between her legs, back and back until his middle finger breached her anus. She cried out and sucked her lip as he pushed up into her. As his finger thrust and stroked, he pressed the flat of his hand up tight between her spread labia, up flush against her pussy.

Her eyelids fluttered and she sat on his palm, shifting and sliding. 'She feels that?'

'Oh yes.'

'Bet she likes it,' she breathed. The strain of pleasure on her face was exquisite, and the slippery wetness of her flood against the palm of his hand made his balls feel leaden and hot.

'She does.' He shifted so the heel of his palm raked her clit hard and she came, nearly collapsing against his palm. 'She liked that too.'

Tara's breasts rose and fell in her effort to catch her breath. 'Bet she'd like it even better if you'd fuck me really hard.' She moaned her protest as he pulled his hand free, cupped her bottom in both palms and lifted her. He was treated to a tantalizing view of her wet pout before she closed her legs around his waist, shifted her hips and expertly sheathed his cock in her warm, tight grip.

'Oh Goddess, yes,' he hissed between his teeth. 'She likes that. She likes that a lot. And so do I. Jesus, Tara! So do I.' She took his mouth like he was lunch and she was starving and he returned the favour. Inside him what was happening with Lucia was no longer a visible thing, no longer a thing he

155

could even define. He felt her spread along his nervous system like electricity in high-tension wires, he felt her coursing through his blood stream like the water in Aira Force after a heavy storm. And Tara felt her. For a second Tara's eyes fluttered wildly. She arched against the wall as though her back were breaking. She pulled oxygen into her lungs as though she were drowning. And then she dug her knuckles into his shoulders and fucked him as hard as he fucked her. Her eyes were locked on his, the fire in them slightly brighter, and the surprise, the awe tinged with fear made them seem large and deep and wild, like they filled the room, the cottage, the whole Borrowdale Valley and beyond. And Goddess, he wanted her all over him, all inside him, filling every pore of him almost like Lucia did. But what Tara did to him, she did in the real world, in the world of flesh and blood and lust and love.

He never wanted it to end, but there was no stopping it, no controlling the power set in motion. They both exploded in an orgasm that felt like it breached the boundaries of the Dream World and the Ether. What must have surely been Lucia's version of coming sizzled through them both like fast-moving lightning. The water had gone from hot to tepid, and gooseflesh was breaking on Tara's shoulders as she reached to turn off the tap.

As he settled her on to her feet again, she planted a kiss on his left nipple. 'She fucks good, your demon.' Then she reached up and stroked his cheek. 'And you're not so bad either.'

Anderson and Cassandra lay on the big four-poster bed both fully clothed. The dappled sunlight of the waning afternoon shone through the lace curtains. Her back was to him. He gently stroked her shoulder, but otherwise he did not touch her. She did not wish it.

'My love, if it is just a little privacy that you desire to help you digest all that has happened to you, then of course I shall grant you that. I do understand that your experience has been most traumatic, but I am loath to leave you alone at this time. Surely you must understand.'

The shaking of her shoulder told him that she wept. And he felt the most miserable of men beholding her pain and being unable to ease it, unable to offer comfort. He moved closer and curled around her in a spoon position, but she shrugged him off.

Reluctantly he pulled away and sat on the edge of the bed, watching her helplessly. She would not talk to him about what had transpired in the Dream World, and he knew it was not wise to press her. However at this moment he was certain he could rip Deacon's demon heart from his chest and force him to eat it whilst it still beat. And in truth, he knew what made him most angry was that he had not been able to protect Cassandra, and in the end he could not, without the help of others, even mount a proper rescue. This, he was certain, Deacon had carefully calculated when he had taken Cassandra into the Dream World rather than the Ether. This was, no doubt, Deacon's revenge for the role Anderson had played in his recapture. No doubt, Deacon had not counted on Lucia bringing him home from the Ether. That he'd had to rely on a demon to be restored to his coven family had left Anderson feeling uneasy, and yet he certainly would have not refused Lucia's help. But now that he was home and more helpless than he could ever remember feeling, the struggle with simply navigating the Ether seemed bliss.

Anderson could not recall ever having felt such impotent miserable rage, and it was all he could do to bear the sight of his beloved suffering so.

The lunch meeting had been the most painful he had ever attended. Cassandra had not been herself. She carefully told the details of her abduction without so much as a mention of anything Deacon had said to her, and when pressed, all she would say was that she did not remember. Anderson knew that she was not being truthful, and he was certain that if he knew, the rest of the coven knew as well. The worry he felt for her was like a sharp pain in his heart. Whatever had happened was most certainly unimaginably horrible for her to have reacted in such a way, and he felt her suffering more deeply than if it had been his own.

At last she dragged herself upright in the bed, wiped her eyes on the backs of her hands and turned to face him, forcing a smile. 'Please, Anderson, I really do want to be by myself for a while. No one can harm me here. You know that.' The ravaged look of her tore at him, and he could barely control the urge to take her in his arms and hold her, against her will, if need be, until she relented, until she let him comfort her.

He kissed her gently on the cheek. 'As you wish, my love, but I am never more than a heartbeat away from you if you need me.'

Her eyes welled again. She swallowed hard and nodded.

All of the willpower he had was needed to prevent him from lingering in the room in non-corporeal form, but she would know. She was more sensitive to his comings and goings than even Tara was. The depth of their bond still astounded him, and he knew that it was that depth that ravaged him at the moment and made him the most miserable of men.

Perhaps he would ask Sky to watch over her. Though Cassandra was very close to Sky, there was not the bond between them that she and Anderson shared, and Sky was gifted in making herself as though she did not exist if she so desired. Yes, he would send Sky. They were all worried about her and, even in the safety of Elemental Cottage, he did not want to leave her unguarded.

Downstairs Anderson found Tara alone in her study. He knew that Kennet had gone with Marie and Tim to reinforce the protection spells on the boundaries of Lacewing Farm and Elemental Cottage.

When Tara saw him she closed the battered leather book she had been perusing and came into his arms. He held her tightly to him, feeling comforted at the touch of his friend. She kissed him gently and pulled away. 'How's Cassandra?' she asked.

'She will not talk to me. She will not let me touch her. How can I help her to heal if I am not allowed to touch her?'

'The bastard,' Tara hissed. 'If wishing could make it true, he would have been destroyed a thousand times over today alone.'

'Nay, my darling, he would have been destroyed a million times over this day alone, and in my own mind I have thought of the most hideous means for his demise and felt pleasure in the worst of them, felt desire that they should be prolonged, that he should suffer endlessly as he has caused those I love to suffer.' As he spoke, he reached to stroke her cheek.

'I have never seen Cassandra so, even in the beginning when she would not suffer the touch of another. Even then, there was a brightness, a brashness about her spirit that shone like the sun. It is as though Deacon has taken that away from her.'

'She's dream sensitive, Anderson,' Tara said, pouring him a cup of coffee and motioning him to sit on the sofa next to her. 'Even more so than I am, way more so than I am. It's a part of her succubus nature. Has she discussed her dreams with you, recently?' she asked.

He held the cup between his hands, relishing the warmth of it. 'She has had dreams of her mother, unpleasant dreams, dreams of herself still in the womb, of her mother raging at someone Cassandra never sees, dreams of her mother calling the babe in her belly a monster.' It hurt Anderson to even say such words out loud when they concerned his beloved Cassandra. And the thought of her enduring such an assault in the Dream World made his insides roil.

Tara cursed under her breath. 'It's a good bet if you know that, Deacon knows that. We can't keep him from the Dream World now that he's free again. We can't keep him from anywhere but Elemental Cottage.' She shook her head sadly. 'And he still finds a way into the heart of us.'

He brought his fist down on the table with such impact that coffee sloshed onto the wooden surface. 'This must end, Tara! I do not want him in a cage, I do not want him trapped in his own skin. I want him destroyed, completely and utterly destroyed so that he may no longer damage those I love.'

She took his hand and squeezed it hard. 'Believe me, my dear, dear friend, no one wants that more than I do.'

The front doorbell rang, and they could both hear Fiori's enthusiastic greeting. A minute later, she appeared at the study door with Ferris in tow. Ferris was the strange caretaker of Cassandra's property in Surrey. Though he was not a ghost, Anderson was pretty sure he was not wholly human either. He wielded powerful magic, and he held no memory of how he had come to be in Cassandra's service. He came with the property she mysteriously inherited, and he had an uncanny gift for arriving unbidden just when his mistress needed him most. Certainly Anderson would not argue that this was one of those times, Would that the caretaker could help her.

After offering both Tara and Anderson a warm handshake with a cold hand, Ferris said without preamble, 'I've come to take Cassandra back to Storm Croft.'

Tara blinked. 'There must be some mistake.'

'No mistake,' Ferris said. 'I received her call to come and fetch her home several hours ago. As it turns out, I was already on business in Birmingham, therefore it was not a difficult journey for me to make.'

Anderson felt as though he had taken a blow to the stomach. 'I do not understand. This is her home now. Why would she want to leave?'

'I don't know, Anderson. All I know is that she called me and asked me to take her home. And this, as you know, is a part of my responsibility toward her.' He shifted nervously, as though he were contemplating something uncomfortable. 'I will say that I don't feel good about her leaving. I don't feel good in my gut, but I am duty bound to do as she asks, as you know.'

Anderson vanished into thin air and reappeared instantly in Cassandra's room, where she was placing the last of her clothes into a battered suitcase on the bed. His sudden appearance caused her to yelp with a start, and she dropped the stack of T-shirts she had just taken from the chest of drawers.

'Ferris has arrived.'

'I heard the doorbell,' she said, kneeling to pick up the shirts, which she then set about refolding as though it were the most important task ever assigned her. 'I figured that might be him.'

'He has informed Tara and myself that he is here to return you to Surrey.'

'For the moment, yes. Though I probably won't stay there. I never do.' Her voice was cold, distant. 'I just think it's better this way.'

For a moment he did not speak, feeling as though his whole world were collapsing around him, feeling even more despair than he had when Deacon had cast him into the deep Ether. When he found his voice, his words came with great difficulty. 'I am sorry, my love. It grieves me to the very core of my being that I have not protected you as I should, that I was not –'

'Anderson? No!' She turned with such violence that she nearly knocked the T-shirts back onto the floor. 'You've done nothing wrong. You've done everything right. No one in my life has ever been as wonderful as you are. It's not you.' She fought back a sob. 'I've known all along deep down that I don't belong here, that I'm only pretending to be normal.' She wiped tears with the backs of her hands. 'We all know it's only a matter of time before I hurt someone seriously.'

'That is rubbish, my darling! We most certainly do not know that, for it is not the truth. Please, my love –' he grabbed her arm and pulled her to him '– this is Deacon speaking, not you. My dearest Cassandra, my beautiful powerful Cassandra knows full well that this is her home, that her power compliments and enhances the power of this coven.'

She pulled away. 'Anderson, please don't make this any more difficult than it already is. I knew. I've always known, just as my mother and my grandmother knew. Sooner or later

161

someone will get hurt. If I go now, I can prevent that from happening. I can keep those I care about safe.'

Tara knocked on the door and came in without waiting for an acknowledgment. 'If you're going to leave, you're going to tell it to the whole coven, not slink out like some coward.'

Anderson bristled but Tara raised a hand before he could say anything, her gaze locked on Cassandra. 'You owe us all that much. Downstairs in the library as soon as Tim, Marie and Kennet get back from reinforcing the protection spells. Are we clear?'

Cassandra swallowed hard then nodded.

'Good. Anderson, come with me – I need you downstairs.' She grabbed him by the hand, not allowing him the opportunity to protest.

'So that's it, then,' Tim said, holding Cassandra in a cold stare. 'Things get a little rough and you bolt like a deer.'

Anderson stiffened, but said nothing. He sat across the room from Cassandra, who sat straight backed on the love seat next to Ferris, who looked as cool and neutral as he always did. She, on the other hand, felt as though she were on trial, and she certainly couldn't blame everyone for being upset. It must feel like such a betrayal to them. But that didn't matter. What mattered was keeping them safe. She was a fool to ever think she could live like a normal person. 'It's better for everyone if I go,' she said. Her words were clipped and tightly controlled. 'Now that Anderson's back he can finish training you and Marie in ethereal magic,' she said to Tim. 'He's more experienced at it than I am anyway.'

Marie sat with her arms folded defiantly across her chest. 'You're lying, Cassandra. We all know you are. We all know you're keeping secrets, not telling the truth about what happened in the Dream World. Look, everyone here's had a run-in with that bastard, and it's always a train wreck. But everything you keep from us he can use against us, you can't be so naïve as to not see that.'

Cassandra's mouth felt dry as a desert. They were seated

in the formal sitting room and this time Fiori hadn't served up the usual tea and homemade biscuits. She was being interrogated, and there was no doubt about it. 'Surely you can see how dangerous I am, how I put everybody at risk just by being here. Look at what happened earlier.'

'What happened is that you tried to save me.' Alice spoke softly from where she sat on a ladder-back chair near the door. 'You did nothing dangerous. You did nothing that any other person in this coven wouldn't have done. You were trying to protect me. Just like Deacon knew you would.'

For a moment the room was silent. All eyes were locked on Cassandra, but she squared her shoulders and looked down at her hands folded in her lap. She knew all their arguments. She had always known all of their arguments, and for a glorious few months, she had believed them. 'I'm sorry,' she said, knowing that there was no real words that would make any of them understand. They hadn't felt her delight in Danny's death, and if they had, they'd know what a monster she really was. 'I can't stay. I have to go.'

'We won't be able to protect you once you leave Elemental Cottage.' Tara said.

'I'll be fine. I'll be with Ferris.'

'He can't protect you and you both know it,' Sky said. 'In case you've forgotten what happened last time.'

Ferris shifted uncomfortably on his chair, or at least as uncomfortably as she ever saw him. 'I have taken precautions. Deacon won't be able to pull me into the Ether again. And –' he offered an enormous shrug '– I don't dream, so he can't defile my dream space.'

That was news to Cassandra, and clearly to everyone in the room, but Sky's full attention was still on her. 'Why are you doing this?' she asked.

'I'm doing this because I don't want to put anyone here at risk any longer, and if Ferris can't protect me, and Deacon comes for me, then he's not coming for someone else.' The argument sounded weak even to her, but it was the best she could do at the moment, in an uncomfortable situation that she would have given anything to avoid.

'At least not until he's tortured you sufficiently, until you bore him enough for him to let you die,' Tara said. 'Then he'll come for whoever he considers next on the list. Don't you see? He's ripping my coven apart and you're the place he's beginning.'

'My darling, you must know that Tara is right.' Anderson sat on the very edge of his chair, as though at any minute he would spring to his feet, take her in his arms and make everything all right. And, dear Goddess, she wished that could happen. He continued. 'We are your family. You are stronger, we are all stronger when you are with us, when you are a part of us.'

'You at least owe us an explanation, a real one,' Fiori said. 'Everyone in this coven bears scars from Deacon. You're not the only one. What, did you think because he hurt you once he wouldn't do it again?'

'Fiori.' Anderson's voice was a low warning.

But the redhead raised her hand to deflect him and continued. 'Why do you think you're special? Why do you think you can cut and run when he hurts you? I'm dead, for fuck's sake! And you have no idea what he put me through before I died. Do you want him to do this to someone else?' As she spoke her physical body faded, and Alice gasped, still not quite used to the proclivities of the ghosts at Elemental Cottage. 'What makes you Miss Delicate and Dainty? What makes your responsibility to this coven's safety any less?'

'I kill people!' Cassandra blurted. She came to her feet trembling, and the room flashed bright with her rage. 'My love kills people!

'Bullshit!' Fiori said. 'You've never killed anybody. You couldn't. It's not in you; I don't care what you say. You've lived like a nun to keep from it. And that's unbelievable discipline. But here, in this coven, you've finally had the training you need so that you can love. We're all still alive, aren't we, and we've all loved you?'

'I'm a succubus.' She took a deep breath and it all spilled out, all the vile, ugliness she had wanted to hide from them. 'In my dreams I kill my lovers. In my dreams I take from my lovers, and I take from them, and I take from them until I feel their last breath, the last bit of their essence pass into me.' She breathed a sob. 'And when I'm done, when they're dead next to me, I revel in the feel of their life force coursing through me, and I crave more. I always crave more. In my dreams I can't get enough, and I wake and I'm always, always hungry.' Angrily she wiped tears from her eyes. 'I am a monster, just like my mother said, thanks to some demon who couldn't keep his cock to himself.' She turned to Ferris. 'Please let's go,' she said.

Ferris was barely to his feet before the room shook so violently that he fell back onto the love seat, and Cassandra was tossed to the floor. Kennet, who sat next to Tara on the sofa, uttered a startled gasp and arched back onto the cushion in a violent spasm. Tara grabbed for him in alarm, but his thrashing knocked her onto the carpet before he could brace himself with both hands pressed hard against the couch. The world flashed blindingly bright, and suddenly Lucia stood in front of them, robes flaming, stellar-brilliant gaze levelled at Cassandra where she had fallen on the floor. And yet strangely, Cassandra was able to meet that gaze.

Anderson catapulted off his seat toward Cassandra, but Lucia raised a hand, and he fell back into the chair from a force that was almost physical. Cassandra crab-walked away from the demon until her back was pressed up against the love seat, and there was no place else for her to go.

Lucia stood above her for a long moment, holding her in her fiery gaze. The room was suddenly airless, breathless and utterly silent, suspended in time, time that was locked in the gaze of the demon. It was a gaze Cassandra met with angry defiance in spite of feeling as though her whole body were imploding in Lucia's presence. And just when it felt like the very fabric of time itself would split in two with the stretch of it, Lucia swept aside the hem of her robe and knelt next to

Cassandra, studying her as though she had never seen the like before. At last she spoke in a voice that felt like it vibrated the very core of Elemental Cottage and everyone in it. 'Did Deacon tell you these things, Cassandra Larkin? Did he tell you that you would never be sated but in the death of your lover? Did he tell you that your father was a demon, that your mother was weak? My dearest girl, have you not yet learned what a liar he is?'

Cassandra could do nothing but gasp and blink. No one else in the room so much as moved, though she was pretty sure no one could have if they'd wanted to.

'Shall I tell you the truth, then, my darling girl? The truth that I was not inclined to tell you until now, until I had seen all that I have seen. Your father was not a demon. Your father was a man of property and enough wealth to make sure, when properly persuaded, that his daughter was well cared for and protected. He made a blood oath to your mother that all of your needs would be met and your secrets would be kept safe, safe even from you. This one –' she nodded to Ferris '– is responsible for the keeping of those secrets and is bound by magic to do so. This one is also responsible for the fire that destroyed your grandmother's books of shadows, though he remembers it not. It was done not to keep their secrets from you, but to keep them from Deacon for a little longer.' She lifted her hand to Ferris who uttered a gasp, shook his head and blinked as though he had just come out of a deep sleep. 'That secret, Ferris, you no longer need keep. And when the time is full and Deacon is destroyed, you may be released from the others as well.'

She turned her attention back to Cassandra. 'The demon was not your father, Cassandra Larkin. The demon was your mother.'

A collective gasp shattered the silence that had fallen the minute Lucia appeared in the room and took control. Cassandra felt a wave of vertigo, the kind she used to feel as a child when she fell back into her body after riding the Ether. 'How can that be?' She forced the words up the incredibly long distance from her throat out into the tense atmosphere of the demon-possessed room.

'I possessed Celia, the woman in whose womb you grew, the woman whom your psyche has twisted into the angry pathetic creature in your dreams. I possessed her in much the same way I now possess Kennet. In fact, since her, I have possessed no other until Kennet. She should not have been able to conceive while I possessed her. But she was an extraordinary woman, Celia, and not the weak woman who walks your dreams. When I saw that it might be possible, when I saw that her egg might be capable of carrying my spark, I had to know. We both did. Unlike your twisted dreams, my darling, Celia Dalton knew from the beginning of the amazing child growing in her belly. It was your power in the womb that she chose to carry, that she chose to bring to fruition, knowing what an extraordinary being she carried. I am sorry, my dear girl, her death I could not prevent. I cannot tell you how that fact still grieves me. We did not intuit exactly what your gifts would be, but it was never our intention for you to bear the weight of those gifts on your own.'

Anderson had somehow escaped the demon's thrall and came to Cassandra's side, helping her onto the love seat and cradling her next to him.

'You're my mother?' Cassandra's voice was barely more than a whisper. In fact she was amazed she could speak at all. She felt as though the world that only seconds ago threatened to crush her had been replaced with a vastness far greater than the Ether. For a second, she wondered if she were still upstairs asleep in Anderson's arms, dreaming.

'As much as Celia was your mother, yes, I am also. I suppose you could say that you have three parents, my darling, and one of them is a demon, but most definitely not your father. Your dreams of your mother's loathing are only the dreams of a child who did not know, a child who did not understand what really happened and sadly was never taught because there was no one still living in her life who knew. And though your grandmother loved you deeply, she was not

167

privy to the secrets of your birth. Fortunately for you, she was a deeply intelligent, intuitive witch and pieced a great deal of the mystery of her extraordinary granddaughter together. Her death drew the attention of Deacon, and we feared for you, thus the destruction of her books of shadows. Those dreams that plague you, my darling girl, they mean nothing, and Deacon knows this, though he does not know the truth. That is why I could not protect your mother when you were born. The bastard discovered my dwelling place. He would have gladly killed your mother and you, though he believed I had possessed her simply because I had a taste for experiencing motherhood in the flesh, a misconception I was glad to let him have. You were put in the orphanage to protect your identity, to protect you from Deacon. It was not my intention to wait so long before your grandmother found you, but there were extenuating circumstances, once again involving Deacon. It was the best way I knew to protect you. In that time I drew his attention to me, and his desire for my death kept him from noticing the child of a mortal whom I had once possessed, who was tucked away anonymously in an orphanage.'

'Why did you possess Celia in the first place?' Tara said.

'Because she asked it of me, Tara Stone. Never have I taken the possession of flesh without the permission of the possessed. Always that taking is with mutual consent. I do not tread where I am not welcome.'

'And her father?' Anderson asked. 'Why did he not take his child and raise her as the heiress she is?'

'That is the other part of the story,' Lucia said. 'Cassandra's father was Celia's lover when I possessed her. He was a man of wealth. He loved Celia, and I believe he would have married her if the situation had been different. He knew nothing of her pact with me. Though I must confess it was my doing that made certain you were very well provided for, my dear Cassandra, and that your secret was kept. He is dead now, your father. Another of Deacon's atrocities, destroyed when he discovered that the man was the lover of the one I possessed.'

168

She smiled up at Tara. 'I understand the enmity between you and Deacon, for he has made every effort to thwart me. He has taken from me any I cared about, as he will Kennet if he is allowed, as he has tried to do to Cassandra.' She turned her attention back to Cassandra. 'It is my fault that he came for you. I could not hide my anger when his thoughts turned to you, when he lusted for your power. I am afraid I could not hide my rage from him, and though he perhaps thought I desired to possess you, he is not easily fooled.'

'How do I know what you say is any more true than what Deacon says?' Cassandra asked.

'That is a valid question, my darling, and one I shall with pleasure answer for you.' She turned her attention to Anderson. 'Be my filter, ghost. Other than Tara Stone, you are the eldest here among the coven, and you will not be lied to, especially not when it involves your beloved. Let me possess you but for a moment and you will see.'

Tara shifted nervously next to Kennet, but both Kennet and Anderson offered her nods of reassurance. Anderson opened his arms wide and Lucia came into his embrace and nestled into his chest. He caught his breath as though ice water had been dumped down his spine. His head jerked, his eyes widened, then it was as though his face were cupped in invisible hands and gently, but firmly forced to focus on Cassandra. His chest rose and fell rapidly like bellows and he nodded. 'I see,' he whispered. 'I understand.' Then he reached out and took Cassandra's hand, and the energy that passed between the three of them was much like what Cassandra felt when she took deeply from a lover. A sob caught in her chest, and her lip quivered. 'I see,' she repeated, her voice weak and trembling. 'Then it's true.' This time her voice was strong and full of amazement. She closed her eyes and breathed deeply as though she were breathing in the fresh fell air after being locked too long in a foetid room.

Lucia stepped back from Anderson, who slumped for a second, gasped, then moved to take Cassandra protectively in his arms.

'It's true then,' Marie whispered. 'Wow!'

Lucia nodded. 'It is indeed true, Marie Warren.' Then she turned her full attention once again on her daughter. 'Cassandra, for all that has happened to you I am to blame. But you must believe me when I tell you that what Deacon has wrought in your dreams, in your thoughts, none of it is true. None of it. Your dreams are only what you fear, they are your neuroses manifest just as they are for anyone. It is only that your dreams are more vivid and you have so many doubts and so many unanswered questions. Even the dream that you will only be sated in the death of a lover, I promise you, my darling, is not true. Has any sated you such as this one has?' She nodded to Anderson who still held her protectively.

Cassandra blinked back tears and shook her head, clinging to him. 'Have any loved you as he has, as these have? Have any held you in higher esteem, honoured you more, mourned with you and comforted you more than these present here in this place?' She looked around the room at the other coven members. 'Do you not understand that it is this very thing Deacon wishes to rip from you, to rip from every single person in this room? He wishes to take from you all that comforts you, all that gives you a sense of place and belonging, all that gives you well-being and purpose, all that maintains and sustains this place, this coven in the unbreakable bond of love. I promise you, Deacon wants Tara Stone laid bare, Deacon wants Tara Stone completely at his mercy. Deacon wants Tara Stone for himself alone, and though he will delight in making you suffer, he cannot have what he desires while any of you live.'

Cassandra pushed herself up from Anderson's arms to stand in front of Lucia. 'Then perhaps it's time you did what you promised to do and helped us get rid of Deacon for good.'

Lucia moved so close to Cassandra that the illusion of her fiery robe threatened to consume her. 'I do not believe you inherited your sharp tongue from me, my daughter. That was most certainly Celia's gift to you. But if these who love you so well can tolerate it, then so shall I. And yes, I shall keep my promise as has been my plan from the beginning.' Without another word, Lucia returned to Kennet, who opened his arms to her in an embrace that ended in her seemingly vanishing into his chest.

Cassandra was left standing in the middle of the library in a daze.

'Then you're staying, are you?' Tim said, the tiniest quirk of a smile on his lips.

'This is your home, my darling, surely you cannot doubt that,' Anderson said, coming to her side and slipping an arm around her.

She leaned into his embrace and nodded. 'I'm staying. This is my home. And I'm sorry that I doubted it.'

'It's a lot for you to take in,' Tara said. 'A lot for all of us to take in. You're moving from strength to strength, Cassandra, as you've always done, as you always will do. And there's no place like home to do that. That's as true now as it will be in the future when Deacon's gone and you're forced to worry about mundane things like growing enough basil for Fiori's kitchen.'

Surely it must have been there before but suddenly, from down the hall in the kitchen, the aroma of the rack of lamb Fiori was preparing for dinner was mouth-watering, and they all seemed to smell it at the same time.

'I for one would welcome such mundane times,' Fiori said. She stood and motioned to Sky. 'Come on, hon, help me get dinner on. I don't know about anyone else, but I'm starving.'

Chapter Seventeen

Perhaps it was the release from the stress of nearly losing one of their dear family, but dinner was accompanied with a very large serving of lust. Before the meal was served, Cassandra changed from her travelling clothes into a thin cashmere top the colour of dog roses. It caressed and displayed her proud bosoms, which were free of a brassiere, in such a way that Anderson could scarce keep from pressing the cup of his hand to their fullness. The very sight made his member swell as she settled in next to him at the table, deliberately brushing against him as she did so. He reckoned that under the full sway of her spring skirt, her womanhood was also unhindered by the confinement of undergarments, and indeed he could smell the rising scent of her sweetness even above the delicious aroma of Fiori's dinner – and he was at least as ravenous for Cassandra, especially after having come so close to losing her. The very thought still made him shudder.

Anderson struggled to focus his attention on the conversation at the table rather than on thoughts of Cassandra's lovely sex. With the approach of Full Moon tomorrow, Tim Meriwether was asking if it were possible to repair the scrying mirror prison as, at least, a holding cell until they could figure a way to destroy Deacon.

'I don't fancy an execution,' Tara said, 'but I'll do it if I have to. Best let's try to repair it. I want to be as ready as we can be.'

As dinner progressed, Cassandra's hand had gone from Anderson's knee up to the inside of his thigh to rest on his penis, now pressing most urgently against the closure of his trousers. She managed her exploratory touch and stroke while eating tender young carrots which Fiori had picked from the greenhouse early beds that morning. She ate them with her tongue and her lips with the same relish she applied to his manhood when she pleasured it with her mouth. He had no doubt her act was deliberate, and her actions placed him in exquisite agony, even more so as she guided his hand up under her skirt and opened her legs wide to his probing. The valley of her sex was heavily dewed and deeply cleft with her need, and the grip and release of her around his finger as he pressed it upward into her sex was nearly his undoing, right there at the dinner table. Dear Goddess, he was not sure that he would be able to manage proper table etiquette until after dessert and coffee were served. In fact, such was his lust that he had visions of throwing the woman over his shoulder, taking her upstairs and ravishing her until she was unable to walk properly. And he was certain that not a person at the table would be offended by his actions, not even Fiori, who would, in her efforts to make sure each coven member was well-nourished, surely send a tray of delectables up for them to enjoy when they were sated and famished from their lovemaking.

It was only as Ferris got up to help Fiori clear plates from the main course that Anderson noticed the man struggled with the swelling insistence of his own member. The touch of his hand low on Fiori's slender back as though he were rushing her along to the kitchen convinced Anderson that there would be at least a little time for digesting while Fiori and Ferris served up the dessert. Sky immediately excused herself to help and shanghaied a surprised Alice into the kitchen as well. Anderson smiled at the thought of the pleasuring that would, no doubt, happen there before the serving up of the tarte au citron, and he raked the seat of Cassandra's pleasure with the pad of his thumb causing her to gasp and shift her womanhood closer to his hand in a sudden delicious flood of wetness. There was a wave of giggles from the kitchen followed in short order by a startled gasp from Marie as Tim leaned in and kissed her ear. The tips of her bosoms were tightly budded and pressing anxiously against a pale cream top thin enough to show intimations of the darkened colour of that budding.

The sounds coming from the kitchen became soft grunts and moans. Pleasure was never a thing kept hidden at Elemental Cottage. It was always rejoiced in and celebrated. Across the table, Kennet was clearly fumbling with the opening of his jeans and Tara breathed as though she had been doing hard physical labour. She was the coven leader, and no one was more sensitive to the needs of her coven that Tara Stone. Kennet pushed back from the table just enough for her to lift her skirt and settle on his lap. His breath hitched, her eyelids fluttered as she eased down onto him, still facing the table as though she were simply seated there on his lap waiting for the next course. But the way Kennet shifted slowly, rhythmically, hypnotically beneath her, the way Tara caught her breath and sucked at her bottom lip made it clear that she had sheathed him deeply. His hand eased up under her black vest to caress and knead her bosoms which swayed freely beneath.

There was a rattle of pots and pans in the kitchen and a squeal of pleasure, followed by another wave of giggles.

Tim slid beneath the table and Marie gasped and made no effort to hide her own moans of pleasure at what Anderson could well imagine Tim was doing to her sweet sex poised there between her lovely legs.

'Fuck!' Cassandra breathed. 'I can't take this any more. I feel like my cunt's on fire.' She forced Anderson's chair back, ripped open his trousers and mounted him with the rough, carefree spirit he so loved in her, and he so rejoiced in the return of it. She sheathed him face to face, catching her heels on the legs of the chair for better leverage. Anderson could do little more than moan his ecstasy into her mouth as she ravaged his tongue with hers. 'My dear woman,' he breathed, 'I completely surrender. My heart, my body, all of my being belongs to you.'

'Then we surrender to each other,' she whispered with a little sob.

Tim rose from beneath the table, his face wet with Marie's pleasure. Then he hunched over her and pushed up into her, her skirt sliding back to expose her silken thighs and rounded bottom as he pulled her onto him and she wrapped her legs around him in a breathless frenzy of grunts and shoves.

The room felt as though it could barely contain the lust or the magic that rose around the table and emanated with equal power from the kitchen.

'This is what he wants to take from us,' Tara spoke, her voice tight with her approaching release. 'But it's not his to take, not now not ever. Not now. Not ever.'

The release was simultaneous, as only the Elemental Coven could manage. Anderson felt like his own emission could fill the sea and Cassandra's trembling womanhood gripping him so tightly coaxed him to convulse and release again and again even as the nip of her succubus nature passed over him, feeling like the caress of the Goddess herself. The accompanying explosion from the kitchen was guttural and ecstatic, and then there came, once again, the sounds of polite conversation.

By the time the tarte au citron was served with freshly whipped cream, everyone was once again properly tucked and attired for dessert.

Anderson was never quite sure how much of such wonderful shared lovemaking in the Elemental Coven was spontaneous and how much happened because Tara intuited the need for it. No doubt the coven, by its nature, by the nature of each of its members and by the gifts and passions they brought into the circle had its own magic, driven by the bond between all of them. He contemplated these things as he lay curled around his Cassandra, whom he had done his very best to pleasure until she could not walk properly. The thought made him smile. The challenge of so sating a succubus was, no doubt, a long-term challenge that he was looking forward to taking

175

upon himself. But the power of the magic that had been woven by the day-in, day-out living, working and loving together of the Elemental Coven was surely now autonomous after generations of such magic being woven by myriad witches and their lovers.

The magical fabric of the coven was something he had never contemplated, but in truth, as he now did so, he was not sure that it was even in Deacon's power to destroy such a thing, to desecrate such magic. The fabric of the Elemental Coven, though beautifully, exquisitely woven with the lives and lusts and dreams and hopes and loves of so many people, was not a delicate fabric at all. It was not a tapestry, nor was it fine silk. It was a powerful weave that had resulted in a fabric that might very well be indestructible, a fabric that made steel seem fragile.

He cupped Cassandra's sex and kissed her shoulder, and she moved against him in her sleep, moaning softly. As she did so, his insides leapt with excitement that was more than the desire for the woman he loved, it was for the first time an understanding that the power, the weapon, the very thing needed to destroy Deacon was already within their grasp. All they lacked was an understanding of how to wield it.

He pulled back the duvet and quietly crept from bed. He needed to think about this moment of clarity and what it meant. He was halfway dressed when he felt Lucia's presence in the room. He understood. She would not invade her daughter's privacy while he was in her bed, but now that she had declared her link to Cassandra and especially after the near loss of her, Lucia would not have her left alone. Anderson had known this the moment she had possessed him, and it gave him a sense of relief for which he scarce had words.

He tiptoed quietly into the now silent hallway. The lust had dissipated into post-coital bliss only a short while ago. Marie and Tim, lustful as they were, made no attempt to return to Lacewing Farm for the night but took up residence in the room reserved for them, inviting Alice to share their bed. Anderson was sure Ferris had been well-pleasured by Fiori and Sky. And Tara and Kennet had retired to Tara's study, where he was certain they were not being studious at all. He and Cassandra had made their excuses and returned to Cassandra's suite. At some point he though he heard Tara and Kennet stumble upstairs to bed. By then the sounds and the power of lust were thick in Elemental Cottage, weaving yet another layer to the powerful magic of its fabric.

He was still contemplating the fabric of the Elemental Coven when he realised he was not the only one who was not now sleeping. He expected it would be Sky wandering about in the kitchen doing a few tinctures in the wee hours, since Sky seldom slept. Unlike Fiori and himself, she took no pleasure in it. But to his surprise, it was not Sky.

Kennet stood naked to the waist in the darkened kitchen with a cup of Fiori's hot cocoa cradled in his hands. He watched the heavy moon casting silver shadows on the back garden and wondered what it must be like to see the waxing and waning of the moon season-in, season-out from this place, filled with such exquisite magic and such amazing people. Filled with so much love. The ache that he felt at knowing he would never have that experience was heavy. He didn't understand how it could hurt so much, how he could miss what he'd never had, what he never expected to have. His thoughts were interrupted by Anderson's silent footfalls, and he had to admit, he wasn't sorry for the interruption.

'The kettle's still hot if you want some cocoa.' He spoke without looking as Anderson entered the room. Years of living with a demon had sharpened his senses to the point that even a ghost, even one as stealthy as Anderson, couldn't sneak up on him. The ghost nodded his greeting, then helped himself to a mug.

Kennet heard the pouring of the water, the mixing of the cocoa, and the following silence, in which he knew Anderson was watching him, studying him. He waited until, at last, the ghost drew a deep breath and said, 'I know that you are alone, as your Lucia is now keeping watch over Cassandra while I am away from her bed.' He smiled, no doubt thinking of the woman he loved tucked safely beneath the duvet under the watchful eye of her mother. Her mother. The thought still unnerved Kennet. He would have considered Lucia a lot of things, but motherly wasn't one of them. That the story she had shared with the Elemental Coven only a few hours ago seemed totally preposterous made it no less true. Such a thing was not something Lucia would lie about. Lucia was not a good liar under the best of circumstances. It was a human subterfuge she had no desire to master. 'Though Cassandra is well protected in this place,' Anderson continued, 'I am much comforted by Lucia's presence after the events of the past day.'

Kennet nodded. 'I can certainly understand that.'

There was companionable silence, as there often was among men, who were usually less inclined to be verbally communicative than women. And yet Kennet was certain Anderson had something on his mind and was not likely to remain silent. When at last he did speak, Kennet wished he hadn't.

'It is true that your life is forfeit to Lucia, then?'

Kennet turned away from the silver shimmer of the back garden to face the ghost. This was not a topic he wanted to talk about in Tara Stone's house. It was not a topic he wanted to talk about at all. 'How did you know?' he asked.

'I saw the bargain you made with her when she possessed me and used me as a filter of truth earlier today. She was not particularly careful about shielding that area of her consciousness from me.' His smile was self-deprecating, his shrug Gallic. 'Perhaps she does not consider humans, in whatever stage of existence we may be, of any concern to her.'

'That's not true,' Kennet said. 'She considers humans deeply fascinating. She would never tell you that, of course. Though I wish this had been one of the times she had been more discreet. She wanted you to know about our agreement

178

or you wouldn't have known. Lucia doesn't take anything for granted, not even her superiority to us humans, in whatever our stage of existence.' There was the tiniest hint of bitterness in his voice. He hoped Anderson didn't notice, but he knew that the ghost was notorious for catching every nuance. He added quickly, almost apologetically, 'The one thing Lucia is not is petty. Unlike Deacon, she has a code of honour – albeit different from what you or I might have, she does have one. She's been on me since the first time I showed up at Elemental Cottage to tell Tara, to tell her that my life is not my own and to protect both of us from the folly of our hearts, as she puts it.'

'But you haven't,' Anderson said, leaning back against the breakfast bar. 'You haven't told Tara.'

'I hinted at it very strongly, I skirted the issue very closely a couple of times, but I don't know. It almost seems worse to tell her than to just let it happen.'

Anderson held his gaze until Kennet shifted uncomfortably. 'It is clear to me that you do not mean that, and that you are as much of a coward as any man is when he must confront the woman he loves with bad news.'

The woman he loved. The knot that tightened around Kennet's heart was nearly painful. He could deny it all he wanted, but that made it no less true. He wondered if it were that obvious or if the ghost were just perceptive and had picked up on the subtleties. What subtleties? It didn't take much of a brain to see that he couldn't get enough of Tara Stone. She filled his every waking thought and a good few of his dreams as well.

He sat his cup down and scrubbed a hand over his face. 'This wasn't supposed to happen. I wasn't supposed to feel … this way. When I made the pact with Lucia seven years ago, I was dying anyway. Everyone I loved was dead. That my life would be forfeit to a demon seemed like a moot point back then. Back then I could have never imagined that I would –' he swallowed hard and shook his head '– that I could ever feel this way. Ever.'

'It is no hardship to love Tara Stone,' Anderson said. 'I have loved her deeply all my long existence, and all of that time I have striven to be worthy of her love, for truly she is the best of humanity.'

'I know I'm not worthy of her love, Anderson. That makes what I feel all the more difficult, and that she returns my feelings –' he forced a tight laugh '– I surely must be dreaming. It can't be real.'

Anderson moved closer to stand next to him, his gaze now turned at the heavy moon. 'My dear man, I did not mean to imply that you were not worthy, though of course in my opinion no one is worthy of such a woman as she. Tara Stone makes wise choices, and I believe that she chooses wisely in matters of the heart as well, but you must tell her. She must know the truth, and perhaps there is hope yet. Perhaps there is some bargain she may broker with Lucia. Perhaps if we all work together then perhaps we may –'

'No!' Kennet said. 'No one else must know. Lucia told you and only you. She could have made it public knowledge if she'd wanted to. No. The secret is mine to share or not.'

Anderson shrugged, then drank his cocoa to the dregs. 'Very well, if that is the way you wish it, it shall not be made coven knowledge. However –' he held Kennet's gaze in a look that made Kennet feel chilled to the bone '– if you do not tell Tara, I shall. She needs to know and you have had ample opportunity to inform her.'

'Inform me of what? What's going on?'

Kennet's insides twisted at the sight of Tara. She was dressed in a black silk robe tied carelessly around her waist, gaping dangerously across her lovely breasts. Her hair was mussed from sleep and from their lovemaking. She looked like some sacred apparition bathed in the silver flood of moonlight. He wanted to take her in his arms, to fold her close to him and keep her safe. He wanted to make love to her in the moonlight and never stop until the moon had waxed and waned and waxed again. But, dear Goddess, what he knew must happen next was none of those things, and he could hardly bear the thought of it. The ghost, however, didn't really care what Kennet wanted. His concern was for Tara and rightly so.

Tara came into the kitchen wiping sleepily at her eyes. She kissed Anderson on the mouth with a gentle brush of her lips and ran a hand over the tight trim of his beard. Then she settled an arm around Kennet's waist, and his insides felt hungry for the warmth of the woman in his arms. 'Tell me what?' she asked again, looking from one man to the other.

Anderson still held Kennet in his unyielding gaze. 'Kennet has something to tell you, my darling, and I shall speak to you tomorrow as well, but for now I have the sudden desire to return to the succubus's bed and ravish her once more.' He kissed Tara on the cheek, and embraced her, shooting Kennet a look of warning over her shoulder. Then he turned and left Kennet alone with the weight of a secret he wished he didn't have.

She leaned up into his arms and he felt the delicious press of her body, still warm from sleep as she kissed him, her tongue lingering to leisurely explore his mouth. Before she pulled away, she spoke against his lips. 'Tell me. What is it you need me to know?'

'I'm going to die.' He blurted the words out with none of the grace and finesse he had hoped for, and she just blinked and stared at him.

'What do you mean you're going to die? Kennet, what are you talking about?' There was an edge in her voice that made her whole countenance seem a little more dangerous, a little more feral.

'I told you from the beginning that I'm already dead. I wasn't joking, Tara, though I can't tell you how much I wish that I were.'

She pulled away and stepped back, holding his hand tightly. 'Kennet, I don't like this. I don't like this at all. Come clean. Now.'

And he did. He told her everything, he told her about using the last of his strength to get into the Dream World in hope of

181

finding Lucia, he told her about his loss, his rage, his pain, his mourning, he told her about how he'd argued with Lucia, how he'd done everything but throw himself at her, and he supposed, in all honesty, he had done that too. He told her about waking up in the hospital morgue to find he was no longer alone in his body, nor would he ever be again as long as he lived.

When he was done they both sat on the stools at the breakfast bar. For a long time there was silence between them, the tracks of tears on her cheeks were quicksilver, and they made him ache even more than he had when Lucia had done her worst, forcing him to release Deacon.

At last she wiped her eyes on the backs of her hands, sniffed, and spoke calmly. 'We have only until Deacon's defeated?'

He lifted her hand which still clenched his tightly and kissed her knuckles. 'He killed everyone I loved, Tara. I would have done anything. Anything.'

She nodded, but said nothing.

'I never imagined in my wildest dreams back then there would be you, and that I would ... that I would feel this way for you.'

She stood and paced in front of him. 'I won't accept this.' Her voice was fierce, her eyes wide in the moonlight. 'I will not accept this. There has to be another way.'

'There is no other way, Tara. It's my part of the bargain, and you know as well as I do it'll be worth it to rid the world of Deacon once and for all.' He stood to pull her into his arms but she slapped him away.

'The fuck there isn't! There is! There has to be. Where's Lucia? Where is she? There has to be another way.'

'Tara.' He pulled her to him and wrapped his arms tightly around her as she struggled to pull away. 'A demon lives in me. I invited her. I agreed to the price. It wasn't negotiable.'

'Then let her take me. If all she needs is a human sacrifice, let her take me. Goddess knows I've lived too long anyway ... where the hell is she? Let her take me.'

'She's not here right now, and even if she were, she would never agree to that, Tara.' He kissed the top of her head and swallowed back his own tears. 'And even if she would, I wouldn't. The role you play in this horrible game is too important. Me, I'm just a cheap-arsed witch-hack who didn't have the smarts to keep my nose out of my mother's book of shadows. You matter too much to too many people, darling.'

'No I don't. I don't matter. I'm the one who caused all of this nightmare. If it weren't for me all of this suffering could have been prevented, but I just keep on living and living and living.' Her knees gave and she settled onto the floor, and he settled with her, holding her. When her anger and her sobs had calmed, he lifted her into his arms and carried her back to her bed. As he climbed in next to her, she came into his arms and kissed him. Then she said, in a voice already filling up with sleep, 'I won't let it happen, Kennet Lucian. I'll find another way. I'll find another way.'

As Tara drifted into sleep, Lucia settled warm and heavy into the place reserved for her 'I am sorry, my darling boy. Would that there were another way.'

Chapter Eighteen

Tara went hunting Lucia. It was dark. She wasn't sure how long she scoured the borders of the Dream World, but the moon, which had been nearly full, had waned to the tiniest of slivers sprawled like a bright horseshoe above Derwentwater. The demon should have been easy to find under the circumstances. Now she was bound so tightly to the Elemental Coven and Cassandra it should have been a doddle, and yet Tara's search through the Dream World, through all of the haunts where Lucia might have hung out when she wasn't residing inside Kennet, turned up no sign of her.

She was on the top of High Spy looking down into Grisdale Tarn when she felt his presence, like a cold mist settling around her. For a long time he said nothing, for a long time he didn't even take corporeal form. He only lingered, and the mist warmed around her.

When she didn't acknowledge him, he groaned softly and took form, shimmering in moonlight that wasn't there. 'Please do not be angry at me for my visit with the succubus yesterday. Surely you must understand what a fascinating creature she is, unique in all the world.' When Tara made no response, he continued. 'I understand that her kiss has the power to weaken even me. I could not have imagined such a thing, and I was so longing to discover for myself. Please do not think that my desire for her was anything beyond academic. I am, by nature, a curious being. Surely you must know that, my darling.'

When she still didn't speak, he moved behind her, pulled her hair to one side and settled a kiss on her nape. The feeling that passed through her was peace, bliss, as though all of her cares had been lifted, as though the weight of all the past years was suddenly gone from her shoulders. In spite of her efforts to ignore him, to keep him at a distance, she couldn't stop the sigh that escaped her throat.

'There. You see how good it will be, my darling.' He curled his fingers in her hair and pulled her head back to rest against his chest, then ran a splayed hand up her stomach to settle just below her breasts and press her tightly against him, against the wild pounding of his heart. 'When there are no more distractions, when you have let all things go that interfere with your peace, then we shall feel such bliss as you have never imagined.' He nibbled her earlobe gently. 'For all of the succubus's uniqueness, my love, she is but a little girl compared to you. Your magnificence outshines all of those lesser beings you have striven so needlessly to protect. And each time one of them suffers, each time I take one of them from you, you become more exquisite, more beautiful, more irresistible until I can scarce contain my desire for you.' When she shuddered, his hand moved up to cup her breasts and she felt as though her heart would leap from her chest to participate in such a caress.

'Have you not always known this truth in your heart of hearts, my lovely?' He moved in closer and she could feel his erection pressing naked against her naked bottom. How could she have not noticed that they were both undressed? He continued. 'Have you not always felt my refining fire transforming you, purifying you, creating in you the perfection that you are now, the epitome of female power and beauty?' His hand moved away from her breasts, down over her belly and in between her swollen folds, fingers probing into her, thumb raking at her clit. There was nothing she could do but moan out loud and arch back against him. He offered a satisfied grunt at her response. 'Have you not known from the beginning that you have been my driving force? You are the thread that binds me, the fire the draws me. All that I have ever done I have done for you.'

He settled her onto the soft moss and eased her legs open

with the flat of his hand, his gaze holding her in brightness she had never noticed before. He took her mouth in a deep kiss that felt smothering until she stopped struggling. Then it felt as though he breathed for her, the very in and out of the flow of oxygen was his to offer, was his to serve up to her with his lips, his tongue, his teeth. And how she hungered for it, hungered for it as though she had never breathed until his kiss, hungered for it as though she had never felt until he touched her.

'That's it my darling. Take from me. Take all that you need. No one can give you what I can, no one can fulfil you as I can. Our lives are woven so tightly together.' He raised above her and in her peripheral vision she saw the enormity of his need, saw the weight of his erection, felt for the briefest of seconds his sense of urgency. 'I can wait but a little longer, my beauty. Then I shall finish the rest, and we will be free of their tangled web, free to weave our own perfection around each other as it has always been intended from the very beginning, from the very moment our eyes first met.' He pulled her to him raising her hips so that she was ready. 'Let me but penetrate you this once, my love, let me but fill you with my lust and you will understand at last. You will understand everything. You will see why all that binds you here to this place, to this coven must pass for you to rise to heights you cannot yet imagine. And you shall do so at my side, as it was always, from the beginning, intended to be.' He settled one last kiss on her lips, and as he did so, fire, death and destruction flashed behind her closed eyes. The death of Rayna in the winter chill of Derwentwater, the torture of her husband, the death of her sister, all at Deacon's hand. And at last, her own hands delivering the final blow to poor tortured Fiori, offering up to her dear coven sister death and release, even as her heart died a little in the offering.

She woke with a startled gasp, cold sweat sheened her body, and yet lust roiled low in her belly, curled tightly around the revulsion that shook her. She would not masturbate. She absolutely would not masturbate to thoughts of Deacon. The very idea made her feel ill, wrong-footed, horribly guilty, as though she had just broken the most forbidden of taboos.

Next to her, Kennet slept undisturbed. She laid her hand on his chest and felt the slow even beating of his heart, and their conversation in the kitchen came flooding back to her in painful waves. As she watched the rise and fall of his chest, Lucia rose from him like mist on the fells, glanced at Tara, then moved onto the balcony outside the French doors. Tara fumbled into her robe and scrambled to join her.

The first breath of night air was sweet and cleansing, the second, soaked with perspiration as she was, made her shiver. Lucia watched her for a moment, shook her head, then the flames from her robe felt suddenly physically warm. 'There, that is better is it not?' she said as the shivering dissipated. 'Kennet will not thank me if you catch your death,' Lucia added.

'Take me,' Tara blurted, not even offering a thank you for the warmth. 'Spare Kennet and take me instead. Please.'

Lucia didn't answer. Instead, she looked out over the fields, just greying with the coming dawn and spoke as unbothered as if Tara had asked her for the time. 'Deacon has been visiting you in your dreams, has he not?' She didn't wait for a reply. 'How long has this been happening?'

Her question took Tara aback, and she stopped to think. 'I don't know, a couple of weeks maybe. It started happening not long before you returned Anderson.'

'And yet you are unequalled among those who practise dream magic. It should not be possible for him to penetrate your dreams, should it, my darling?'

Tara shook her head.

Lucia turned her gaze full on her and, for a second, Tara felt as though she would disintegrate in the heat of it. 'The dreams, they arouse you, do they not?'

Tara shivered at the thought of how close she had come to letting him take her. 'They're just dreams, the inner workings of a very neurotic unconscious. Everyone has one, you know,

187

and mine's more neurotic that most.'

'Though I cannot fault your logic,' Lucia said, 'we both know that it is false. We both know that they are far more than dreams, and it would be wise if you would tell me about them since, if I am not mistaken, you have shared them with no one because they embarrass you, because they make you uncomfortable, because you are ashamed that you cannot control them, and that Deacon is the sexual centre of them.'

Tara felt a sense of relief at offloading the dreams, at finding someone she could tell without feeling that she'd somehow betrayed them. There was no logic to any of those feelings, and in the beginning she would have given anything to have been able to share them with Anderson, but Anderson hadn't been there, had he? Lucia listened without comment, so much so that Tara wondered from time to time if she was paying attention. When at last she spoke, however, it was obvious she'd missed nothing.

'Deacon has hated me simply because I am another demon.' She shrugged. 'Well, that and the fact that I have from time to time tried to kill him, but of course you can understand why. He is an aberration even among demons, and he is hell-bent on bringing about as much destruction as he can. However, while it is true that he hates me, it is with a neutral hate, the kind of hate that one would expect between two predators competing for the same territory. It has never been personal with Deacon and me, at least not until Cassandra came into the world, but he does not know that. His feelings for you, however, are on another level altogether and, while I have no doubt that he hated your mother for what she and her coven did to him, he has never hated you.'

Tara grunted and chafed her arms, even though she was no longer cold. 'What the hell do you call it, then?'

Lucia raised a golden eyebrow. 'My darling Tara, I would have thought that would be obvious. Deacon does not hate you. Deacon loves you. He loves you with a jealous love that will tolerate no one else near you, no one else that will take your complete focus away from him and him only.'

'That's ridiculous!' But even as Tara said it, the dreams were evidence to the contrary.

'Deacon sees that the end is nigh, Tara. But he cannot see that the end he senses could be his very own. Deacon is prideful, very prideful. In his mind there has never been a scenario where you and he do not end up together. In his mind, there has never been a scenario where ultimately he does not destroy everything and everyone around you so that he and he alone will be the centre of your world.'

'That's insane.' Tara spoke, her voice barely a whisper.

'Deacon understands what most mortals do not, Tara. Deacon understands just how closely hate and love nestle together in the human breast. Your dreams should leave you in no doubt of that fact. Have you not wanted him, lusted for him, fantasised in the deepest part of yourself what it would feel like to be penetrated by him, to feel the full impact of his lust inside your flesh?'

Tara shivered with a rage that was as much at herself as it was at Deacon. 'I want him gone. I want him destroyed completely and utterly, gone from all realms, destroyed as though he'd never been. That, Lucia, is all I want from Deacon.' Her whole body trembled with her anger, with all the memories of pain and helplessness, with all the years of longing to end Deacon's horrible scourge. She pulled an icy breath into her lungs and continued. 'I will not rest until I've achieved that end, no matter how many lifetimes it takes me. I will not stop.'

Lucia reached out a hand and stroked Tara's face and for the briefest of seconds the hand felt as though it were solid warm flesh. 'Then you understand already why I cannot grant your wish. The desire of your heart is as mine, is as Kennet's, to end Deacon's monstrous existence once and for all. No matter how many lifetimes it takes. Your fate is tied to Deacon's more so than is the fate of anyone else on this plane of existence. Whether or not Kennet and I succeed, your fate is tied to Deacon. But Kennet's fate, of his own choosing, is tied to me, and his life is and always has been the nonnegotiable price. I am terribly sorry, Tara, my darling girl, truly I am. As I have never been sorry before, I am sorry. But I cannot exchange Kennet for you, and even if I could, I would not. You are the heart of this coven. You are the source of power that drives the events in which we are now in the midst, and drive them you must.

'I tried to dissuade Kennet from getting too close to you, for I knew when he saw your heart he would love you as he has never known love but, alas, he is as stubborn as you are my darling. And such power as the two of you wield could not but be drawn to each other.'

'I won't accept this. There has to be a way, and I'll find it because I won't accept this,' Tara woke in mid-sentence with Kennet gently shaking her.

'It's only a dream, Tara. It's just a dream. I'm here. It's all right.'

'But last night in the kitchen,' she said. 'That wasn't a dream, was it?'

He shook his head. 'No my darling, that wasn't a dream.' He pulled her to him and kissed her, and she felt his morning erection against her thigh, and the want in her was like nothing she had ever felt before.

She pushed him onto his back and mounted him, guiding him between her legs with one hand while the other rested on his chest. The minute she sheathed him she became aware of Lucia's presence, curled at some nebulous place close to his centre. 'I need to come, Kennet Lucian,' she said. 'I need you to make me come.'

'I think I can manage that.' He offered her a sleepy smile, cupped her breasts then moved one hand to rest on her pubis so that his thumb could circle and rake her clit, and she flooded him with her lust.

It was early morning, the responses of the man beneath her were more instinct than finesse, shoving up into her, then letting her grind him back down into the mattress, cupping and kneading and touching and fondling with early morning awkwardness, awkwardness that had less to do with magic than to do with just plain physical need, just the deep need to be connected. But then again, was there anything more magical than that need to be connected?

As his body tightened beneath her with the nearness of his ejaculation, as her grip tightened around him and as her clit raked against his body each time she settled onto him harder than the time before, everything fell away but the moment. Everything fell away but the rise and fall, the grip and release, the next breath in and out, flesh and blood – human, alive, lusting, needing, loving. And they both came, her knees squeezing up tight against his ribs, his hands gripping her hips bruise-deep. They came until she fell forward against the rise and fall of his chest, felt his hurried breath on the back of her shoulder as she spoke into his ear. 'I won't let you go, Kennet Lucian. I won't. I'll find another way.'

Chapter Nineteen

'I found her as you see her, sleeping peacefully, or so I thought. But I was unable to wake her,' Anderson said.

Tara leaned over the big bed next to Fiori who, for all practical purposes, looked to be in a deep sleep. Fiori always dozed in the moonlight before a Full Moon Circle, especially when it was a cloudless night like this one. It made her dreams more powerful, she said. Tara smoothed the hair away from the sleeping witch's face and cursed softly. 'She's dreaming.' She nodded to the rapid movement of Fiori's eyes beneath her lids. Almost as though to prove the point, Fiori shifted on the bed and moaned, then uttered a few words in Old Gaelic, a language that, in her long existence, she had all but forgotten in the Waking World.

Lucia appeared in the room like a wisp of mist and bent so close to the sleeping Fiori's face that for a second Tara thought she would possess her. Then she pronounced what they all dreaded. 'He has taken her.'

'What do you mean he's taken her?' Tim said. 'He can't have taken her. He can't get into Elemental Cottage. The Cottage and Lacewing Farm have been the only places where we've always all been safe. How the hell could he have taken her? He can't have breached the perimeter.'

'Oh, he did not breach your perimeter, Tim Meriwether. The perimeter is intact.' Lucia's gaze locked accusingly on Tara. 'Do you not yet know what has happened, Tara Stone?'

'What is it?' Tim asked. 'What the hell is she talking about? Tara?'

The whole coven now crowded in and around the door to

Fiori's room, along with Alice and Ferris. They were all robed and ready to begin the Full Moon Ritual. It was only as they gathered in the Room of Reflection that they realised Fiori had not prepared the candles and the altar, as it was her turn to do. And now, all eyes were on Tara.

Last night's dream rushed back to her in a wave of vertigo. 'Oh dear Goddess.' Tara's words were barely more than a whisper. And in truth for a second she feared if she opened her mouth further, she would vomit. The world tilted and the sound that filled her ears was of beating wings and slapping waves. 'No. It can't be. How can it possibly be?' She shook her head and everything around her drifted in and out of focus. 'No this can't be happening. Not like this. Dear Goddess, please not like this.' Her knees gave from under her and she would have fallen if Kennet hadn't stepped forward to support her.

'What is it, my darling?' Anderson asked. 'Do not fret. Only tell us what ...' His words died in his throat, and he blinked as though he had just awakened from a dream. Then he sucked in a deep breath he did not need. 'But surely this cannot be.'

'It is the truth,' Lucia said. 'And Tara knows in her heart of hearts that it is.'

'What?' Cassandra asked.

'It's me.' Tara spoke with an effort that felt as though each word coming from her mouth was weighted with lead. 'This is because of me, what happened to Fiori. I'm the reason Deacon can get in.' She pulled away from Kennet and turned to face everyone, feeling as though her world were falling away from her even as she spoke. 'The Dream Knot – Kennet's right. I can't bond with him as long as he's Lucia's possession.' She settled onto the edge of the bed, once more fighting back the urge to vomit. 'But the bond does exist. It's not a myth.' She viewed everyone, through a mist, all of those she had loved and struggled to protect and now had inadvertently betrayed. 'And though I don't know how it happened, it seems that it exists between Deacon and me.'

'Fuck,' Marie whispered. 'Jesus! How could the bastard do that? How?'

Alice swallowed back a gasp of shock. 'Then you have to leave,' she said, her words trembling and thinning to near-hysteria. 'No one here is safe until you leave. You can go, and you'll be safe – you said it yourself, he won't hurt you. And then you can plan a way to get rid of him, like you did before. You have to leave.'

Cassandra placed an arm around the hysterical woman to comfort her. 'It doesn't matter where she goes, Alice, the link with all of us is a dream link, and the Dream World knows no distance.'

'Then what are we doing to do?' Alice asked. 'What are we going to do?'

Tim squared his shoulders, blew out a sharp breath and said, 'Stay awake. That's what we're going to do. Stay awake and figure out how to kick the fucker's arse once and for all.'

Kennet settled onto the edge of the bed next to Tara and took her hand. 'We still need to do the Full Moon Ritual. It's a powerful time, we need the strength it'll lend us.' He shook her gently. 'Tara. Tara, don't you go away, don't you go anywhere but right here and right now. We need you. We all need you now more than ever.' There was a nod of agreement among the coven. 'It's time for us to do what you said, take the battle to Deacon, and destroy him.' His eyes were brighter than the fire that filled Lucia's, and his gaze helped her focus, helped her clear the mist of despair that threatened to overwhelm her. 'I've waited seven long years for this –' he shot a look at Lucia, whose visage still wavered near the bed '– it's time we did what we came to do. It's time we ended it for good.'

There was a unison nod of agreement.

A shiver ran down Tara's spine at what that meant, to Kennet, to end it for good. And yet it had come down to this. Her hand had been forced, and neither she nor Kennet were left with any other choice. She would not lose anyone else, and her own heart would have to sacrifice. After all, she was ultimately to blame. 'All right, we'll do the Full Moon Ritual, but we'll regroup first. I want everyone in the library in 30 minutes for a coven meeting. We won't go into this circle unprepared.'

Tara was in her study sorting through a stack of books of shadows that she felt might have relevant information in them when Anderson knocked. As he stepped inside and shut the door behind him, she came into his arms. Dear Goddess, how she had missed his embrace, his wisdom, his calming influence. He held her for a long time, his strong arms enfolding her tightly as though he would never let her go, as though he would do everything in his power to keep her safe from the horrors outside his embrace. But the horrors were inside her, and even Anderson could not make them go away. She fought back tears that were more of helpless rage than anything else. 'I can't bear the thought of that bastard torturing Fiori again, not after all she's been through, not after I … what I did.' The thought of Fiori's death at her hand, even though it had been an act of mercy, was now even more unbearable than it always was.

'Do not you worry, my darling Tara,' Anderson said. 'We shall make him pay for every hair on every head of every person he has ever harmed. We shall end Deacon's reign of terror once and for all. This … this violation of our beloved high priestess, at the very heart of this coven, this is an atrocity, a violation none of us shall tolerate.' He kissed her and pulled away, still holding her hands. 'The others are in the library doing what they can, just as you have requested. Sky has taken up Fiori's role for the moment and has served coffee.' He offered her a wry smile. 'Very strong coffee, indeed. I am sure it is in an effort to keep us all awake, and none are complaining, though I fear Fiori would be appalled at the desecration of her fine Sumatran dark roast.'

In spite of herself, Tara smiled at the thought.

Anderson continued. 'My darling, I must talk to you before we meet together with the coven. There is a thought that came to me last night as I lay watching Cassandra sleep. It is something that in my heart of hearts I know is important, though I do not know how, but perhaps with all of us working together we may figure it out.'

'If you think it'll help, Anderson, then tell me everything.' Tara motioned him to the sofa, and for the next few minutes, he told her about the autonomous power he believed the Elemental Coven had woven with all the magic it had done through the years, with all of the loving and living and laughing. 'But the fabric of the Elemental Coven, though exquisitely woven, is by no means delicate,' he said at last. 'The weave of it is powerful and in my very marrow I believe that the fabric of the Elemental Coven might very well be indestructible. I do not mean its individual members, but I do mean the power of their lust, their love, their magic, their lives all woven together over such a long time. I believe that it is in that power we shall find the key to defeating Deacon.' He raised a hand. 'I am very aware that it is a vague notion, and that it may seem like so many words in the wind at the moment and, yet, I am persuaded that there is truth in these words and ... Tara? What is it, my love? Are you all right?'

Tara scrambled to her feet and shuffled through the books of shadow until she found the one she was looking for. Then she opened it with trembling fingers. 'Anderson, you're brilliant,' she said, barely able to speak around the pounding of her heart. She read out loud.

Thrice bound and once released. The spell shall reverse what was not meant to be, so shall it be done.
Thrice bound and once released. Banish the demon, the smoke and the flame, as above so below.
Thrice bound and once released. The reflection of reflection. His seed passed to dust as though he'd never been. So completes the circle, so begins again.

'What if the translation is wrong, Anderson?' she said. 'You know how things are sometimes muddled when they've been channelled.'

He leaned over her to look at the words and the catch of his breath assured her that he got it, just as she had.

'What if the translation is "Thrice woven and once unravelled?" Tara whispered. 'It would be such an easy mistake to make, and it changes the meaning entirely.'

'Then though what Kennet and Lucia believe to be the proper interpretation of the passage is closer than what we originally believed, it is still not right,' Anderson said.

She looked up into the eyes of her dear friend and shook her head. 'Not right at all. I'm the reset button, Anderson. All I have to do is stay awake until I can go into the Dream World on my own terms.'

Even before she could call for her, Lucia appeared next to her making the room flash and shimmer as though it were on fire.

'Anderson,' Tara said, squeezing his hand. 'I need to speak to Lucia, then I'll join you and the others.' As he turned to go, she pulled him back into her arms and hugged him fiercely. 'I have missed you so very much, my dear friend,' she whispered against his ear. 'There are so many things I wish I could have told you.' She ignored the look of question on his face and turned her attention to the Lucia.

When Anderson was gone, she spoke. 'Lucia, if you want to defeat Deacon, then you need to release Kennet and possess me.'

Though the ham sandwiches Sky slapped together with Alice's help were a far cry from the elegant fare Fiori would have served up at such a time, they weren't bad and, in spite of the shock of the last few hours, or maybe because of the shock, everyone was famished.

'I've done what I can to make sure Fiori's comfortable,' Sky said. 'Sadly, when she's already dreaming, there's little I can do to affect her dreams with herbs or tinctures. I've enfleshed Lisette to keep watch over her, so she won't be left alone. In the meantime, we have no way of knowing what

Deacon's putting her through in the Dream World. We can hope that he's taken her only to get our attention and that her dreams are no more than what she would dream in any given sleep cycle.'

Tara certainly hoped so, but she had no more faith that it was true than she figured anyone else in the room did.

'Clearly those of us who are ghosts, and of course Lucia, will not be affected by the need for sleep, therefore we should be able to avoid Deacon's dream trap as long as we stay awake. However, I am worried about those who walk permanently among the living.' Anderson nodded to Alice, who sat with her arms wrapped around herself looking as if she had already been plunged into her worst nightmare.

'Since I do not dream, I have little need for sleep,' Ferris said. 'I'll be all right. Don't worry about me.'

'Aren't there spells we can do, or something?' Marie asked. 'You know, just something to keep us alert as long as possible?'

'Yes,' Tara said. 'We can do spells that'll keep all of us awake, but the longer the spells are in place the more dangerous the side effects become. Even magic can only hold the symptoms of sleep deprivation at bay for so long and with what we're facing now, we can't afford not to be at the top of our game.'

'Perhaps not,' Tim said, 'but I don't see how we have much choice in the matter under the circumstances.'

'We have choices – choices Deacon doesn't know about. Choices that won't involve us staying awake.' Tara moved to stand in front of the fire Tim had built in the hearth. 'I know what we need to do to unweave the spell that binds Deacon to this realm. I know what we need to do to unweave Deacon.'

The room was deadly silent. The only sound was the crackling of the fire, as though no one dared to hope, Tara thought. Well, she could certainly understand that after all the bastard had put them through.

Kennet glanced at Lucia, and Tara caught the slight nod of the demon's head and the determined set of Kennet's jaw.

'Tell us,' he said.

Tara returned to sit next to him. 'We won't wait for him to pick off the living one by one when they can no longer stay awake. We'll take the battle to him in the Dream World.'

Marie blinked. 'We're going to deliberately go into the Dream World?'

'We have a heavy proportion of people within this coven who are skilled in dream magic,' Tara said. 'We'll go in the front door, and we'll go in fighting.'

'What about those who aren't skilled in dream magic?' Cassandra said, nodding to Alice, who looked only slightly less than terrified.

'Sky has several tinctures that are strong stimulants and will keep you awake.' Tara spoke to Alice. Then she turned her attention to Ferris. 'I need you to stay with her.' She held his gaze. 'And I need you to make love to her. When we begin the dream magic, Ferris, I need you to make love to her. Alice, you'll be very high, thanks to Sky's herbs, do you understand?'

Alice nodded.

'What the two of you do will keep you safe and enhance our magic. When the dream begins, Ferris, I need you to make love to Alice, and I need you to keep her on the very edge, but don't let her come, do you understand?'

Alice blushed and so did Ferris. 'I understand,' he said.' And when Cassandra shot him a questioning look, he offered her an embarrassed smile. 'You're not the only one from Storm Croft who practises sex magic, Cassandra Larkin.'

Anderson told the coven about his epiphany and about the retranslation of the passage from the book of shadows. It had the result Tara had hoped for. The excitement of the coven was sharp-edged and morale was suddenly higher with the feeling of the night before battle. Exactly what it was, Tara thought.

'And you know this spell of unravelling,' Marie said.

Tara nodded. 'I know it. It's a spell only I can do because it was my mother whose spell trapped Deacon as he is, therefore it falls to my mother's blood, the one Deacon has sought vengeance upon all these years, to do the unravelling. It'll be the job of the rest of the coven to make sure I get that opportunity. Is that clear?'

Everyone nodded.

'What about her?' Tim gestured to Lucia. 'I thought with a demon on our side she would at least have some task besides just turning Deacon loose on us.'

Tara shot Lucia a quick glance, but if Tim's comment had offended her, she didn't show it. 'I promise you, Lucia will be doing her part, without which I won't be able to do mine.'

Tim looked doubtful, but said no more.

'Just so you all understand what you're getting into,' Tara said, 'with the dream magic we'll be doing tonight, we'll be opening the floodgates to our worst nightmares and that's exactly where Deacon will attack us. He'll find the place of pain and make it hurt worse than you've ever imagined. If there's anything in your deepest self you want to keep hidden, he'll parade it out for the world to see. He'll make you feel despair you never knew existed, so don't go in expecting anything else, and don't go in expecting to be heroes. Just endure it, only for a little while endure it. And keep yourselves safe. Once I'm close enough to him, once I have his attention, it'll be over very quickly, and we'll be back in time for breakfast and Fiori's Swedish pancakes.'

Marie blew out a heavy breath. 'Just another day at the office.'

'We won't be doing the circle in the Room of Reflection tonight,' Tara said. 'We'll need the Dream Cave. Since it's dream magic we'll be doing, I want every possible advantage.'

Anderson nodded. 'Very well, since it is unprepared, Cassandra and I shall make it ready, and to speed along those preparations, if I may, I shall ask Marie and Tim to aid us.' He held Tara's gaze. 'We will need an hour, after which time you and Kennet may join us.' There was no mistaking his meaning.

200

Sky nodded agreement. 'In the meantime, I think for the kind of magic you two'll be doing –' she smiled a reassuring smile at Alice and Ferris '– we'll take the big suite. The bed will give you more room for pleasuring.'

Tara and Kennet stood rooted in front of the fireplace in the library until they could no longer hear Sky with Alice and Ferris, as they ascended the stairs to the privacy of the big suite; until they could no longer hear the engine of Tim's Land Rover heading off to the Dream Cave. Then Kennet folded Tara in his arms with a deep sigh. 'I'd hoped we'd have more time.' He nuzzled her nape. 'So much more time.' He kissed her ear and then took her mouth hungrily. Curled next to the beating of his heart, Tara felt Lucia. Her presence had gone from being invasive and unwelcome to being a comforting reassurance in a time when Tara could use all the comfort and reassurance she could get.

When he pulled away, he smiled down at her apologetically. 'A threesome, then?'

'I've never known you without her,' Tara said. She fought back a sob. 'Strange that I can no longer remember what it felt like not to know you, not to love you.'

He kissed her again and ran his hands over the curve up her hips. 'I love you, Tara Stone, and I never thought I'd love again. Ever. In spite of Lucia's warnings, I'm not sorry, even now, I'm not sorry.' He closed his eyes tight, and the pain on his face abraded some place inside Tara that she'd kept hidden and secret and pushed away from herself for so many years it had forgotten what real pain felt like. It had forgotten what anything felt like. 'I want it over,' he whispered. 'I want him gone so he can't hurt you any more.' Then he held her gaze, eyes wide and bright in the firelight. 'You sent them away, didn't you? You sent them out of harm's way.'

Strange that it was Lucia who nodded, and she saw it, as did he, as clearly as if Lucia had stood in the room next to them. 'In the end it is we three who must destroy Deacon,' Lucia said. 'Kennet, you have always known this, and Tara,

I believe you now understand also, as do I. There shall be no harming of the innocent this time. Those whom Tara Stone has loved and protected shall be kept safe from the battle we must fight. In the meantime, until we are engaged in that battle, this I shall give you now at the end of our time together as a gift of my esteem.'

The library fell away with a fluttering of Lucia's fiery robes like the wind in the sails of a ship. Then, hand in hand, Kennet and Tara traversed the path down into the depths. They followed Lucia deep into the fire cave where they had both first met her, what now seemed like lifetimes ago. With each step of descent, the power of her presence became heavier, thicker around them. Tara felt the hairs on the back of her neck prickle and her pulse raced like a terrified animal in her throat. She found herself wondering how she had ever endured being in the presence of such power and how Kennet had endured being the vessel for it all of these years.

Each step of descent became more and more difficult until at last, when they reached the place where the cave opened into a vast chamber, Tara found that she could no longer move. She could do nothing but drop to her knees. Next to her Kennet did the same. For a terrifying moment, she thought she would suffocate. Then her chest expanded as though oxygen had suddenly exploded into her lungs and rushed outward to fill every cell of her body. At the same time every part of who she was collapsed in on itself under the intense weight of her own being. It was then she realised she was naked, clenching Kennet's hand in a bone-crunching grip. She was suddenly unable to raise her eyes, but she could see enough of Kennet to tell that he was also naked. And erect.

'I've been here before,' Kennet whispered. 'Back when I was broken. So broken. And you healed me.'

'And you shall be broken again, Kennet Birch,' Lucia said. 'This time I shall not be there to heal you, but others shall be.'

'I don't understand,' he said.

But Lucia offered no explanation.

Then Tara was suddenly free to move, free to see the naked Lucia lift one foot onto a rock that suddenly appeared at just the right place, then she opened one burnished thigh to reveal the split of her, and Tara couldn't take her eyes off the exquisite protrusion of her clit. The cave was suddenly awash in the honeyed-earth scent of female arousal, sweeter than any scent Tara had ever smelled. With one hand the demon parted the swell of herself and, with the other, she tenderly cupped the base of Kennet's neck. Gently, she guided him to her and tilted her hips to open the pathway still further as Kennet's tongue found the hard node and the deep valley of her, and he moaned breathlessly into her. Tara could barely hold back the desire to push him aside and take the demon's sweetness for herself.

Lucia's soft laughter sounded like the tinkle of bells. 'Come, Tara Stone.' She took Tara by the hand and helped her to her feet. 'You shall not be deprived of pleasure. We three shall be well sated when we go into battle. She guided Tara's hand to the rounded hillocks of her breasts, heavily crowned with the tight pucker of nipples mounted high atop straining areolae. Tara cupped and stroked until Lucia curled her fingers in her hair and pulled her first into a hungry kiss that was a tangle of tongue and lips and teeth, then she guided her down to nurse. The sounds coming from Tara's throat were not unlike those of a happily suckling babe. As though it knew its way, as though it didn't need her permission, Tara's hand slid down to rest in Kennet's hair, and the feel of it, damp with the heat of lovemaking and curled in loose mussed locks made her ache for all that would now never be. And the moan in her throat became a different kind of need.

In her peripheral vision she could see Kennet's hand resting on the clenching muscles of Lucia's bottom, and Tara's breath caught in her chest as his other hand came to rest on her pubis. First he caressed and fondled the tight curls that protected it and then he eased in with a rake of her clit that made her drench him before he slid his middle finger up inside her. Once the finger had made itself at home, he

203

wriggled another in next to it and let her grip at him, all swollen and tight and wet, while he probed. Lucia's hand slid down from Tara's head over her back and found her anus. At first, she caressed it and circled it with the heavy press of the pad of her thumb. Then with Tara pushing back in anticipation, she worried the tight pucker open and shoved in knuckle-deep. And Tara came, trembling like the fire that danced on the walls of the cave, wetting Kennet's hand even further.

'There, that's better now, isn't it, darling?' Lucia said, then she lifted Tara's face for a lingering kiss. She gave Kennet's erect cock one tugging stroke, and he grunted his semen into the cup of her hand. 'Better for both of you,' she breathed. 'In this place, my dear man, as you well know, recovery time is unnecessary. And sure enough, Kennet's erection didn't wane.

Lucia stepped back from both of them and wiped Kennet's semen up over the flat plane of her belly and onto her breasts. Then she stuck a still glistening finger into Tara's mouth and Tara came again just from the taste of Kennet on her lips. 'And you too, my darling, Tara,' Lucia said. 'You may orgasm until you lose consciousness –' she cupped her chin in her hand and held her gaze '– but then you would wake up in a place not nearly so pleasant, and we shall all be there soon enough, shall we not?'

'Now, I believe that Kennet's needs are for more than to empty himself in my hand, and yours is the sex he has dreamed of even before he knew it was you, Tara Stone.'

Kennet, who was still on his knees, his face shining with the wetness of Lucia's cunt, pulled Tara down onto the floor of the cave. She rolled onto her back letting her legs fall open, lifting her hips and writhing impatiently as he kissed the inside of each of her thighs.

'Is hers not a lovely pussy, my darling boy?' Lucia asked. 'It is the only gateway that has taken you to the heart of your dream, the only gateway that has taken you to the heart of yourself.'

As she spoke, Kennet lowered his face to Tara's swollen

splay and suckled and nibbled his way up to her clit to reverence the Keystone.

'That's it my darling,' Lucia said. 'Take what your heart desires and we three shall celebrate the strength of our lust and our love.' The cave buzzed with the raise of power that Tara felt to the very marrow of her bones. Never had she felt the power of earth and the power of fire so strongly linked.

Then Kennet rose above her and took her mouth, his erection pressing at the gateway. 'I love you, Tara Stone, as I have never loved, as I never dreamed I could. Please don't forget that.' He held her gaze, eyes wide, pupils dilated. 'Don't forget me.'

'Never,' she sobbed. 'Never in a thousand lifetimes. Never.' Then she wrapped her legs around him and thrust up to meet him.

She threw her arms around him with a fierceness that cracked joints and strained ligaments, as though she would hold him to her for ever, as though she were the one who would now possess him, as though she would never let him go. But she would. And she would do it willingly.

'Soon now, my darling girl,' Lucia whispered in her ear, and Tara realised with a start that for the first time in seven years, Kennet could no longer hear Lucia. 'It shall happen when he comes, and you shall feel it and you shall know exactly the instant when it happens and so shall he, and he will not be pleased.'

He'd be alive, and that's all that matters, Tara thought. He would be alive and so would those she loved. 'I love you, Kennet. I love you, Kennet. I love you, Kennet.' She willed herself to focus, to ride the wave, to grip him inside her as she had never gripped him before, to love him as he had never known love, even as she dreaded the tensing of his muscles, the tight thrusting of his buttocks, the holding of his breath, as he drew nearer. 'I love you, Kennet. I love you, Kennet. Dear Goddess, remember that always.'

His grip tightened on her hips, he shoved as though he wanted nothing so badly as to crawl up inside her and she wanted that too.

And then it happened. She felt him convulse, felt him flood her, felt his lips ravishing hers as he whispered her name. And the cave flashed brighter than the sun and suddenly she was falling away and he was screaming, raging, 'Damn you, Lucia! Damn you! Don't you do this, don't you take her. She has to live! She has to live!'

But take her she did, and suddenly every space within Tara that she had not known was there was filled with Lucia. And suddenly the space within her that had loved felt empty and desolate, with a desolation deeper than any she had ever known. But even that didn't matter in the end. Kennet would live and the Elemental Coven would suffer no more. And they would heal him. They would heal each other.

'We must go now.' Lucia spoke from the place where she now settled, below Tara's sternum. We have a demon to destroy, and he is waiting for you, my love. He is waiting for you. And do not worry, my darling girl, he will not know I am within you until we are ready.'

Chapter Twenty

Kennet roared into consciousness on the floor in the library with Tara clutched to his chest. 'Don't you do this to me! Don't you dare do this to me!' He shook her, even slapped her face, but there was no response. It was then he realised that Anderson and Tim Meriwether were standing in the doorway of the library.

'What the hell happened?' Tim asked, pushing his way in right behind Anderson who was across the floor and kneeling next to Tara in a heartbeat.

'She's gone and so's Lucia. They've gone into the Dream World.' He scrambled to his feet and lifted Tara gently onto the sofa then knelt next to her just as Marie and Cassandra shoved in and Sky materialised by the fireplace.

As everything came rushing back to him, he clutched his stomach and bent over himself feeling suddenly, deeply empty.

'What the hell happened?' Tim repeated.

When Kennet straightened up, still kneeling next to Tara, all eyes were on him. 'Lucia left me.'

'Left you?' Marie said. 'What do you mean left you? She leaves you all the time.'

'I mean –' he took a deep breath '– she no longer possesses me, and I think …' He could barely bring himself to voice his fears because the longer he was back in the Waking World, the more certain he was that they were true. 'I think she's possessed Tara and the two have gone after Deacon.'

'You fucking bastard!' Tim launched himself at Kennet, grabbed him by the front of his shirt and pulled him to his feet. 'We were all right till you two showed up. We had everything under control, and now this!' He nodded to where Tara moaned softly and thrashed, on some dream journey none of them could see, but for sure it wouldn't be a pleasant one if Deacon were in charge.

Anderson pulled Tim off Kennet with way more ease than should have been possible. 'Tim, this is not helpful to our situation. You must calm down. We need Kennet if we are to find Tara and Lucia. He is well versed in dream magic.'

'Why did she do this? Why? Doesn't she know we all want a piece of Deacon?' Tim raged. 'Doesn't she know we'd do anything to protect her?'

'You have answered your own question,' Anderson said. 'Tara knows all of these things, and she would do anything to protect her coven family, those she loves.' He held Kennet's gaze. 'She also knows that we, none of us, would have ever agreed to such foolhardiness, so she chose simply not to tell us.'

'Well, what are we going to do, then?' Marie said. 'We can't let her face him alone.'

'We have to go to her,' Cassandra said. 'The cave's ready, but I think we can do what we need to in the Room of Reflection and save time.'

Anderson still held Kennet's gaze. 'You are certain she has allowed Lucia to possess her.'

Kennet nodded. 'I felt her leave me, and it wasn't the same as it feels when she takes a lady's night out. She's gone.' Anderson alone knew what that meant, and Kennet couldn't bear to think about it, so he turned his attention to everyone else. 'I'm a strong dreamer. I can get in easily enough. Getting into the Dream World is no problem, but finding which nightmare Deacon has her in is another matter.'

Anderson reached down and stroked Tara's face. 'Do not worry, Kennet. I know which nightmare she is in. She will be in the same one with Fiori.' Tim and Marie and Sky all nodded their agreement. They uniformly wore an expression of dark horror, and Kennet felt his insides turn to ice.

208

Even as Tara entered the dream, she fought the urge to break and run. They were in a cave, not unlike the Dream Cave. In fact it was the Dream Cave until it had been too badly desecrated to ever be cleansed, and Fiori's death had been that desecration – Fiori's death at her hand.

'What you have told your coven, you must now remember, Tara Luciana.'

Tara knew Lucia was right, but hearing Fiori's cries of pain was nearly her undoing. On the ledge only slightly raised from where she now stood was Fiori held in Deacon's embrace, one large hand fondling her breasts, the other stroking the side of her face and her exposed neck.

Tara squared her shoulders and felt as though Lucia were doing the same inside her. 'Fiori,' she called out. 'It's just a dream, Fiori. You're sleeping soundly back home in Elemental Cottage, and when I'm done here you'll wake up as though nothing has happened. Try not to worry.'

'I know,' Fiori gasped. 'I know. I'm trying. I know it'll be OK.'

'It'll be OK?' Deacon squeezed Fiori's breast until she flinched. 'I do believe that is a strange statement to make to the woman who killed you, my dear Fiori.'

'Let her go, Deacon.' Tara said, sounding a lot calmer than she felt. 'I've come, as you wanted. You don't need her. Let her go.'

'Oh, but I have not called you, my darling Tara. I am not yet ready for you, my Bondsmate in the Dream World. If I had called you, since we are so bound together, then you would have had no choice but to come to me.' His chuckle was low and without humour. 'It still mystifies you, does it not? That we are now so bound in the World of Dreams? Shall I tell you how it happened?' He vanished, leaving Fiori, who slumped with a gasp onto the floor of the cave. Then he materialised instantly next to Tara. Before she could step back, he took her face in his hands and kissed her hard and deeply and, in spite of the horror of the situation, it took all the willpower she had to keep from flinging her arms around him in response. Then he pulled away and whispered in her ear, 'It was the kiss, my darling.' He offered her a hurt frown when she couldn't recall. 'Surely you remember?' He drew his fingers to his lips and touched them gently with a quirk of a smile. 'When you came to rescue the she demon's plaything?' He offered a deep sigh. 'Of course I understood that he was your lover, and that you would come for him.' He leaned in close to her. 'But it was me you kissed, my darling, and to say that your lips are magic – well, that is a bit of an understatement, my beauty. I took from you the link, the bond that you would have settled on one so much less worthy of it than I. But then he was already bound to the she demon and unable to accept your generous offering. Surely you did not think I would have so easily relinquished Lucia's toy to you if there had been nothing in the exchange for me. And oh, such a treasure it is, my darling, the ultimate gift from your mouth to mine. You have given me the keys to the kingdom.' He lifted her chin and brushed another kiss across her lips, this time almost gentle and fleeting, 'And in time, you will also give me the keys to your heart. You will see. In time you shall understand the bond that has always been ours. In time you shall –' He stopped mid-sentence and the look on his face was suddenly dark. With a roar that felt as though it would split the world, he backhanded Tara, and the impact sent her sprawling onto the cave floor, cracking bone and knocking the breath out of her. She was certain her shoulder had been dislocated in his efforts.

'You dare to play the whore with the she demon in my presence?' He pulled her to her feet with such force that her neck popped and for a second she was certain he had broken it. But in an instant, she felt Lucia's healing touch, just before she was yanked from her body like surgical tape from a wound and Tara screamed in more pain that she could ever remember feeling – and she had felt a lot.

'We are bonded in the Dream World, Tara Stone. Surely you did not think you could keep this cunt of a demon a secret from me.' For a brief second, Lucia stood by her side, and then with an upward thrust of Deacon's hand, she vanished and the cave was deathly silent except for Deacon's angry breath like a gale against her face. And then his countenance softened, or at least he offered her a smile, but his eyes were still deadly. 'My darling Tara, it has always been in my mind that you, being far superior to all others I have known of your sex, should be my consort and walk by my side and not merely be my helpmeet to serve my needs. But in spite of my desire toward you, in spite of my longing to elevate you to a high place, I have always known that a woman of such haughty parentage, a woman who has set herself to rule unnaturally over men, would have to be disciplined, refined through fire, as it were, to become worthy of me. But I had never thought you were the type to whore yourself to another when you surely must have known that you were always mine. Always!'

'What have you done with Lucia? Where have you sent her?' she said, trying to sound calm.

He shrugged. 'Somewhere in the Dream World. It is much better organised than the Ether, no doubt, but that makes it no less difficult to navigate, my darling. And there are no maps.'

He dragged her bodily up the rock ledge and shoved her onto her knees next to Fiori. 'I think that the best lesson I can teach you is a lesson through suffering, my lovely.' He dragged Fiori to her feet by her hair. He offered a chuckle as he twisted his hand tighter against her scalp. 'Of course, not your own suffering, my dearest Tara. You are royalty. You are my consort. No hand shall be laid upon you. No, I think it best that for you, I shall make use of a whipping boy, as kings did for princes in the days of old. Or in this case, a whipping girl will do just fine, since I already happen to have one at my disposal. And this time you shall not offer her the coup de grace. I shall make certain of that.' He ran an open palm up Fiori's bare belly, and she screamed.

Dear Goddess, how Fiori screamed, and no matter how hard Tara tried to remind herself that they were both only just dreaming, she knew that Fiori was still suffering, and her one sure chance at destroying Deacon for ever had been taken from her when Deacon had cast Lucia out of the dream. She had to think. Damn it, she had to be able to think, and Fiori kept screaming. From where she lay crumpled on the ground, she managed to reach out and touch Fiori's bare foot. It was the simplest of calming spells, and yet to Tara's surprise it worked. At her touch Fiori slumped in Deacon's arms.

He shoved her to the ground and straightened his waistcoat with a breath of satisfaction. 'I shall give you two some girl time, then, while I go to find the demon whore. Do not think that she shall escape unscathed after she has led you astray, my love,' he said. And then he vanished.

Struggling to protect her dislocated shoulder, Tara pulled Fiori into her lap with her good arm and slapped her face none too gently. She didn't know how much time they had, but it couldn't be long. 'Fiori! Fiori! Wake up. I need you, do you hear me?'

The woman's eyes fluttered and she opened them and caught a sob of oxygen into her lungs, then coughed and gagged, pushing her way into a sitting position so that she could breathe. 'Fiori, listen to me. We don't have much time.' Tara took her chin in her hand, holding her gaze. 'I think I can send you back to the Waking World. Don't talk, just listen. If I'm bonded to him in the dream world, then I should be able to undo what he's done and send you home. If I'm able to send you home, there's something you must do for me. You won't like it, but if you want this to end, if you want Deacon to end, if you want the suffering to end for ever, then you have to do this for me.'

Trembling from her injuries and fighting back tears, Fiori nodded.

'Good.' Tara hugged her tightly, ignoring her own pain and the little gasp that escaped the throat of her sister witch. 'You said once you hoped that if the time ever came you would have the courage to return the favour.'

The sob and the wild-eyed nod that Fiori offered assured

212

Tara that she knew exactly what she meant.

'Now I'm asking you – no, I'm begging you, Fiori. You must return the favour. I can end this for ever, but now that Lucia's gone, I need your help.' She whispered the words she couldn't bring herself to say out loud into Fiori's ear and saw horror flood the woman's dark eyes.

But only for a moment. Then her bottom lip trembled, she sat up straight and nodded, looking into Tara's eyes. 'I promise,' she whispered. 'I promise.'

Tara felt her heart soar, for the briefest of moments. Then she leaned in and kissed Fiori on the mouth. 'Thank you, my dear sister.' Then she kissed her again, this time deeper and still deeper until the woman gave a little whimper and vanished from her arms. And Tara fell sobbing with relief against the floor of the cave. All she had to do now was hold on. Just hold on. She would know. She would know when it happened, and after that it would all be over.

In her bed in Elemental Cottage, Fiori woke up just as the rest of the coven, sequestered in the Room of Reflection, slipped into the Dream World. She felt them go. For a second she lay very still with her eyes closed, sensing the world around her. Lisette sat in the chair next to her bed keeping watch, and the ghost practically fluttered with excitement when Fiori sat up.

'They're all in the Room of Reflection except for Alice and Ferris and those two are in the big suite fucking because that's what Tara said would keep them away from the Dream World. Frankly I think they got the best job of all. Apparently she let Lucia possess her and she has some plan to kill Deacon and now you're back and…'

Fiori laid a finger across her mouth. 'Tara sent me back and it's urgent that I get into the Room of Reflection.'

Lisette blinked and moved Fiori's finger away from her mouth. 'You're a member of the coven, why are you telling me this? You know how to cut a door into a magic circle.' She smiled sweetly, and Fiori's stomach clenched. She was sure there would be no sweetness if Lisette knew what she

213

was about to do. In anger, she had once told Tim that what Tara had done for her in the taking of her life was an act of kindness, an act of mercy. She had told him that she hoped if she ever had to do the same, she would be as courageous. And now for Tara, for the coven she loved, she must be, even though she couldn't bear to think about the pain and the sorrow that would follow. She dressed quickly in her ceremonial robe and was standing before the Room of Reflection almost before she knew it. She cut a door into the magic that buzzed and hummed over her body the second she stepped into the darkened room. She did not dare linger for a second lest her courage falter.

Candles flickered brightly on the altar, the flames leaping high and reflecting back through each of the mirrors that surrounded the perimeter of the Room of Reflection. Fiori recognised immediately the feel of dream magic, and the dreamers on their journey to find Tara and bring her back had not long passed through the Gateway into the Dream World. Three couples lay in each other's arms, Marie and Tim, Cassandra and Anderson, and Kennet and Sky. That they had made their preparations in a hurry was shown in the fact that they lay on the bare wood floor rather on the sumptuous cushions that would have usually been laid out for dream magic. She looked around the room, her heart pounding with the powerful backwash of magic from the opening of the Gateway and from the overwhelming weight of the task set before her. There on the floor at the foot of the altar lay Tara. Only she lay on a bed of soft cushions, only she lay covered in a soft throw that Rayna had made back when she lived, back before Deacon drowned her in the cold winter waters of Derwentwater. He had taken so much from them for so long. Tim thrashed on the floor in Marie's arms, yet another reminder of what had been taken from them. But for Deacon it might have been her in Tim's arms, it might have been she who received his adoring looks when he thought no one noticed. She loved Marie, as they all did, but their lives had been lived in the wake of Deacon's destruction, always a long list of what might have been, and never a moment of looking to the future without fear of what he might do next. And even as her heart broke, she did not falter. After all, her heart had broken long ago, more times that she dared contemplate now, and there had been no forgetting, no healing, no leaving the past behind. The past had followed every single member of the Elemental Coven from the time of Deacon's death and possession until now. And now it would end, and maybe her heart would only have to break this one last time.

All around her the moans and thrashings of the dreamers began in earnest. She knew now that they were truly approaching the world of nightmares, and sadly she would bring them all back to one last nightmare before it would all end for good.

She settled onto the floor next to Tara so that her beloved high priestess's head was cradled in her lap. Then she bent and kissed her, feeling the sweet in and out of her breath as she did so, remembering the long journey they had walked together. In the end she was possessed by Lucia, so she would not return as a ghost, and in truth Fiori didn't think she could endure the sight of one so full of life adjusting to existence with no life. No one knew how hard it had been, how long she had struggled to adjust. Perhaps she would follow in Tara's footsteps. There were ways she could end her existence, and certainly there would be no need to continue after Deacon was gone. Not only would there be no need, but she would not have the heart for it after what she was about to do.

In her arms Tara cried out and thrashed violently and Fiori cradled her until she calmed. Then she kissed her one more time and took her head between her hands. The snapping of a neck was easy with strong hands, Anderson had said. She had always hoped she would never have to find out, but then she had hoped a lot of things. She took a deep breath and braced herself. She didn't notice the mist of a figure rising behind her.

Chapter Twenty-one

'Dear Goddess, please tell me we're getting close,' Tim said.

'We will be there before any of us is ready, I fear,' Anderson replied.

'I don't care. I just want to get Tara and Fiori back from that bastard, then we can regroup to fight another day, if we have to.'

Kennet walked silently next to Anderson, who was himself silent except when spoken to. With the weight of what they both knew, neither of them was in the mood for conversation.

'Is there no other way?' Kennet asked at last when he felt he could speak to Anderson without anyone overhearing.

'You have said not. She believes not or she would not have done what she did.'

'And you're OK with that?' Kennet said.

Anderson shot him an acid glance. 'You know that I am not. She has been the heart and soul of all of us for a long time, and I –'

Suddenly the world shifted around them to the nightmare they all knew and dreaded. Deacon stood in the cave on the ledge with Tara in his embrace. Fiori was no place in sight.

'Ah, your friends have come to our party, my darling. What an unexpected surprise.' Deacon raked a fist through her hair and spoke next to her ear. 'Well, perhaps not that unexpected, not really. My goodness, but they are loyal to you, and that one –' he nodded to Kennet '– that one has such a hard-on for you.' He caressed her breast and pulled her to him so that her back was pressed up tight against his front. 'You'll have to tell him that you belong to me now, my darling. I don't want another man's lust on what is rightfully mine, and I shall make extra sure that he suffers long for pawing at you as he has.'

'Perhaps you will make me suffer, Deacon.' Kennet leapt onto the ledge where the two stood and it was only then Tara saw the sword he hefted. 'But you won't do it before I return the favour. And I promise you,' he said, 'you will never in a thousand lifetimes be worthy of the love of Tara Stone.'

As Kennet raised the sword and the others climbed onto the ledge surrounding Deacon in a semicircle, Deacon released Tara and turned to face Kennet, smiling as though he were welcoming his best mate to dinner. 'Surely you know, my dear fellow, that you cannot harm me with that toy.' He nodded to the sword.

'Tara did,' Tim said, stepping to flank Kennet. 'Don't you recognise that sword, Deacon? Tara used it to tear you a new one on Raven Crag when you were bullying poor Serina. Ah, but you knew it from before, didn't you? When Tara's mother used it to call a Circle of Power for the Stone Coven. What was it Tara told me? Ah, yes. It's the protector of boundaries, and the banisher of anything that defiles a sacred space. You remember it well, don't you? It's the same sword Rayna Stone used to cast you out of her coven.'

Before Deacon could react to Tim's revelation, Anderson slid his arms around Tara and pulled her to him. 'This one shall never belong to you, demon. She is ours.'

Before he could do more than attempt to bellow his rage, Cassandra stepped forward. 'As I recall, you have dreams about kissing a succubus, demon. Well, I'm here to make your dreams come true.' She curled strong fingers into his hair and pulled him close. 'I do know your dreams, demon, and I'm especially fond of the nightmares, remember?' She kissed him long and hard, forcing him back against the wall of the cave with his arms flailing, even as he struggled to grip her, to hang on to her.

Tara was crushed between Kennet and Anderson. 'I shall be very cross with you when we have returned you safely to

Elemental Cottage,' Anderson said. Kennet just kissed her, then stepped forward and raised the sword.

Tara stayed his hand. 'The sword won't kill him and neither will Cassandra's kiss. There's only one way to end him for ever.'

There was a deafening clap of thunder, the cave shook, and a chasm opened in the roof above them. When the dust settled, what was left looked like a jagged-edged pane of glass with a view into the Room of Reflection at Elemental Cottage.

'That's Fiori,' Marie said. 'She's awake, and what's Lucia doing with her? I thought she was with Tara.'

Suddenly all eyes were on Fiori as she placed a firm hand on either side of the sleeping Tara's face.

'What the hell is she doing?' Tim said

Tara nearly fainted with relief.

Cassandra had lost her footing with the trembling of the cave floor. Deacon pushed her aside and stepped forward, laughing robustly. 'Do not you worry, my darling Tara. I now know exactly where to find your Fiori and the demon bitch at whose teat you suckle. And I promise they shall provide you with countless hours of entertainment.'

'Tara, what the fuck is she up to?' Marie yelled.

'This is his doing, this is Deacon's fault,' Cassandra was saying. But it all fell away as background noise. Tara had very little time. She stepped forward and kissed Anderson. 'Thank you, my dearest friend. You've been my sanity and my humanity.' Then she took Kennet into her arms and kissed him as hard as she could in the little time that was left to her. 'I love you, Kennet. Never forget that.' Then she turned to the others. 'You are the very heart of me, all of you. You are worthy, so very worthy of all that's good and honourable and filled with love.'

Then she took a deep breath, which felt like the first she'd taken in a long, long time, and turned her attention to Deacon. 'Thrice woven and once unravelled. That's the proper translation of the passage that so haunts you, Deacon, that so

218

haunts all of us. Thrice woven and once unravelled. And this day I shall unravel you as though you have never been.'

But Deacon was only half-listening. His gaze was locked on what was happening in the Room of Reflection. 'What is that witch doing? Fiori, what is she doing? What vile magic is this that she works?' But even as he asked, the full impact became clear to him. 'Make her stop it now, Tara Stone, or I shall cause you suffering such as you have never known.'

'You will cause no one suffering ever again, Deacon.' Even as she spoke Tara felt as though the heart of her were being hollowed out in her chest.

'Dear Goddess,' Marie gasped. 'What the hell is happening? What the hell is happening? It's all leaving, it's all disappearing ...'

'Being undone.' Cassandra spoke with a sob. 'It's all being undone, unravelled. As Deacon is undone, so's Elemental Coven. We're all connected to him.' Anderson reached out and pulled Cassandra and Marie and Tim to him, and there was silence except for a sniffle and an occasional sob.

'Let us discuss this, my dear Tara.' Deacon forced a nervous chuckle. 'It is quite clear to me now that I have misunderstood the depth of our bond, the depth of my bond to the Elemental Coven, and if you allow me, I will raise your coven to heights none of you has ever imagined, if you will but offer me such a chance.'

'You have nothing that we want, demon,' Tara said, resting a hand on her throat, waiting for the final snap, wondering if it would hurt. In her mind's eye she had already begun the spell of unravelling, and as she did so, for the first time she understood that Deacon would not be the only one undone. How many lifetimes had her existence and the existence of the Elemental Coven been completely and totally intertwined with Deacon's? How many lifetimes had they battled him, suffered his vileness, endured agonising losses at his hand? How many lifetimes had it been their purpose, almost their sole purpose to destroy him? And in this fabric of survival, they had, out of necessity, also woven the sickness and the vileness of living only to destroy, of living only to avenge. How could she not know that as she unravelled him, so would she unravel herself and her own beloved coven?

Deacon roared like an angry lion and swept up a hand to include all of the coven. 'They will all be undone as I am. Have you not told them? Do they not know? Will you do this to your own coven, to those you so love?'

It was Tim who spoke, clinging tightly to Marie and Cassandra, who clung to Anderson and Kennet and Sky. 'If we're undone, then we're undone, demon, but you won't plague anyone else ever again, and it'll be our honour to be undone in the service of Tara Stone.'

'You cannot let this happen, Tara, my dear heart, you cannot let this happen! Have I not loved only you? Have I not been loyal to only you all of these many years? You cannot esteem that love so lightly, or the power that I may offer up with it.' When she made no answer, he stomped and raged and the rock beneath his feet split in two. 'I shall not allow it! This cannot be, you little cunt! You are a cunt as was your mother before you, and this I will not allow!'

Even as Deacon raged, the scene in the Room of Reflection brightened like the sun and expanded to fill the whole universe. 'Please, Tara Stone, I beg you to reconsider. There is so much I can offer you and your coven, please do not do this thing. I now understand the error of my ways, and I shall from this day forth be transformed.'

In the tiny space left to the living, Kennet stepped forward and took Tara in his arms, and the Elemental Coven moved as one into a tight circle around the two of them, each feeling an unravelling that was personal and intimate with a bitter-sweet agony for all that had been lost and all that could never be restored. As all they had known, all they had loved, all that had held them together fell away, they clung on to each other.

Back home in Elemental Cottage Fiori took a deep breath, steadied her grip and gave one sharp twist.

The cave trembled and shuddered and the rocks

themselves split with a deafening crack. Deacon roared louder than thunder, a roar that seemed to go on for ever, then became a sickening shriek fading finally, painfully to a begging whimper before it died into silence.

And it was as though he had never been.

For a shining moment the world felt like a fresh breath of air on the high fells, then they awoke to the sound of heart wrenching sobs and found Fiori cradling Tara's lifeless body in her arms.

Kennet crawled across the floor and ran a trembling hand along Tara's cold cheek, then he turned on Lucia. 'You bring her back! You bring her back now. This was not the way it was supposed to happen – you lied! It was supposed to be me. It was supposed to be me!' He elbowed Fiori out of the way and took Tara in his arms.

'It was never supposed to be you, my darling boy.' Lucia said. 'It was always supposed to be her. I didn't know it. She didn't even know it until only a few hours ago.'

'I don't care. You bring her back. Now! You don't know the price she paid, the unravelling, you don't know the price they all paid.' He nodded to the rest of the coven. 'They need her. I need her. You fucking bring her back!'

Lucia stood unmoving beside the altar, the look on her face like that of a graveyard angel. 'What has been unmade can be remade, without Deacon's vileness distorting it. They shall heal and all shall be rewoven afresh. They still have each other, and now you have them. But, my dear boy, I cannot interfere. The price Tara Stone bargained was the same one you bargained. She knew as did you.'

'Bullshit!' Cassandra pushed to her feet and moved past the altar with such force that the candles flickered and went out. 'You didn't keep your part of bargain. You didn't keep your bargain to any of us. You released Deacon promising to make it all better. And you didn't, did you? Tara did. And now she's dead! And you didn't even do that yourself. You made poor Fiori do your dirty work.'

Anderson grabbed for her hand but she jerked free.

'You're why I didn't want to know my parentage. I'm the child of a coward, a user, a manipulator who toys with other people's lives. Well, this is my real family. Not you.' She opened her arms to include the others in the Room of Reflection. 'This is my family! You bring her back or you're not my mother. Do you understand me? You bring her back now! Right now!' She stomped her foot and wiped angrily at her tears.

The room was silent except for sniffles and sobs. Then Lucia knelt next to Tara's body. She studied her as though she were a problem to be solved, and then she spoke slowly. 'This is very unconventional. Not a part of the plan at all.' She brushed the hair away from Tara's face and caressed her pale cheek. 'I have never done such a thing, and if I do it, I shall have to reside in her, at least until I am sure that she can be self-sustaining again. That could take a while.'

'Then do it,' Cassandra and Kennet said at the same time.

Lucia settled onto the cushions next to Tara's body, still studying her closely. 'Technically she is still my possession, mine to do with what I wish, and truly the world will be a sadder place without her in it.' As she spoke, she lay down on the pillows next to Tara, as though she intended to embrace her, and then as she pressed in close to Tara's chest, she simply disappeared as though she had crawled inside. For a painfully long moment nothing happened. No one uttered a breath. It was as though time itself were stretched to the breaking point. Then Tara gasped a desperate breath and sat up with a little cry of surprise. She looked around her and blinked. 'He's gone.' Her voice was barely more than a whisper. 'Deacon's really gone. He no longer exists, and you're all here. All of you still together.' She laid a hand on her chest. 'And I'm ...' A single tear slid down her cheek. 'I'm still alive.'

The room erupted in chaos and Tara Luciana Stone was buried alive in an avalanche of affectionate hugs and kisses.

Chapter Twenty-two

Four Months Later

Tara woke in the middle of her bed, wrapped around Kennet, her head resting on his chest. The late summer sun had risen above the fells just enough to streak the duvet in golden light. For a moment she basked in the silence of Saturday morning at Elemental Cottage, a Saturday morning when the whole coven was present after the Full Moon Circle last night. She smiled and wriggled closer to the man she loved, revelling in the steady powerful beat of his heart. In the undefined space inside her where Lucia now resided, the demon mirrored her feelings. Without a doubt it was contentment that she felt, and it still took some getting used to. Even after four months, occasionally she awoke fearing what the day would bring, until she remembered that he was gone. Deacon was truly gone for good.

Everyone in the Elemental Coven had suffered nightmares after Deacon's destruction, but they were real, human nightmares, and they had been shared and comforted away. No one slept alone, no one suffered alone, and slowly but surely the fabric of the Elemental Coven, that which was woven anew each day, was the fabric of everyday coven life, the fabric of the ebb and flow of the seasons, the fabric of the waxing and waning of the moon, the fabric of magic worked for good and wholesome reasons. And slowly but surely, healing was taking place.

Suddenly she remembered the best thing about the morning after Full Moon Circle. She stretched and sighed, then she kissed Kennet and nibbled his neck until he opened one eye. 'Fiori's making Swedish pancakes,' she whispered against his ear. Then she nipped him on the right pec just above his nipple as she wriggled free of his embrace and grabbed for her robe. He quickly followed suit.

They hurried down the stairs only to discover Marie and Tim peeking in the window at the top of the kitchen's swinging doors. Kennet stood on his tiptoes for a peek of his own and offered a little gasp of approval. 'Wow. I didn't know you could do that with whipped cream.'

'Never mind the whipped cream,' Tim whispered. 'What a way to eat strawberries.'

As the two women pushed forward for a better view, the doors swung open and the Kitchen Brigade, as Fiori, Sky, Alice and Ferris were now affectionately called, found themselves exposed.

Fiori sat on the granite work island in the middle of the huge kitchen with her skirt and her apron pushed up over her hips and her bare feet resting on Ferris's shoulders. He had just applied a good, sloppy squirt of canned whipped cream between her legs. He raked fresh strawberries deep into her frothy folds before feeding them to Sky who was kneeling on the floor sucking his cock between bites of strawberry. With another can of whipped cream, Alice happily decorated Fiori's exposed breasts. Her heavy nipples poking up through the white fluff were not unlike succulent berries. In turn Fiori was fingering Alice beneath the rudely gaping hem of her robe. No one even paused except Fiori, who motioned them all in. 'Breakfast is going to be a little late,' she spoke around a tiny yelp as Ferris nipped her clit. 'Help yourself to fresh fruit and whipped cream.'

Kennet picked up a strawberry from the bowl sitting next to Fiori and popped it into Tara's mouth. 'Will there be any whipped cream left for the pancakes?' he asked.

'Oh, the canned stuff is just for play,' Fiori said. 'The good stuff was just delivered from Tim's neighbour's dairy ten minutes ago.' She lifted her hips off the table and Ferris went down deep into a soft landing of whipped cream and Fiori. 'I'll whip that myself,' she managed around a wave of giggles.

Tara could just make out the tip of Kennet's erection poking from between the folds of his robe. She slipped her hand inside and cupped him, then stroked, and when he opened his mouth with a groan, she took advantage and offered him back some of the sweet strawberry pulp with a push and a press of her tongue. In her peripheral vision, she could already see that Tim had squirted a thick trail of whipped cream from Marie's clit all the way back, and he didn't mind being a sloppy eater as he plopped Marie down on one of the high kitchen stools to enjoy their breakfast appetiser.

Just then Cassandra and Anderson shoved their way into the kitchen, already showered and dressed. Anderson took in the situation and gave both Tara and Marie a lazy tongue-kiss before giving Tim's balls a casual fondling. 'What do you think, my dear Cassandra?' He settled onto a stool and unzipping his fly to take out his nearly permanent erection. 'Shall we watch while breakfast is being prepared?'

'That's a great idea,' Cassandra said, lifting her skirt and wriggling her pantiless bottom onto his lap until she sheathed him. Then she moaned her satisfaction. 'I've always wanted to know how Fiori does it.'

Anderson reached up under her spring jumper and began to stroke her nipples. 'My darling, Cassandra, I do not know anyone who has more culinary finesse than our Fiori. We could all learn a great deal from her.'

'Now you know why I spend so much time in the kitchen,' Fiori giggled, just as Ferris pulled her to the edge of the counter, pushed up into her and began to thrust. Sky turned her attention to Alice, who was only too happy to reciprocate, and Cassandra strained her neck to offer Anderson a sloppy tongue kiss. 'He'll have all three of their pussies, Ferris will,' she managed with a chuckle. 'Who knew he was so insatiable?'

225

Cupping Tara's bottom, Kennet lifted her onto the oak table by the window then thrust into her leisurely. It was their morning fuck. It seldom lasted long, but it was way more satisfying than the first shot of caffeine. Lucia stirred inside her, revelling in so much sex so often. The morning sunshine streamed through the window onto Kennet's hair, streaking it bronze and gold, and Tara marvelled that they had so quickly found their routine, that even in spite of their mutual long stretches of aloneness, they were at home in each other, as though they had always been together. And Lucia – well, Lucia had taken a bit more getting used to, but she could definitely make their sex life kinky when she wanted to, and she wanted to a lot. She was also more than happy to play with other members of the coven whenever there was an invite, and there often was. She and Cassandra were working hard at getting to know each other, and as a result of knowing her parentage and understanding what that meant, Cassandra's skills and magic were growing exponentially.

As the Elemental Coven healed, Deacon became more and more like a bad dream, and together they got on with the peaceful business of their lives. The herb and potion shop in Keswick was making more money than ever since Marie had taken over managing it. It was also getting a new look. No one could have ever imagined that Ferris had a head for DIY. And Anderson – well, Anderson was more of a renaissance man than a romantic. He and Cassandra were building a telescope to be housed in a refurbished garden shed behind Elemental Cottage, and his skill as a naturalist and an artist were quite impressive. Though he didn't share Cassandra's and Tara's love for gardening, he spent more than his fair share of time in the greenhouse enjoying the gardeners. Kennet had been a farmer before his world had fallen apart, and he and Tim were expanding Lacewing Farm to experiment with heritage breeds of sheep and a few cattle. Alice was in the process of selling her bungalow and settling in with Ferris in his frequent journeys between Surrey and Elemental Cottage. She had come to grips with her gift for ethereal magic and was finally allowing Cassandra to train her. Cassandra still hadn't decided what to do about Storm Croft, though it already belonged to the Elemental Coven as far as she was concerned. After all, they were her family.

The sounds of orgasm erupted in the kitchen in a wave of pleasure, a wave of magic that everyone felt, and everyone took into themselves and gave back to each other.

Tara pulled Kennet to her in a tight embrace and buried her face in his neck, breathing in the desert-heat scent of him. 'I love you, Kennet Birch.'

'I love you, Tara Luciana Stone.' He replied, holding her almost too tight for breath.

Later, as they all sat around the breakfast table feasting on Fiori's Swedish pancakes and Cumberland sausage from a farm over by Seathwaite, Tim and Kennet talked about their plans to add another barn out at Lacewing Farm next spring. Cassandra talked about her latest discoveries of ancient ethereal spells in one of the old books of shadows written in bastard Latin. Alice happily told everyone about her rain-drenched first triumph of Scafell Pike. As Kennet's fingers curled around hers beneath the table, Tara realised that Anderson was right. The fabric of the Elemental Coven was a strong fabric indeed, beautifully and powerfully woven. It had been put to the test in terrible ways, but at its core, at its heart and soul it had held, and all that had been unwoven was now being remade stronger and more beautiful each day, each hour, each moment that they all lived and laughed and loved together as a coven family.

The End

First in the *Lakeland Heatwave* trilogy

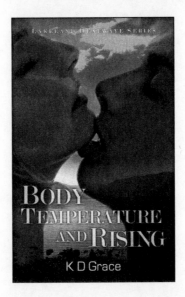

Body Temperature and Rising

Can the power of lust overcome deadly intentions?

A voyeuristic encounter on the fells ends in sex with a charming ghost for American Marie Warren who realises she has the ability to unleash demons. Her powers bring her to a coven of witches who practise rare sex magic that allows ghosts access to pleasures of the flesh. As ancient grudges unfold, Deacon, the demon Marie has unleashed will stop at nothing to destroy everything the coven's high priestess holds dear, including Marie and her landlord, Tim Meriwether. Only the power of lust Marie and Tim share can stop Deacon before the coven is destroyed and innocent people die?

ISBN   9781908086877